THE PLAYER + THE PACT = I DO

LOUISE BAY

Published by Louise Bay 2024

ISBN – 978-1-80456-037-2

BOOKS BY LOUISE BAY

New York City Billionaires

The Boss + The Maid = Chemistry

The Player + The Pact = I Do

The Hero + Vegas = No Regrets

The Doctors Series

Dr. Off Limits

Dr. Perfect

Dr. CEO

Dr. Fake Fiancé

Dr. Single Dad

The Mister Series

Mr. Mayfair

Mr. Knightsbridge

Mr. Smithfield

Mr. Park Lane

Mr. Bloomsbury

Mr. Notting Hill

The Christmas Collection

The 14 Days of Christmas

The Player Series

International Player

Private Player

Dr. Off Limits

<u>Standalones</u>

Hollywood Scandal

Love Unexpected

Hopeful

The Empire State Series

<u>Gentleman Series</u>

The Wrong Gentleman

The Ruthless Gentleman

<u>The Royals Series</u>

The Earl of London

The British Knight

Duke of Manhattan

Park Avenue Prince

King of Wall Street

<u>The Nights Series</u>

Indigo Nights

Promised Nights

Parisian Nights

Faithful

Sign up to the Louise Bay mailing list at
www.louisebay/mailinglist

Read more at www.louisebay.com

PROLOGUE

Jules

When I'm on my deathbed, I wonder if I'll look back on tonight as the most embarrassing night of my life. Turning up in costume to a party that your best friend-slash-roommate *told* you was a costume party shouldn't be embarrassing. In fact, if this actually *had* been a costume party, I'm pretty sure I would have gotten a medal, or at least been crowned queen.

Because I've gone all out.

All. Out.

Sadly, this party is just a regular party and I'm the only one in a costume.

It isn't *slightly* embarrassing. Unlike my roommate, I can't take off my top hat and jacket and voila, I'm no longer a ringmaster from the circus, just someone who's a little overdressed. Nope, that honor goes to Sophia. And I'm not in a costume that at least makes me look hot, a la Bridget Jones dressed up as a Playboy bunny. Nope. I'm dressed as

Mystique from the X-Men. Not the hot-as-fuck movie Mystique, either. I'm the comic-book version: less hot but more authentic.

With my long white dress—slits to my thighs on either side, of course—long white gloves and a circle of small skulls as my belt, I might have been able to get away with, "This isn't a costume, I'm just an eccentric dresser," but I'm *blue.* Blue and overly proud of my belt. I made it myself. In a city where you can find almost anything, four-inch skulls proved difficult. But as the saying goes, *Ask and you shall receive.* Especially when you ask the Internet. Specifically, www.skullsdirect.co.uk. I had to get the goddamn things shipped from the UK, but my skull belt does not disappoint.

All to say, I'm not just embarrassed—I'm pissed. So much of my effort has gone to waste. New York isn't really a costume party place. In fact, this was supposed to be my first-ever adult costume party and call me pathetic, but I've been excited.

If it wasn't for Sophia, I would have fled as soon as I realized it wasn't a costume party. But she's here to accidently bump into a guy she works with, who she's convinced is the love of her life, so I have to stick around. I stand on my tiptoes to see if she's heading back with our drinks or if I've been abandoned.

She owes me for this.

"You thought this was a fancy dress party?" a male British voice says from behind me.

I spin around and have to tilt back my head to see his face. The guy in front of me looks like he just woke up. His hair is a mess of disobedient brown curls that fall over his eyes. He's got a sexy smile that makes me feel like we're both in on a joke.

"Fancy what?" I ask.

He nods at me. "You're dressed as Mystique. Comic-book Mystique though. I like the belt. Very authentic."

I bite back a smile, but I'm secretly impressed that he knows who I'm supposed to be. "Comic-book nerd, huh?"

He shrugs. "I had a minor Mystique obsession when I was younger."

I sigh. "Me too."

"You're the first girl I've met who's into comics."

"Woman. I'm the first woman you've ever met. And anyway, I'm not. Not anymore." My dad left a few comics behind when he bailed on us for the last time. When I found them, I stashed them under my bed and pulled them out occasionally. Mystique was the only character who stuck in my brain. She was hot and fierce and powerful and everything I wanted to feel when I read those comics, wondering if my dad realized he'd left them behind. If he cared as little for those colorful stories as he did for me. "Are you one of those guys who spends all his disposable income tracking down and finding rare editions?"

He grins at me and there's a corresponding clunk in my chest, like his smile just unbolted something in me. "I'm not. Although that sounds like fun." Our gazes lock and I exhale, feeling a little more relaxed than I have since our arrival.

"If this had been a costume party, what would you have come as?" I ask him.

"Ahhh, good question." His gaze doesn't leave mine and it takes everything I have not to shiver. "Maybe Wolverine? He and Mystique were friends for a while, weren't they?"

Friends *for a while*? What does that mean? I shrug. "I can't remember," I say. But I know Wolverine and Mystique weren't friends. Not in any of the comics my dad left. Mystique didn't have any friends in the comics I had.

"Maybe Batman," he says. "I can see some crossover

potential." He grins, and I focus on his teeth and how perfectly white and straight they are. His lips look pillowy soft. A Batman mask would frame his mouth beautifully.

Before I can stop it, a small laugh escapes. "Crossover potential?" I ask.

"I think Batman could tame Mystique," he says.

I raise my eyebrows. "Tame her?"

"She just needs to be loved," he says, and there's that grin again.

"That's how you see her?"

"That's how she is," he says, as one of his curls falls across his face. Just before I reach for it, he pushes it back. I'm mesmerized, completely under his spell. He could tell me anything right now and I'd believe him. I want to hear everything he has to say.

"You're British," I say.

"I like you," he replies. An answering smile curls around my lips.

"You don't know me," I say, still grinning. I want him to like me.

"I want to know more," he says, and his eyes do this sparkly, sexy, flirty thing. I find myself nodding.

"What do you want to know?"

"Your number," he says, pulling out his phone.

I laugh. "I've known you five seconds. Why would I give you my number?"

"We've got the start of something beautiful here. I know you feel it. Why *wouldn't* you give me your number?"

There's definitely something in the air between us. A buzz of connection or attraction or chemistry. But he's so handsome. So confident. How many numbers has this guy already gathered tonight? He's probably in competition with his friends for who can get the most numbers.

"How's life across the pond?"

"I was born there, but been stateside since I was fifteen. New York feels like home." He freezes and frowns for the first time since we started speaking. "Not just home, but destiny."

"Wow. Destiny? That's a very un-New York kinda thing to say."

He laughs, the sound reaching every molecule of his body. "Maybe New Yorkers don't realize how lucky they are if they're born into this city. Are you a native?"

"I grew up in Jersey," I reply. "Still live there. Travel across for work. Tell me your top three favorite things about the city."

He pulls in a breath and his chest lifts. I fight the urge to sweep my hand across it. "I don't know where to start. I can only have three?"

"Start with three," I say.

"Early mornings. There's a different vibe and it feels like a secret city. People talk about New York at night—Broadway, clubs, the Empire State Building lit up in different colors. That's cool and everything, but for me, New York is at its best in the early morning. I love to hear the clank of delivery trucks opening their back doors. I like to go on a run through Midtown when the streets are deserted and imagine the tens of thousands of tourists tucked up in their hotel bedrooms in the buildings around me. I love the fact I can hide from the sun entirely because the buildings dictate where it shines—"

"Wait, you like that the buildings block out the sun?"

"They don't *block* it, but the architecture and engineering protect people from the heat as much as they can. It's a city that celebrates human innovation and progress. It tells you that even on a tiny island, great things can happen."

"Huh. That's an interesting take."

"What about you? You like the city?"

"I'm not sure I've given it as much thought as you."

He laughs. "Spoken like someone who was raised in Jersey. See, you've taken it for granted. It's the best city on earth and you've always known it's just across the river, tempting you with every opportunity you could ever wish for."

This guy is so positive, it's difficult to see an opposing point of view. Is this how cults start? If he asked me right now, I'd probably sign up to whatever he was selling.

"I like the idea of being tempted with possibility," I say.

He grins at me like he's just watched me unwrap a Christmas present. "I meant it when I said I like you. If you're not going to give me your number, will you take mine? I'd really like to take you to dinner. See if this chemistry is..."

"Destiny?"

He laughs. "What a very un-New York thing that would be."

I should walk away. He's talking chemistry and destiny and I *know* it's all bullshit. I know it in my head, but there's a tiny piece of my heart that's sucking it up like he's pouring water into the mouth of a parched camel.

I hand him my phone.

He looks down to key in the number, and honestly, the shift of his gaze is like the sun passing behind the Empire State Building. The room has gone from spring to winter in the blink of an eye.

Did this guy slip something into my drink? It's like I'm bewitched. I realize I don't even know his name.

"Leo Hart," he says as he types, as if he's answering the question I just asked in my head. "By the end of the evening, I really hope I've convinced you to call me, Mystique."

"You want me to call you Mystique?" I ask.

His eyes slice to mine. "I only ever want you to call me Leo."

We talk as if we're on a stopwatch and we have to learn everything about each other before Midnight or the spell floating between us will be broken.

"I have to go to the restroom," I say eventually. I've been trying to avoid it for as long as possible, but I do not want to pee myself in front of this guy. I like him. I can't remember ever feeling chemistry with a guy like I do with this one after just an hour or two getting to know them. Maybe I need a beat. I need to take a step back and see if I still like him after a five-minute time-out.

"Really?" he asks. "Shall I wait here? Or are you just being polite and you're actually trying to get rid of me."

I laugh. "Really." I need a minute, but there's something about this chemistry—about this *potential destiny*—that I want to come back to.

"Okay. Well, I'm only going to wait here in this exact spot for about four or five hours. So don't take too long."

I laugh again and head to the restroom. In line, I'm behind a guy who barely looks twelve. I know that he's trying to figure out who I'm supposed to be. He keeps glancing at me, and I fiddle with my belt to give him a clue, which he clearly doesn't decipher. Not like Leo Hart.

It takes me about ten minutes to get back to the spot where Leo and I were exploring our potential destiny. But he's nowhere to be seen.

Damn.

I mean, of course he was joking about waiting for me for five or six hours, but I was hoping for ten minutes.

Part of me wonders if he took the opportunity to get another drink. Or if he went to use another restroom. I try and subtly glance around to see if I can spot him. It's difficult for me to do anything without attracting attention. I spot Sophia in the corner with some guy. They look like they're about to kiss, so I guess if that's not the guy from work, she's still having a great time.

And then I see Leo. He's laughing, and I can't help but smile. I glance at who he's talking to. It's a beautiful brunette woman—more Jean Grey than Mystique. She looks polished, with a slick bob and a red lip. She's the type of woman who, even if I'd come as myself tonight, would still make me feel like a blue mutant.

He says something to her. She nods, and then he hands her his phone and she begins to type.

My stomach lurches. It's like our conversation, which felt so light and exciting, has turned to lead inside me.

I'm an idiot.

Leo Hart is just some guy at a party trying to get laid by talking about destiny. And I fell for it. I bet he gets a dozen numbers tonight. He's probably the type of guy who doesn't need to commit to a lease because he's in a different woman's bed every night.

He's exactly the kind of guy I'm absolutely determined won't be part of my destiny.

I interrupt Sophia almost dry-humping her co-worker and tell her I'm not feeling well. She offers to leave with me, but I'd rather be alone. I need to go home and scrub off my blue skin and send it down the drain, together with any memories of my conversation with Leo Hart.

I'm done. Men always disappoint me, yet I still keep

hoping one of them is going to be different. Tonight, I learned my lesson.

Again.

As I head for the door, I promise myself it will be the last time.

TWO YEARS LATER

ONE

Leo

I'm laughing so hard I almost miss the call I've been waiting for since I started my career. I don't recognize the number, but something makes me swipe accept. I push my seat out from the table where I've been sitting with my five best friends.

"Just gotta take this," I say as they ignore me. I step away but don't leave the private room Worth has arranged for tonight's dinner.

"Leo Hart," I say as a pretty waitress enters carrying some of our appetizers. She's cute. Blonde. Short. Full red lips and a nice arse. I make a mental note to find her later and see if she wants to get a late-night drink, and by drink, I mean come back to my place and get naked.

"It's Jonathan from *Property International*," the caller on the other end of the phone says. *Property International* is a trade journal for people in the real estate business, and Jonathan is the longtime editor. They've done some interviews with me, but I'm not expecting a call from them.

"Hey, Jonathan," I say, flashing a smile at the waitress. She smiles back and the glint in her eye tells me I know what—or rather, who—I'll be doing later. "It's been a while. How's things?"

"I'm going to cut to the chase. I know you're a busy man. As you know, the *Property International* annual awards are coming up next month." My mind races ahead. He wants to tell me I'm nominated for Developer of the Year. Because I'm *always* nominated for Developer of the Year. I've won it more times than I've lost it.

"Awards season," I say with a chuckle.

"We're awarding you Developer of the Decade. Thought I'd give you plenty of warning so you can get your speech prepared."

My breath catches for just a second, and I compose myself. "Wow," I say. "Is this a new thing? I'm not sure I remember a Developer of the Decade award before."

"Ten years ago, you weren't a thing."

It's true. Ten years ago, I was buying and flipping one-bedroom apartments in New Jersey. Life looks different with a bit of runway in front of me and a few risky decisions that paid off behind me.

"Well, I'm very flattered. When's the ceremony?"

"October," Jonathan says. "It's at the Plaza. We're expecting it to sell out. Only 600 tickets and we have a new lead sponsor who's really publicizing to their connections."

Of course the announcement of my award comes with a not-so-subtle sales pitch. This awards ceremony is a money maker for the magazine, because everyone who's nominated will buy a table for the low, low price of ten thousand dollars.

"Well, sign me up for a table of ten as usual." I always bring members of my team.

"Great news," Jonathan says. "And congratulations. You're doing amazing things."

"Er, thanks." What other reaction is there to praise like that? I might have lived in America for nearly twenty years, but the British inside me still can't take a compliment. I know I'm good at what I do. I know I started with nothing and now dominate Manhattan real estate development. I'm not quite sure how to react when someone plays that back to me.

We hang up and I go back to the table.

"Everything okay?" Bennett asks from beside me.

"Yeah, that was a guy who organizes the property industry awards. He called to tell me I'm going to be awarded Developer of the Decade."

Bennett pats me on the back. "Congratulations, my friend."

Fisher's on the other side of me. "It's not Hotelier of the Decade, that's for sure. Bennett is whipping our asses at the moment."

"He was living in the fucking hotel for months," Jack says. "We still haven't decided whether that was a breach of competition rules."

I chuckle to myself at the lack of airtime my award gets me among my friends. It's oddly comforting to know that nothing any of us can do will leave the others in awe. We're equals. We don't pander, we don't flatter and we don't lie to each other.

The six of us met at business school, where we set up an app to deliver prescription medicines to people's homes as part of a group project. It made each of us a literal fortune. It meant I went from flipping tiny apartments in New Jersey to building tower blocks in Manhattan. When we sold out, we each bought a hotel as a side hustle so we had a continued connection and a way of competing that kept us bound together.

Problem is, Bennett's hotel has been dominating for the last few years. I need to switch out the manager at my place. He's old and tired. But he's a safe pair of hands and I'm so busy, I don't want to spend precious time overseeing someone new who's more of a risk. It's a problem for another day.

"That's great," Worth says. "Congratulations."

"Thanks," I say.

"You taking a date?" Bennett asks.

I know he's low-key worried about me since the last woman I dated turned out not to be who she said she was, but I'm more than over it. I'm not lacking for female company.

"Nah, it's a work thing. I'll take the team." *And I doubt I'll leave alone*, I don't add.

"What's that?" Byron calls from the other side of the table, where he's been engrossed in his phone. "I feel like I missed something."

"Leo is being awarded Developer of the Decade at the *Property International* Awards," Bennett says.

"Leo," he says in a chastising tone. "Did you create these awards?"

"You're a bloody comedian, Byron," I answer. "You should actually give up your day job and start touring with that act."

"Looks legit," Jack says, holding out his phone to the table. It's the awards web page. "Wow, the sponsor is Hammonds." He shoots me a glance. I try to ignore the shiver that passes through my body every time I hear that name.

Hammonds is the new sponsor?

Why would they sponsor the awards? Frank Hammond never spends money on stuff like that. He's an archetypal Scrooge. I unclench my jaw and shrug. "They try to win my business from time to time," I say.

"Do you laugh in their face?" Jack asks.

I shake my head. "I enjoy their wasted efforts."

Bennett chuckles.

"Have I missed something?" Fisher asks. "I feel like I'm not in on the joke."

"Well, first, it wouldn't be the first time," Bennett says. "And second, it's not a joke."

I see Jack nudge Fisher, but he doesn't get the hint that he's meant to be shutting up to spare my feelings. But it's fine. I think. It's been a long time. I don't need my feelings spared.

"Hammonds is Caroline Hammond's father's real estate agency," I say to Fisher.

"Ohhh," Fisher says. "Sorry, mate. I didn't do the math."

"It's fine."

"You won't have to deal with them, will you?" Bennett asks.

I shake my head. "No, they're just the sponsor. And anyway, I run into Mr. Hammond every now and then. He has no clue who I am." Or maybe he does and he likes to pretend he doesn't. I might have dated his daughter for two years but we were never officially introduced.

"Really?" Bennett asks. "You ever want to tell him?"

I think about it for a second. "No. I'd much prefer he thought I was a developer he or his firm might do business with at some point. I quite like the way he sucks up. It's not subtle."

"The ultimate revenge," Fisher says, grinning.

But it doesn't feel like revenge. There's no satisfaction

in seeing the man who made me feel two inches tall from my current vantage point. Despite dating his daughter for nearly two years, I never met him when I was younger. The closest we ever came to a face-to-face meeting was when I told his minion to fuck off after he offered me money—on Frank's behalf—to get out of his daughter's life.

Now, whenever I run into him, I still get a physical urge to punch the man. But it wouldn't achieve anything. All I'd prove to him is that I'm still the boy he *thought* I was at eighteen. And I'm not that boy. I never was. I was better than Frank Hammond then, and I'm better than him now.

And his daughter never deserved me.

TWO

Jules

If I were a betting woman, I'd wager that for most people reeling off their top ten most life-changing films, *Pretty Woman* doesn't make the cut.

In my personal top ten, it's the only entry.

I've replayed the scene when Vivian describes herself as a bum magnet a thousand times. Nothing had ever resonated so hard with me. I watched that film at twenty-five and immediately ditched my on-again-off-again boyfriend/late-night booty call.

Of course, the difference between me and Vivian is that I'm not a bum magnet, I'm an *asshole* magnet. Show me a guy who's too handsome for his own good, has serious commitment issues and an inability to be faithful, and there I'll be, pawing at him like a dog desperate for a scratch behind the ears.

On the flip side, if you're a sweet, kind, faithful guy, I'll happily go on a couple of dates with you, but soon enough, you'll be giving me the ick when you pull out my chair or insist on getting the check.

I'm a mess.

From what I can see, there's no cure, so I've resigned myself to a life of celibacy. Sort of. Maybe *celibacy* isn't the right description. I can do the sex bit. I quite like sex. But actually try and have a committed relationship? Nope. I'm officially out.

All of that should make working for Leo Hart a lot easier than it actually is.

It's not like I'm looking for a partner, a mate, a boyfriend. I'm absolutely not. The problem is, Leo is still as attractive as he was when I first met him at the party. Still dazzling. Still easy to get sucked into his vortex of bullshit if I'm not on high alert at all times.

He doesn't remember me. He doesn't realize that he's the reason I spent the day after the party on the couch watching *Pretty Woman*. That's the day I came to the conclusion that until I get de-magnetized from the assholes, I'm not interested in dating.

But thank god he doesn't recognize me. If he did, there's no way I'd have gotten this job. And this job—as Leo's administrative assistant—is the job I need so I can get the job I *really* want.

My cell buzzes in my bag. I quickly check it—it's a message from my mom, telling me she loves me. She sends the same message every day, and has since the first day I got a phone. She knows I won't respond at work, but she tells me anyway. Her message is a reminder to keep my eyes on the prize, since, like her, I've spent the last decade working in hotels. I started in housekeeping, cleaning rooms in five-star hotels, just like her. I worked my way up to become deputy housekeeper before moving to events, then reception, where I eventually headed up the team.

I've worked concierge, waitressing, behind the bar. There's no aspect of hotel work I don't enjoy, no aspect of the business I haven't studied up close and personal. I've seen it all—which is why I can see The Mayfair hurtling toward the drain if someone doesn't replace the manager.

A little research revealed that Leo owns the place. After getting over the initial shock of finding out the guy I needed something from was the same guy who'd blown me off two years ago, I put my bruised ego to the side and got to work. I tried numerous times to contact him about taking on the role as manager of The Mayfair. I've emailed my résumé and sent it via snail mail. I've called, even turned up at his office and handed him my materials personally—well, not personally, since security wouldn't let me through the lobby. But I watched someone place the résumé in an interoffice mail envelope and hand it off to a courier, so that's something at least.

None of it has gotten me a response.

I get it; I never made it to college. I don't have any previous experience managing a five-star hotel. But I know I'll be good at the job.

I decided I needed a new way to get Leo's attention. I applied for the open assistant role and sailed through the interview process. My plan is to work hard, gain Leo's trust, then tell him to his face he needs to hire me as the new manager of The Mayfair.

I'm still in phase one of my plan: prove I'm trustworthy and capable.

"Jules," the man in question shouts from his office. I roll my eyes, but stand and pick up my phone. I'm about to round my desk and go into his office when he bursts out the door, looking like he's just gotten out of bed. His hair is ruffled, his shirt a little crumpled. The urge to nuzzle into his hard chest hits me like a bottle of Clorox to the head.

Fuck. I hate him. And I hate that I find him so completely attractive.

Eyes on the prize, Jules. Eyes on the prize.

"Have you heard anything about Hammonds?" he asks.

"The agency? You never deal with them. Were you expecting a call?"

He shakes his head. "I'm going to be awarded Developer of the Decade at the PI Awards and they're sponsoring it. Which reminds me, can you call up *Property International* and get us a table? Then figure out which of the team is going to go."

"A table for the awards ceremony. Got it," I say. Leo only ever gives me half the information I need for any project he tosses in my direction, but I've gotten used to it over the last few months since I started. "And there are nine spaces for the team. Let me know who you want to attend and I'll let them know."

"Eight," he corrects me. "Because you're on the list." He flashes me a smile that makes my insides melt like a bowl of ice cream abandoned in the sun. I look away, pretending I'm not affected at all.

I know he thinks he's being a good boss by inviting me to an awards ceremony, but in fact he's being the exact opposite. The last thing I want is to be anywhere near Leo Hart when I'm dressed up in heels and a tight dress. I definitely don't want to see him in a tux. Day-to-day business casual is bad enough. But once we're both dressed to the nines, I don't trust myself not to do something embarrassing, like throw myself at him. Not in the slightest. I can handle it in the office. He's a professional and so am I. There is definitely no flirting going on. And the job I want is always on my mind when I'm behind my desk.

But outside the office? I can't really think about that.

I both appreciate and slightly resent Leo for being professional enough not to flirt with me. In the same way that I'm hardwired to be attracted to men like him—players, playboys, womanizers, philanderers—he's hardwired to flirt, to reel women in, to make them feel good, to feel special, to *want* him. I should know. Flirting is Leo Hart's superpower, even when he's not the one in a superhero costume.

It's good that he looks through me rather than at me. Yes, sometimes it's a blow to my ego, but this is the way it has to be. If I want to keep this job—which I do, until I get the job I really want—I have to be just another non-sexualized cog in the wheel of Leo's professional life. Like a desk chair with a heartbeat or day planner with a mind as sharp as a tack.

"So, there's nothing about Hammonds in there?" Leo nods toward the open copy of *Property International* on my desk.

I have no interest in property development, but I need Leo to see that I'm great at my job, so I always scour the magazine to make sure I'm up-to-date with industry news. "It only just came this morning, so I haven't had a chance to go through it all." Why they send a hard copy of this thing, I have no idea. I also get a daily email.

Leo continues to stare at the magazine before stalking over to my desk, bringing with him the scent of freshly mown grass and crackling fires—totally incongruous with our location in the center of Manhattan. I'm sure whatever he needs is online. Must he need to come so close? "Did you do an online search?" I ask, hoping the idea will send him back into his office.

He stands next to my desk and flips through the pages of the magazine. "I'm not sure what I'm looking for," he replies like it makes sense. "There's just something in my gut that says... something over there has changed."

"Oh," I say, looking at the page he just turned to. "The awards." A two-page spread on the awards ceremony is at the center of the magazine. Leo's name is under Developer of the Decade and the Hammonds logo is front and center.

"Surely a different agency sponsors the awards every time?" I ask.

"Absolutely. But it's never Hammonds because they're too cheap."

"Does it matter?" I ask.

He flips the page and takes a step back. I follow his eyeline, but it's just more sponsored material about Hammonds. About how the CEO is retiring.

"Can you read it?" he asks, thrusting his hands into his pockets. He starts to pace in front of my desk.

I pick up the magazine, eyeing Leo, wondering whether he's about to have some kind of breakdown. I've never seen him so ruffled. He's usually put together, charming, unflappable.

"'Hammonds CEO to step down in a changing of the guard,'" I say, reading the headline. I pause, and Leo glances up from his pacing. I continue: "'Frank Hammond is retiring from the firm he founded in 1984. Grant Boden, his son-in-law, will relocate to New York from California, where he runs the West Coast office, to take over. Husband of Mr. Hammond's eldest daughter, Caroline Hammond, Grant has worked at Hammonds since—'"

I don't get to finish my sentence before Leo turns back to his office and closes the door behind him.

Is Grant Boden some kind of rival? Archenemy? Have I stumbled on to some kind of real estate war?

I skim over the rest of the article, but it doesn't say much. It's basically a puff piece about how Hammonds is a vital part of the industry and has done loads of high-ticket deals. Who cares?

Apparently my asshole, overly attractive boss does. Which means I do. I need to solve whatever problem this creates for Leo. But first I need to find out what the problem actually is.

THREE

Leo

As I message Bennett to tell him I'm coming over, I don't mention that I've asked Worth to come too. In the lobby of Bennett and Efa's building, I see Byron and Fisher. Apparently word has gotten around that I'm rattled.

"Hey," I say, joining them by the elevators. I sign in at the huge reception desk, which apparently now involves an iris scan. Bennett's still fucking paranoid about security. Byron holds the elevator doors open and Fisher and I step through.

"It's not such a big deal," I say. "Worth didn't need to call you." Granted, it's unusual for one of us to reach out and request counsel. So when I sent that message to Bennett, I knew it would be a big deal. And it *is* a big deal. I need to find a way through this fucking awards ceremony, or I need someone to tell me not going is the right thing to do.

Bennett opens the door, and after exchanging hellos and hugs, we go through to the bar, which I swear has the same sectional from the hotel suite he stayed at when the paranoid fucker thought Efa was his stalker.

Until we found out it wasn't Efa, but my girlfriend, Nadia. She was using me to get close to Bennett. I shake my head, trying to get rid of the image I have of Nadia in my head.

Wherever the sofa's from, it's comfortable and that's all that matters.

Bennett hands out beers and whiskey and tequila. I take a neat whiskey because it's the first thing offered to me. I down it, slide the empty glass onto the table in front of me, and take the beer Worth offers next.

When we're all seated, the low chatter falls into a lull.

"Developer of the Decade is a big deal," I say. I scrape my hands through my hair and tip my head back, staring at the ceiling. "I'm young to be getting that kind of award, and I want to turn up and accept it, you know?"

"Of course you absolutely should turn up and accept it," Worth says. "You should also know that I bought a fucking table at the ceremony and we're all coming. I'm going to be pissed if skipping it is even on the agenda."

"That was supposed to be a surprise," Bennett says.

"Surprise," Fisher says, waving his jazz hands.

"You're a bunch of dickheads, but thank you," I say, nodding at Worth. He's a good guy. It's nice they're going to be there. If I go, I'm going to need the moral support. And I definitely want to go.

"Why are you even considering not going?" Fisher asks.

I take in a breath. "Caroline will be there."

It feels like nobody speaks for an hour and a half.

"Are you sure?" Worth asks. "Doesn't she live in California?"

"Who the fuck is Caroline?" Fisher asks.

I sigh, resigned that we're going to get into it. It feels like I'm about to reach into a barrel of rotting fish guts and sift through it looking for something I know I'm never going to find. I don't want to do it. There doesn't seem to be any point.

"She was the one Leo got engaged to," Worth says, and in wafts the scent of two-week-old cod. "Way back."

"Do I know about her?" Fisher asks.

My gut twists. Even after nearly fifteen years, what happened with Caroline still churns me up inside. Remembering myself as someone so gullible, so trusting, so completely blinded by love... the memories are physically painful.

I'd been in New York less than a year when I met Caroline Hammond, Upper East Side princess and heiress to the Hammond fortune. We'd come to America from the UK twelve months before, because my dad bought a German bakery over the phone from an eighty-two-year-old man who decided it was time to retire.

I was sixteen. Before school and at the weekends, I'd help my dad with deliveries. One stop we made each day was to the Hammond household on 79th Street—one of my dad's key accounts. I first laid eyes on Caroline as she hung out of an upper-floor window, watching us unload a tray of bread. I remember thinking she was the most beautiful girl I'd ever seen.

"I was in love with her," I say. "Or so I thought. I was sixteen. A kid. I just... don't particularly want to see her again," I confess.

The next time I saw her was a week later. She was in the kitchen, watching me. Saying nothing. She wore black leggings and an oversized Blondie t-shirt pulled off her shoulder. I'd been mesmerized by her bare skin and her lack of smile, the way she leaned her hip against the doorjamb. I'd found everything about her completely fascinating.

The third time I saw her, I'd been looking for her. And there she was, still entirely compelling, her light blue eyes fixed on me as soon as we entered the kitchen. It was Friday, the day my dad got paid, and as he was collecting his check, Caroline came up to me, boldly looked me up and down, and said, "I'll be at Marquee tonight."

"And you definitely know that she's going to be at the ceremony?" Worth asks.

"Yes, her husband is taking over the running of her father's agency. The entire reason they're sponsoring the awards is to introduce him to the industry. He's going to be schmoozing everyone in town. And Caroline's going to be right alongside him. They're going to want to present this as a continuity thing—a Hammond is still at the top of the tree, albeit someone who married into the dynasty."

"Did you know she was married?" Worth asks.

I nod. "It's been a few years." It's not like I have a Google alert set, but I'd be lying if I said I didn't keep tabs on her. Not because I'm still in love with her. I'm not. But because I don't want to be surprised by her ever again. I wanted to be made aware if she ever moved back to town. But she never came back to New York after leaving for Berkeley. And thank god. I think I would have left Manhattan if she had.

"Okay," Fisher says. "So this chick you had a thing for is going to be at some event with her husband. Do you still care? Really? After all these years? Fuck her. You've moved on." He yelps, and I'm pretty sure someone, or maybe everyone, has either pinched him or thrown something at him.

"It's a good question," I say. "You're right, Fisher, it was a long time ago." He's got a point. Why do I care so much?

I'm no longer the boy who would do anything Caroline Hammond asked him to.

Who am I kidding? She didn't even have to ask. I gave her everything willingly. But a lot has happened since then. I'm not the person I was when I proposed to Caroline just before she was about to start NYU. I've become the man her father would want her to marry now, not the one he got his minions to try to bribe to disappear out of her life. I'm not some bread delivery boy who doesn't deserve an Upper East Side princess.

"Some things leave a mark," Bennett says. "No matter how long since the initial hurt."

And that sums it up. What Caroline did is scorched into me like a tattoo.

My father warned me that I was making a mistake when I told him Caroline and I were getting married, and I couldn't help him in the bakery anymore because I was moving across the country to be with her. My mother cried as I left with my backpack and two hundred dollars, thinking I was about to start my life with Caroline in California. We loved each other, and not even the width of an entire country would keep us apart.

When I turned down his ten-thousand-dollar bribe to stay away from Caroline, Frank Hammond sent his daughter to Berkeley to tear us apart. But I knew we were stronger than all those external forces. We were in love. We were going to spend the rest of our lives together.

The first time I saw Caroline in California was also the last. I turned up at her dorm and she looked at me, amused. The image of her condescending smile, offered like I was some doll she'd outgrown, has never left me.

But the memories refocused and sharpened this summer when I discovered the woman I was dating was using me. Not to annoy her father, like Caroline had, but to try to bring down my friend. The deception sliced sharp into my skin just like it had all those years ago, and it opened the coffin of feelings I hoped were dead and buried.

"I want to go to this ceremony and look like I don't give a shit, like I can't even remember Caroline's name let alone recall how she used me as a way to get back at her overly controlling father."

"Hell yeah," Fisher calls out. "Fuck them. You're a good-looking dude who's at least as rich as any of us. You rule Manhattan real estate. Any woman would be lucky to have you."

"Right," I say, grinning at my overenthusiastic friend group.

"So call Tom Ford, get a new tux," Fisher says.

"I have a Tom Ford tux that's almost brand-new," I say. "The tux isn't the issue." *Then what is?* I don't need Caroline to find me attractive. I don't expect her to turn around and tell me how she realized rejecting me was the biggest mistake of her life. We were eighteen. She was never in love with me. I understand that.

"I don't want her to think she's had any impact on my life whatsoever," I announce.

"You're a goddamn billionaire," Fisher says. "And you're freakishly good-looking, or so my sister tells me."

"She told you I was freakishly good-looking?" I ask. "She used the word '*freakishly*'?"

"I'll bring up the text if you like?" he asks.

I shake my head. "You're right. I have nothing to prove. So why does it feel like I do?"

Bennett pulls in a breath. "What you need is the right woman on your arm."

Things slot into place in my head. He's right. I can't go

to the awards ceremony on my own. I don't want to. I don't want there to be any aspect of my life Caroline can point to and think, "I did better than he did."

I know it's ridiculous. I was just a pawn in Caroline Hammond's game. No doubt plenty followed me to the same fate over the years. She probably doesn't even remember me. But if I'm going to see her again, I need every piece of armor I can gather. From the outside, I need it to look like I have the perfect life. Like I'm entirely grateful that she dropped me like a brick on fire because things are so much better without her.

Fisher pulls out his phone. "I can call Vivian Cross. She owes me a favor."

"She's married," I reply. "The entire world knows she got married last year. Why would I want to take a married woman to an awards ceremony as my date?"

"She's actually married to Efa's brother-in-law," Bennett says about his soon-to-be wife.

The entire group groans at the mention of another one of Efa's brothers-in-law. She seems to have about three thousand of them.

"Of course she is," Fisher says. "Someone else famous, then. What about Jada De Lune? I'm just about to sign her. She's up and coming."

I shake my head. "No, I don't want someone flown in to be my girlfriend. That's just weird."

"So, you need a date who isn't famous?" Fisher says. "This is easy." He squints as he thinks.

"Wait—you want someone to pose as your girlfriend?" Bennett asks.

"I don't want to go without a date. And I don't have a girlfriend..." I see a couple of women semi-regularly. As soon as anything feels too familiar, I tend to withdraw. I'm not interested in having a relationship. And I don't want to ask one of them to come with me to the awards, because it will give them the wrong idea.

"He needs a knockout who can pose as his fiancée," Worth says. "Girlfriend's not enough. We're trying to make sure Caroline Hammond knows that being a dick to Leo was the stupidest thing she ever did, and he hasn't looked back."

"Right," I say. "She was a dick."

"What about Efa?" Fisher says. "She's pretty much the perfect woman from what I can see."

"She's about to be my wife," Bennett says. "I'm not lending her to Leo."

At that moment, Efa comes in with a pile of pizza boxes. "Didn't you hear the door?" she asks, holding the pizza in the air like she's a modern-day statue of liberty. "Anyone would think I'm your maid." She shoots Bennett a look, and they both giggle like adorable teenagers.

"Anything else I can do for anyone?" Efa asks. "Drink top-ups? Shoulder massage?"

"You have any friends who'd want to pose as Leo's fiancée?" Fisher asks.

"What do you mean 'pose'?"

"For an evening. He needs someone to be his date. But they need to act like they're really coupled up."

"I can do it," she says without missing a beat.

Bennett growls from the sofa. "Efa."

She shrugs. "What? I'm not offering to sleep with him. I'll stick on a dress and go to a party with him."

"Thanks," I say. "But your engagement is pretty high profile. After the *Forbes* article and everything."

Efa grins, like remembering the way Bennett sacrificed everything for her is still fresh in her mind.

"It's nice that everyone knows he's my man," she says. "But let me think if I know anyone." Her eyebrows pull together in concentration. "I mean, Eira would do it if you were in a real bind. She's over next weekend."

I smile, but shake my head. "Thanks, Efa. I need someone single. Who lives in New York."

"Okay, I'll put my thinking cap on," she says. "What about someone at work?"

"No. I don't shit where I eat," I say.

"Ewww," she replies. "No one's talking about shitting or eating. You're asking someone to pretend to be engaged to you. Someone who works for you would at least have an incentive to say yes."

"True. But I prefer to keep things separate." I have a healthy appetite for sex. But the sex I like is casual, no-strings-attached, minimal-drama sex. I worked out pretty early on that sex with someone you employ is anything but casual or minimally dramatic, so I've always managed to avoid it. There are plenty of women in New York City who don't work for me.

"Okay, so what about you guys? Any of the women you work with available?"

"No way," Bennett says. "We're not asking the women who work for us, because they might feel some kind of obligation to say yes if it's their boss asking."

"Good point," Efa says. "You know you get me so hot when you say stuff like that?"

"I do know that," Bennett says calmly. "We'll deal with that later."

Efa sighs and heads out.

"So not the women any of us work with. Not anyone famous. What about sisters? Worth?"

"I'm going to pretend I didn't hear that," Worth replies.

I don't blame him. If I had a sister, I wouldn't be hiring her out as a fake fiancée anytime soon.

"What about Mary?" Fisher says, suggesting Byron's sister.

"She's in college," I say. "I don't want to look like a dirtbag."

"Even though you *are* a dirtbag?" Worth asks.

"We'll think of someone," Bennett says. "But given that's the plan, do you feel better about things?"

"I suppose," I reply. "I just want to get it over with. The sooner I see her, the sooner I'll be able to be over it. And if my pretend fiancée is fire, that will help the medicine that is Caroline go down."

It's objectively ridiculous to pretend I'm happily engaged so the woman who ripped my heart out fifteen years ago doesn't think she ruined my life, but I'll feel so much better about seeing her if she thinks I have a perfect life. Without her.

FOUR

Jules

I nearly hit the ceiling as I jump in my seat at the sound of my office door opening. Partly, I'm not used to anyone being in the office at this hour—it's only just seven. Also, I'm working on my strategy plan for The Mayfair, and even though it's not office hours for Hart Developments, I still feel like I shouldn't be working on my dream job when I'm at the desk of my *actual* job.

"Good morning," I say as Leo walks in. I've taken my jacket off and I'm wearing a sleeveless white shirt, but I pull my jacket back on so I'm my most professional self in front of Leo. Dress for the job you want and all that.

I straighten my collar as he stops in front of my desk, his eyebrows knitted together as if he wasn't expecting to see me. He looks ridiculously hot today. The shirt he's wearing is my favorite. It's a cool pink, which brings out the blond streaks in his brown hair. It's a color most straight men wouldn't be caught dead in, but I like that Leo doesn't seem to give a shit and just wears what he wants.

I hate that I like it.

"Good morning," he says. He starts to say something else, but decides against it.

"Can I get you a coffee?" I ask, trying to guess what it is he wants but doesn't want to ask for.

He shakes his head. "I'm good. How long have you been in the office?"

I shrug. "An hour. There are a few things I wanted to get a head start on."

He nods, like it's the most interesting thing he's ever heard. He's freaking me out a little. "I have a few tasks for you," he says.

"Fire away," I say and spin my chair around to properly face him. I'm ready to take notes and be the world's most competent, manager-material assistant.

He looks at me like he's about to speak, but again, doesn't say anything. "Let me get settled and I'll be back."

I shrug and turn back to my spreadsheet. I figure I've got another hour before I need to switch to Hart Developments stuff unless someone calls or Leo decides to hand over whatever it is he wants me to do.

This morning's spreadsheet details immediate cost savings I'd make at The Mayfair over the first three months of my tenure as manager. Next, I'll work on revisions to the proposed management structure. At the moment, there are far too many layers of management. I'm pretty sure it's because Louis, the current manager, wants to make sure that no problem the hotel is grappling with actually comes to his attention.

I want to make the department heads my direct reports, with the new title of deputy hotel managers. That way, whenever there's an issue that crops up with a guest, any of the department heads can identify themselves as a deputy manager and resolve it. At the moment, we have four deputy managers and another six shift managers, and on top of that, the department heads. I'm not sure who does what, but we don't need that many people shielding the hotel manager. The hotel manager needs to be on the floor.

Leo's door swings open and he appears in the doorway. "Right," he says. "I have an unusual job for you."

I groan inwardly. I don't like the sound of unusual. It also means I can't work on my plan anymore. Instead, I'm going to be plugging women's numbers into a spreadsheet or stopping by his apartment to ask the woman he left in his bed to vacate the premises. Not that he's ever asked me to do anything that isn't strictly within my job description, but I can't shake the prior knowledge I brought into this job. I can't imagine how many women Leo sleeps with each week. I was only at that party for ten minutes after we finished our conversation, and he'd already gotten a second phone number. I bet nothing much has changed in the last two years.

I plaster on a smile and glance up at him, waiting for him to tell me what this *unusual* job is.

"This awards ceremony at the end of the month. I need a date for that. For business reasons."

"Right," I say, my tone a little guarded. "And by date, you mean a woman to go with you?"

"Exactly. I need someone who's attractive, single, lives in the city and..." He winces.

Please, god, don't be about to say that she needs to sleep with you at the end of the night. I might just vomit.

"She needs to pretend to be engaged. To me."

"What?" I ask, my filter momentarily failing.

"I need you to find me a fake fiancée for the awards

ceremony. Oh, and they can't work for Hart Developments."

I wait for my brain to make sense of what he's saying, and then when it does, for him to correct himself.

But he doesn't correct himself. Not even a little bit.

He's serious.

"Can I ask why you've tasked me with this? Have you slept with every woman in New York City, so now I'm trolling the other boroughs trying to find you dates?"

He pauses, which is when I realize I should have been using my inside voice.

"Sorry, I just—"

"No, it's fine. I, I— This is a big night. I'm not looking for someone to... socialize with. I want someone who can play the part of my fiancée. Someone who can charm everyone, look beautiful, and believably be my fiancée. This is business."

"Oh, you're serious," I say, and immediately put my fingers over my mouth so nothing else slips out. I need to shut the fuck up or I'm going to get myself fired.

"I'm always serious about business," he says. "Please make sure your inquiries are discreet. Like I said, no one who works here, but maybe a friend. Or an acquaintance. Colleague from a previous job. Have a think."

"You're not looking for an... escort?" I ask him.

His eyes slice to mine and my stomach lifts like I've just tipped over the summit of the Cyclone on Coney Island.

"No, Jules, I'm not looking for an escort. I'm looking for a date—" He stops himself. "A date plus. A little more than a date. Like an Uber Premium."

Is he serious? "You want me to find you a woman who's like an Uber."

"That's not what I said," he replies. "I think you know

what I want, Jules." His tone is measured and tight, like he's about to bend me over the desk and show me who's boss. And Jesus Christ, I'd probably let him because he's exactly the kind of man my mother warned me about.

"Okay, let me see if I can come up with anything. Just... one thing. Why don't you take one of the women on your roster?"

He narrows his eyes. "Who says I have a roster?"

Of course he has a roster. "Are you saying you don't?"

He raises his eyebrows, lifts his chin, and I've never seen him look hotter. "I want someone who understands this is a job. This event is important to me. I want it to go smoothly. I want someone who will definitely show up and know what their role is: my devoted fiancée."

"Okay, so you want me to find you a devoted fiancée? No problem." I say it like he's just asked me to buy him a new desk chair or order a pastrami on rye from Joey's Deli.

How the hell am I going to find him a fiancée?

He shuts the door and I sit back in my chair, willing the heat between my legs to disappear. Why oh why oh why?

I knew taking this job was a risk. I thought I had enough self-control to handle it.

Maybe finding him a date for his awards dinner will help me get the ick. If only he could be even slightly less on-brand for me. Less of a... player.

I have no idea who I'm going to find, or how. I mean, Leo is objectively hot, there's no doubt about that. And he's rich. The combination of hot and rich means that any single woman in New York is likely to say yes to a date, especially to a swanky awards ceremony. But he wants Uber *Premium*. He wants a fake *fiancée*—a woman who's going to play a role for the night. A woman who's discreet.

My mind immediately goes to an actress. There must be

a drama student in this town who needs some work. Is the woman supposed to provide her own dress for the event? Can I offer her some kind of incentive, and if so, what's the budget?

I decide I have too many unanswered questions to be able to proceed.

I rarely go into Leo's office. It smells of him and he looks too darn good behind that desk. Powerful or something. But I don't have a choice.

I knock on the door and he shouts, "Come," and for a second I wonder if that's what he says when he's in bed with a woman. And then I realize I'm an idiot because a man like Leo wouldn't be interested in whether the woman beneath him has reached orgasm.

As I open the door, he looks up at me from his desk and my stomach tilts.

Vagina, you're a traitorous bitch!

"I had a couple of questions about your date for the awards."

He pulls in a breath and nods.

"Do you have a budget for a dress or is she expected to bring her own?"

He falls silent, which I've come to realize is Leo thinking. As much as I'd like to dismiss him as some brainless pretty boy, he's actually smart. And strategic. That's why I can't quite understand why he's letting The Mayfair trundle toward the drain. I guess it's not a priority for him.

"I guess we'll provide the dress, right?" he asks me. "That way we can ensure she has the right look."

Does he want a date or a robot? "What would the 'right look' be?" I ask.

"Elegant. Sexy. Expensive. Socialite vibes."

This guy thinks I'm a magician.

"And is there payment for this role you're asking me to cast someone in?"

He shrugs. "If you think that will help."

"What sort of budget were you thinking?" I ask.

"I want the right person. I'm prepared to pay whatever's necessary."

Whatever's necessary? That hardly clarifies.

"This is important to you, huh?"

"Very," he replies.

My mind is whirring, from possible candidates to the amount of money I would be able to offer them. To the complications of having a woman you just met pretend to be your fiancée.

And then I can't stop thinking about how this seems to be the most important thing to Leo... and how the most important thing to me is managing The Mayfair... and how one could be swapped for the other.

I could pose as Leo's fiancée in return for him agreeing to let me manage The Mayfair.

He looks at me, and I realize I've been staring at him, not saying anything.

"I'll get right on it," I say and turn back to the exit.

What a completely ridiculous idea. If I start pretending I'm in love with Leo Hart, it will only be a matter of time until I'm *actually* in love with him. And I refuse to let that happen.

FIVE

Jules

I kick off my shoes as soon as I get inside the apartment, relishing the cool of the AC. "Why is it so hot out there? It's October. Almost."

"Climate change," Sophia calls from the kitchen.

Sophia is the perfect roommate. She's tidy, an excellent cook, works at Saks and gets a twenty percent discount she's more than happy to share, plus she has a long-distance boyfriend who works on yachts, so he's never around.

"I'm making paella. Want some?" she calls.

I sigh contentedly. "There's nothing I want more."

"Apart from a chilled glass of white wine and a job managing The Mayfair?" she suggests.

I step into our combo kitchen-living space. "Oh yeah. And those two tiny things."

She presses a glass of wine into my hand and sweeps her gaze up and down my body, shaking her head. She doesn't approve of my work closet.

"Thank you. Maybe we should get married. I think you're my perfect match."

"I wouldn't marry you because you dress like shit."

I raise my glass and take a sip. "I told you, I want to look older than I am. There aren't many twenty-nine-year-olds managing five-star hotels. Especially ones that don't have college degrees. I need to look older than I am. And more... qualified."

"You're not just dressed older, you're dressed like someone who inherited Hillary Clinton's wardrobe in December 2016."

"Maybe I did." I glance down at myself and the trousers that are too short to wear with anything but flats. "How tall is she?"

"Shorter than you. And several sizes bigger. Not that either of those things is bad. But your work suits don't fit you."

"Sure they do." When I got the interview for the position in Leo's office, I stopped by Goodwill to try to find something to wear. I found a perfect, mid-blue trouser suit. Yes, it was a little on the large side, but I sewed on some belt loops and created a paper-bag waist with my favorite belt I'd saved up and bought from Saks in the spring. Then I'd turned up the sleeves on the jacket and paired it with a high-necked shirt and flats—because the trousers were a little short. I looked cool during the interview, and the outfit still hits today. "I'm giving hipster vibes."

"You're giving Granny not-so-chic vibes. Any minute now you're going to take up crochet."

I tap my finger against my wineglass. "What a great idea. Think of the throws and blankets I could make for our apartment."

She grins. "How's the asshole?"

I slide onto the counter next to the stove where a pan of rice sits. Looks like the paella is coming along nicely. "He's asshole-ish. In fact, he went up a gear today."

She laughs. "Really? Buy himself a new sports car?"

I groan at the thought. I'm not quite sure what he drives, but I bet it's overpriced and over-accessorized. My dad turned up in an old Porsche one time after he'd been gone six weeks. I'd been so excited to see him. And the car. A yellow car seemed like the coolest thing your dad could ever drive. Looking back, my mom's heart probably sank when she saw it. I didn't know it at the time, but she had a hard time making rent when my dad wasn't around to flash whatever cash he had. A Porsche was not on her list of priorities. "Probably. He also wants me to organize a date for him."

"Oh," she says, adding some kind of liquid to the pan. I'm not going to ask what it is, because I absolutely never cook and I'm sure it will taste amazing. "So you have to arrange something romantic for his latest conquest."

"Oh no," I say. "It's much worse than that. I have to find a woman for him."

She glances at me. "I thought you said he was super handsome and rich and charming. Does he have a problem getting women? I mean, you were pretty smitten with him after a couple of hours at that party."

I sigh. I'd thought I met my soul mate that night. "Right. And no, he doesn't have a problem." He's all the things Sophia described. And he also has that thing that you can't put your finger on—he's sexy. Maybe it's confidence. Or maybe it's the way he looks at me like he knows exactly what I'm thinking. Whatever it is, he's got it. "But he wants to go to—" I stop myself. He's asked me to keep this confidential.

"What?" she asks.

I shrug. "It's more of a professional role."

"You've got me intrigued," she says. "You're hiring him a prostitute?"

I groan. "No! Promise not to say anything?" She nods. "He has this awards thing coming up and for some reason he wants a fiancée."

"Did he say why?"

Did he? I can't quite remember. "He says it's for business. Maybe the women he fucks all have some kind of weird tic—I don't know."

"Maybe he thinks he'll get taken more seriously if he has a fiancée. Like more relatable to the older guys, the industry stalwarts. He's young, right?"

"Early thirties," I say. "A couple of years older than us."

"So we have a couple of years to make our billions, then?"

I laugh. "Right." That's the thing with Leo; he doesn't strike me as the kind of cutthroat go-getter I would have thought a self-made billionaire has to be. How did he get so successful so young? Maybe by understanding that an awards ceremony like the one coming up requires a fiancée? Who am I to question his business methods? Apart from when it comes to The Mayfair, which he seems completely disinterested in.

"So... you want some extra cash to be my boss' fake fiancée for one night?" I ask jokingly, but as soon as I catch Sophia's reaction, I regret asking, because she doesn't look horrified.

"Maybe," she replies. "How much cash?"

"He was a bit vague about it. But I figure you could get at least a thousand bucks." Fact is, I'm sure Leo will pay more than that.

She mouths *wow*. "Tell me what I have to do?"

Jealousy twists in my chest. Leo isn't mine. He was never mine, apart from the two hours I spent with him at the party. Leo's exactly who I *don't* want, so me being jealous makes no sense. Sophia would be a perfect fake fiancée for him. "You just have to be charming and sweet to everyone and look pretty. I mean, I don't have a full job description worked up. You just have to be free the night of October twentieth."

"I mean, if I can fake being charming and sweet, I can fake being a fiancée, right?"

"Exactly," I say. "Are you around tomorrow or are you working?" Inexplicably, I want her to be busy.

"I'm around in the morning. I don't go in until noon."

I pick up my phone. I have Leo's calendar on it. "He can see you at ten if that works?"

"See you at ten," she says. She glances head to toe at me again. "What kind of thing should I wear?"

I shrug. "Something that says you're a billionaire's fiancée," I reply, and I can't help but wonder what that might be. Finding Leo a date for the awards is not what I want to be doing with my life. I should be managing The Mayfair. I'd be much better at that job than being Leo's assistant, though I'm pretty damn good at that, too. He knows it. He's seen how hard I work, how efficient I am.

Then what am I waiting for? I hate working so closely with him. Every day is a reminder that I can't hold a man's attention until the end of a party, let alone a lifetime. Maybe I need to ask for the job I want. The job I was born for. The job that means I'm not ten feet away from Leo Hart at all times.

SIX

Jules

Operation: Manage The Mayfair is underway. Sophia is locked and loaded in the Starbucks next door, waiting to be Leo's ten o'clock. Leo's going to realize I can make anything happen. That I'm the most impressive person he's ever worked with, and he's bound to employ me as his hotel's general manager.

But first, I have my first-ever scheduled meeting with my boss.

On cue, Leo crashes out of his office. "I just looked at my calendar. Have we got a meeting now?" he asks. It's understandable he's confused. I've never put a meeting in the calendar for the two of us. He calls me into his office whenever he needs to speak to me, and I go in whenever I need something from him. No scheduling required.

"We do," I say, standing and picking up the papers I have to present to him. "It's just twenty minutes."

"You've gotten me a fiancée?" he asks.

"I've got someone for you to meet. She'll be here in

about twenty minutes. But I wanted to talk to you about something first."

He looks at me and I stare right back, my face blank, like I'm not a little dizzy from the intensity of his gaze. I've really got to get out of here.

"Okay," he says. "What's this about? You after a pay raise?"

"Kinda," I mumble under my breath. "It's about The Mayfair."

He groans. "What's happened now?" He actively avoids calls from Louis, so I'm not quite sure why he's acting like he's constantly bothered by the hotel.

"I want to run through a few things with you."

"You do?" he asks.

I pull in a breath. This is it. This is me shooting my shot. "I don't know if you know this about me, but my background is hotels."

"Right," he says, turning back toward his office. He's not shutting me down, just moving us to a location that will be more comfortable for him. I follow him. "I've had experience in almost all departments, from housekeeping to reception, and I've acted as deputy manager." I don't add that I was one of three deputy managers. It's not unusual in a hotel to have more than one.

"Right," he says again, taking a seat behind his desk and glancing at his computer screen.

"And I've worked at The Mayfair."

That gets his attention, and he finally looks at me. "You did?"

I nod, glancing away as I sit. "And I got to see how things work—and don't work—up close. I have some ideas."

"I don't run the place," he replies. "Speak to Louis. I'm sure he'll appreciate your input."

He's trying to get rid of me, but I'm not going to let him. Right now is about me, not him. "Louis isn't the right manager for The Mayfair."

Leo sighs. He couldn't be less interested in this conversation if he had Margot Robbie in his lap. "But Louis *is* the manager of the hotel."

"But he shouldn't be."

He raises his eyebrows like a warning that I'm about the step over the line. But there's no point in me working this job unless I'm prepared to say what needs to be said.

"You might not want to hear it but it's true, and I think you agree with me. Louis isn't setting the place on fire by any stretch. But he hides from his responsibilities and has no energy to implement new ideas. He's cut the marketing budget to a tenth of what it was in order to improve profitability, and I guess it's kept him in a job until now, but that lack of marketing budget is having an impact. Bookings are down for the third year in a row. He hasn't asked you for any capital investment for refurbishments, despite a significant number of rooms showing signs of wear and tear." I pause, but Leo doesn't respond, so I go on. "He's running the place into the ground and he doesn't care. This is what he does. I've had a look at his history and talked to people in the industry. He's done it at the last three places he's managed."

Leo sighs. "The Mayfair isn't a priority for me."

"Clearly," I say, and immediately wish I hadn't. "Then why don't you sell it?"

"It's complicated. I can't."

"So you're going to watch it get worse and worse until... when?"

"Have you scheduled this entire meeting so you can

complain about Louis, or are you here to propose a solution?"

I pull my shoulders back. "I have a solution for you. It will require some investment and you're not going to see an uptick in profits for two years, but..." I pull out my financial forecast. "After that, you can see that profitability should increase by twenty-three percent in the following two years."

"You think the marketing budget should increase?"

I set in front of him the budget and capital expenditure plans I developed. He starts scanning the numbers, then flips a page and sees my proposals for increasing the use of the event space and refurbishing the rooms to justify higher room rates. "Increasing the marketing budget alone won't do it. We need to do some capital works. We need to be smarter about advertising. Practically everything Louis is doing needs to be done differently."

He takes his time to look through the financials, tracing his fingers down columns and across rows of figures. I sit, watching, pressing my palms together as hard as I can to keep from fidgeting.

"It all looks impressive," he says. "But I don't have the capacity to recruit and oversee a manager. It all takes time, and I've got to put all my focus into the New River development. Maybe I'll be able to think about it when I've gotten through this bottleneck."

I've only worked with Leo three months, but I know he's never getting through this bottleneck, and if he does, he'll go right into another one. He's a self-made billionaire. He didn't manage that by kicking up his heels. I've got his attention now. He knows my ideas are good or this meeting would have ended five minutes ago. I've got to strike while the iron's hot and ask for what I want.

I pull in a breath. "You need to fire Louis."

"Like I said, I don't have the capacity to do that."

"I can help with everything." I'm being vague and hedging my bets. I need to tell him that I'm the person he's looking for.

This is my shot.

"If you made me the manager, you wouldn't have to recruit, train, or oversee me. You already know I'm trustworthy and good at my job. I have plenty of experience in hotels. I want you to fire Louis and make me the manager of The Mayfair."

Leo's full lips press together in a smirk, and I want to punch him in the mouth, then kiss him. "Right," he says sarcastically.

"I'm serious. I'm well-qualified for the job and I've just presented my strategic plan. All I have to do now is execute it."

"And *I'm* serious that I employed you to be my assistant. An assistant is what I need. I *have* a hotel manager."

"I'll find you another assistant. She'll be twice as good as me, and then I can get on with running your hotel."

"No, Jules." He practically growls out the words and then pulls out his cell. "I have to make a call. Let me know when the woman you have for me to meet arrives."

I remain in my seat, numb from the realization I've taken my shot and so completely and utterly missed. What the actual hell do I do now? I don't have a backup plan. He's got my future in the palm of his hand and all the asshole is interested in is his stupid date for the awards.

He widens his eyes as if to ask me when I'm leaving his office. I gather up the papers, trying to swallow down the fist of cotton in my throat. There's no way I'm going to let this asshole see me cry.

I exit Leo's office and my phone buzzes in my hand. I drop all my papers onto my desk and see that it's Sophia.

"Hey," I say softly, blinking away my tears.

"Alright, mate," she squarks in what she thinks is a fake Australian accent, but just makes her sound like she's been drinking all night. "Want me to come up to the office now, mate?" I know she's just trying to make me laugh but I'm not in the mood. I'm not in the mood to solve another problem for Leo. If he's not going to make me manager of The Mayfair, why do I care if he gets a stupid fiancée for his awards ceremony?

But Sophia's my friend, and a thousand dollars means she'll be able to fly down to Florida to see Jamie the next time he's got some time off.

I sigh. "Why not? Just tell reception you're here to see me." If Leo's not going to make me manager of The Mayfair, I'm not sure where I go from here. Should I try again? Should I just give up and get a deputy manager role somewhere else and pray for promotion? I've had my heart set on this job for so long now, it feels like a waste just to walk away.

Fuck. That. Shit.

I can't just accept no from him. *No*? Two letters, one syllable. I'm going to have to change that no to a yes somehow, or these last three months and my bad suits have all been for nothing. I swallow down my bruised pride and resolve to come up with a plan to change his mind.

SEVEN

Leo

Worth never calls me during the working day, so when I see his name flash on the screen of my phone, I pick up, even though I'm just about to meet my fiancée. At least I hope whoever she is turns out to be my fiancée.

"I'm going to cut to the chase," he says before I even have a chance to say hello.

"Please go ahead," I say sarcastically.

"I think this fake fiancée thing is ridiculous."

I sigh because I don't want to have to justify myself to Worth, of all people. He's such an all-around good guy. I trust him. I like him. I want him on board with this idea because it's important to me. There's no way I'm going to the awards alone. Not when I know Caroline will be there.

"Hear me out," he says. "I get the Caroline thing. But it will turn out to be worse if she or her father finds out it's all been faked."

I push my hands into my hair. "They're not going to find out. Don't worry about it. It's not like we do business together. Next time anyone asks, I'll have split up with whoever it is."

"You might not do business directly with Hammonds, but you know New York is a small city. I'm sure real estate is a small business. The grapevine is very real. You don't want to become a laughing stock. You don't want the reputation of a man who faked his engagement."

"Of course I don't, but why would it come to that? The only people who know are you five and my assistant."

"And whoever she's asked to audition for the part. What's that saying? Two can keep a secret when one of them is dead. You're already at six by my count, plus Efa. That's more murder than I think you're comfortable with."

My heart thrashes against my chest. He's right.

"Why don't you just take a date? You don't have to be engaged, do you?"

"If I turn up with a date..." I pause, pushing my fingers through my hair. "It means I haven't found *the one*—haven't met anyone as important as Caroline, since *Caroline*. I'm not prepared to see her in those circumstances."

"Better that than you get found out as a man who has to hire someone to be his fiancée."

I groan. He's right. If anyone was to find out, it would be humiliating.

"Then I can't go. I won't accept the award," I say. "Because there is no other solution."

Silence echoes at the other end of the phone.

Fuck. Why did Caroline have to come back to town now? Why couldn't she stay in California and run the business from there? I can hear her saying "darling!" like it was yesterday. She had this effected, condescending tone that I thought at first was sophisticated, but hindsight makes clear that it was just fucking rude. "Darling, of course I can't *actually* marry you. You know we were never going to be a long-term thing. I'm a Hammond."

It had taken a while for her words to sink in, to understand that I was just a ball of wool to her kitten—something to be toyed with. I was nothing to her.

"I'm just trying to protect you," Worth says.

"I get it. But I want to go and accept this award. The fact that Hammonds is fucking sponsoring it makes me want to go more. I want to stand up there in front of the hotshots of a city where I used to deliver bread and look at everyone who wants to do business with me, wants a little piece of what I have, and have a chance to soak it all in."

"You deserve that, my friend," Worth says.

I swallow, ignoring the way my throat tightens.

"Maybe the answer is to double down," he says. "Maybe you just need to go harder, rather than retreat."

"What does that mean?" I ask.

"I can't believe I'm saying this, but... maybe you need to get your engagement announcement in *The New York Times*. Go full throttle. Why would you risk doing that if it was fake?"

"Because I was losing my grip on reality? And it doesn't solve the problem of a relative stranger knowing a powerful secret about me."

He sighs. It's still a problem.

"Do you know anyone in the UK? What about a friend of Efa's or Eira's? There's a bit of distance there. Less chance of crossover. Less chance of anyone finding out the engagement's not actually real."

"I'll bring it up tonight."

It's Monday, our regular meet-up night. I could get five opinions for the price of one.

"Look, I have a meeting starting in about two minutes."

I don't tell him it's with a potential fiancée, but even so, this meeting suddenly feels like the wrong thing to do.

I hang up and bellow at Jules to come in.

She sticks her head around the door. She's only been working with me for a few months, but I'm impressed at how quickly she's picked things up. She's smart and resourceful and the plan she worked up for The Mayfair was impressive. If I didn't need a good assistant so badly, I'd be tempted to try her out in place of Louis. But I don't want to rock the boat. She's right, Louis isn't great at his job, but better the devil you know as far as I'm concerned.

"This woman you've lined up," I say. "Where does she work?"

"Saks," she says. "She has a boyfriend down in Florida, so you don't even have to worry about her getting expectations or anything. She's my roommate. She totally gets it."

"I'm going to have to cancel. Or press pause at least. I've got a small-scale crisis at New River to worry about."

She sighs like I'm an exasperating little brother and not her boss. I don't know if she's like this with everyone, but it appears she's borderline annoyed with me at least half the time I'm interacting with her. Lucky for me it doesn't seem to impact her job performance.

"What crisis?" she asks suspiciously.

"I'm dealing with it. Don't worry about it."

"So basically you're rejecting her because she works at Saks. I'm officially out. I'm not finding you a fiancée. Find your own future wife."

It's like I've tripped a hidden switch. Sometimes, Jules can be the most helpful woman on the planet, dedicated to making my office the very best it can be. At other times, she's completely inappropriate and, frankly, rude. She's lucky she's good at her job.

She storms out of the office and closes the door behind her. She's probably frustrated at her wasted efforts trying to find me someone to take to the awards.

I turn back to my emails to find Louis, manager of The Mayfair, has messaged. Since Jules started, he's always gone through her, so his correspondence is completely unexpected.

I click open the message and scan the text.

"Jules," I bellow again.

It's like she's been standing behind my door this entire time, because she pokes her head in immediately.

"Leo, how can I help?" she says like she's Mary fucking Poppins.

"What did you do?"

She opens the door a little wider and steps through. "I'm sorry about before. I just had my roommate waiting and I was a little frustrated."

We're talking at cross-purposes. "Did you see the email from Louis?" I ask.

"No. Should I have?"

"Have you spoken to him?" I ask.

"About what?"

"The fact that you want his job?"

Her expression looks like she just smelled sour milk. "No. Why would I do that?"

"When's the last time you spoke to him?" I ask.

"I've never spoken to him."

"But you said you used to work at The Mayfair."

"I did. But I only saw Louis once in the entire time I worked there. He never came out of his office."

I sigh. Jules doesn't strike me as a particularly gifted liar, and she's never given me a reason not to believe she's telling the truth. "So him sending me his resignation just now is a total coincidence?"

"He resigned?" Her eyes are usually barely visible beneath her thick-framed glasses, but they widen in shock. "Are you hiring? I'll do whatever it takes. Hell, *I'll* even be your fiancée for the awards ceremony."

I can't help but laugh. Jules isn't my type. Not even for a night, let alone a lifetime. She dresses like she's ninety, never wears a scrap of makeup and, well, she seems angry a lot of the time.

Jules isn't going to solve my problems right now. I need to find a new manager for The Mayfair and a solution for the awards ceremony. And based on the seething look in Jules' eyes right now, I'm going to have to figure it all out myself.

EIGHT

Jules

Leo Hart doesn't think I'm attractive enough to play his fiancée. I saw it in his eyes when I suggested I take on the role for the awards ceremony. To be fair, I can't blame him. Leo is a very handsome guy. But the fact is, the man hit on me when I was dressed as Mystique, so I'm not completely abhorrent to him. Maybe Sophia's right, and I've been going a bit hard on the Granny-chic style. I just didn't have the money to buy a wardrobe full of new suits that screamed "hotel manager" when I got hired on as Leo's assistant. What I *did* have was enough money to get Ann Taylored to within an inch of my life at my local Goodwill.

Apparently, Leo doesn't think his fiancée would wear slightly too-big suits.

Hence, exhibit A: bright red heels as high as the Empire State Building, click-clacking on the pavement each time I take a step. And exhibit B: a dress that would be tight if I was going out to a bar, let alone sitting behind my desk all day. I even got my hair blow-dried after work yesterday as I formulated my plan for a quid pro quo. It hits my waist even with the ends curled. I'm one hundred percent Jules Moore. Myself squared. Because I'll do whatever it takes to get what I want, including a full-on *Pretty Woman* transformation.

Today I have to convince Leo Hart to take me to the awards ceremony as his fiancée in return for hiring me as the manager of The Mayfair.

"Excuse me, miss," the security guard calls as I get to the turnstiles. "Can I check your ID?"

I hold up my lanyard as I walk toward him. I usually wear it around my neck, but I don't want to spoil the effect.

He looks between me and the picture on my pass. Once, then twice. "Oh, okay, Jules. Didn't recognize you there for a second."

I smile at him. It's the exact kind of reaction I was hoping for. "No problem," I call, giving him a special toss of my hair before I move through the turnstiles and wait for the elevator.

I hope Leo's not early again today. I want to get organized. Rehearse the arguments I'm going to put to him just one more time. Go through the questions I have for him. But I also want to get into the office before the bulk of people arrive. I don't want to deal with people at Hart Developments either asking me why I'm dressed up or awkwardly *not* asking. I can't decide which would be worse.

I get off at the fifty-sixth floor and I have to switch on the lights. That's a good sign. I might get to my desk without anyone but the security guard questioning me. I undo the buttons on my raincoat and head to my desk, which is in Leo's outer office.

Unfortunately for me, Colin is already in. "Morning, Jules," he calls, and then turns, smiling. His smile turns to shock when he takes in my change in office attire. "You look... different," he says, trying to be diplomatic.

"I'll take that as a compliment," I say as I sweep past him. "See you later."

I shrug off my coat. Even though I've had this dress for a couple years and feel totally comfortable in it outside the office, I still feel oddly self-conscious. Maybe it's the heels. I swear I could get arrested for having a deadly weapon. A small sharp swipe and I could definitely poke someone in the heart with these.

Maybe I need to somehow arrange to be bending over the photocopier or printer when Leo arrives.

I log on to my computer, check I have his day pack of materials for his meetings, and tell myself again why it's worth me hiring myself out for the evening. It doesn't make me a prostitute. There will be no sex. Leo is a player, a play-boy, goes through women like they're water and he has a habit of showering three times a day, but he's not an asshole as a boss. He's not going to make a pass at me, even if he does find me attractive. As long as I can hold myself together and not lick his face, I'm golden.

There's no going back now. I'm here, I'm ready. I just need Leo to see that I'm the answer to all his problems. He gets a new manager at The Mayfair and a fiancée. It's a double win for him. And I can find him a good assistant. This job pays good money. I can probably find someone to fill the position in twenty-four hours.

I hear Leo's laugh in the outer office, where all the employees of Hart Developments work except Leo and me. He always stops to chat to people as he arrives. He's a popular guy. People like working for him. I'd like working for him if he was five notches less attractive than he is.

I stand and round my desk, so he can get a head-to-

toe view and really take me in—proof that I'm Leo Hart fiancée material. I'll also be ready to offer him coffee (which he'll turn down) and say good morning to my boss.

"Morning, Jules," he says, bursting through the door beaming. He freezes as he sees me. His eyes dip to my bright red lips, and then he frowns before letting them trail down my body. Then, like he catches himself being office-inappropriate, he shakes his head. "Good to see you. How are you?"

"Good. I have your pack ready." I pick the papers up from my desk and follow him into his office. "Would you like a coffee?"

He takes a seat behind his desk, and when he looks up at me, he startles, then immediately trains his eyes on his computer screen.

The screen that's still dark, because he hasn't turned it on yet.

"No, thank you."

"I've been through your emails," I say. "Nothing urgent has come in overnight. New River architects want a meeting. I've given them some times next week."

"Right," he says, and I can tell he's not concentrating.

"And in between your meetings, I thought we could talk."

His eyes slide to mine, and I get a jolt in my chest like someone's tapping on my sternum with a hammer.

"Talk?" he asks, in a tone like he's concerned he might be just about to step on a landmine and he's trying to be relaxed, despite being in a life-or-death situation.

"Yes, just picking up on some of the things we discussed yesterday. I know you ruled me out being your fiancée, but I think I'd be perfect for the role. Our meet-cute makes sense.

We work together. Boss-employee things happen all the time."

He puts up a hand to stop me. "Meet *what*?"

"How we met. Our meet-cute."

"Is that what the kids are calling it these days?" He groans. "Sometimes I feel so old."

"And it means you don't have to trust a stranger. You're my boss, so I'm not going to go rogue and reveal that our relationship is put on. You sign my paychecks. I've got every incentive to make things as easy and discreet as possible for you."

"So, you're listing all the reasons why you pretending to be my fiancée is completely inappropriate. Is that what you're doing here?"

"It's not inappropriate. It's not like I'm just doing it to please you, to make sure I don't lose my job—"

"No, you're doing it for promotion. So that's fine, then?"

"But we're not *really* going to get engaged. You're not asking me to hightail it to Vegas, have Elvis officiate, and then fuck your brains out."

I cringe at the words I just used. I shouldn't have brought up fucking. To my boss. To my very handsome boss. And is it me or are the tips of his ears burning red?

I clear my throat and continue. "I'm just saying, we both get what we want in this scenario. And it's not like I'm not qualified for the job. I'm supremely qualified. I know the hotel business inside out. More importantly, I know The Mayfair. This job was *made* for me."

He's shaking his head, not close to being convinced. I know this is my last chance to convince him. It's not like I can start every morning like this, pleading for him to fake propose.

"And on top of that, I'm solving two problems for you.

You like to take a backseat as far as The Mayfair is concerned, I get that." It was one of the first things that struck me when I started working for Leo: he has little to no interest in the hotel. I always wondered how Louis got away with being so shit at his job—and having worked for Leo, now I know. Louis had no one holding him accountable and wasn't enough of a self-starter to do it for himself. "But like it or not, your manager just resigned and you're going to have to do something about it." I hold my hands out. "Ta-dah," I sing. "Here I am. Problem number one solved. No résumés to look through. No interviews, no dealing with recruiters trying to sell you their candidates. Here I am, tons of experience. I've fallen into your lap."

He draws in a breath but doesn't interrupt, and I take it as an invitation to go on.

"And you need a fiancée for your awards ceremony thing. Guess what?" I ask. "Ta-dah!" I sing again. "We've worked together for long enough that the origin story of our relationship would be totally believable. I won't embarrass you, I can hold my own at the event, and despite previous evidence to the contrary, I can actually present myself with a bit of polish. Here I am. Problem number two solved." I put my hand on my hip. "I'm really starting to wonder where my award is for Assistant of the Year."

He chuckles. I think it's the first time we've ever interacted for this long, other than our first meeting. But considering only one of us remembers that night...

"Look, Jules," he says, and his tone is mournful. I can tell he's not excited to start executing my brilliant plan.

"No," I say. "Don't say no. Think about it. It's the least you can do. Give it twenty-four hours to marinate. I don't want you to wake up when I get a job at a rival hotel and you're assistant-less, Mayfair manager-less, and fiancée-less, and wonder if you should have taken longer to decide."

He sighs. "So now you're adding blackmail to the mix?" He must see the confusion on my face, as he lifts his chin and says, "You're going to resign if I don't say yes?"

My shoulders drop. "It's not blackmail exactly."

"Then what exactly is it?"

He's asking me to be honest with him, and I owe him that. The reality of the situation is that I'm going to leave this job over the next few months anyway.

"I took this job because I was frustrated with Louis and I didn't understand why he was getting away with being so... underwhelming."

"You took this job because you hated Louis? I'm confused. What does that even mean?"

I sigh, shifting my weight from foot to foot. "I wanted to be your assistant to prove to you how reliable I am. Show how trustworthy and capable I am. And then... show you my résumé and try to convince you to give me Louis' job."

His expression turns dark, and I stifle a shiver.

"I don't like the idea that I've been in the dark about this grand plan of yours, Jules."

"I know. I just wanted a chance to... to get ahead. I don't have a college degree. I haven't studied hospitality and hotel management. What I know is from being on the ground since I left school. I knew if I sent in my résumé, you wouldn't look twice at someone like me. And before you object, you should know that I *did* send my résumé. Multiple times. You or HR or whoever reviews résumés around here never gave me the time of day, because what I can bring to The Mayfair doesn't translate well on paper. But I know that I'd be good for the place. My mom worked there since I was in junior high until she retired last year. It feels like home. And I just want it... I want it to be better."

He's right to be annoyed. But I haven't been trying to deceive him in a bad way. It was for his benefit too, because he'd have a better-managed hotel.

I'm interrupted by a knock on the open door.

I turn and it's Colin, ready for his 9 a.m. meeting. My heart deflates like an untied balloon. I shot my shot. And the bullet went right through my foot.

"Can I get you a coffee, Leo?"

He doesn't look at me as he shakes his head and begins his meeting with Colin. I retreat and close the door. The first thing I do is kick off my killer heels. At least I don't have to spend the day wearing them. What would be the point?

NINE

Leo

I don't know why I'm asking any of my friends for moral guidance. Every one of them has been ordained in the church of I Don't Give A Shit when it comes to religious outlook, though they're all ethical as fuck. I suppose that's what I need. An ethics lesson, because any understanding I had in that area shot out of the roof when I saw Jules in those heels. Worse when I saw her later in the day in bare feet. I don't know why, but she was even sexier padding around the office, her hair down like it was a Sunday afternoon at home, than when she was dressed up like some kind of soap opera vixen.

The steps to Worth's brownstone seem to have gotten steeper as I climb them. I take a breath before I go to ring the bell, try to fill my lungs, but somehow I can't. I need to get my arse to the gym. I'm turning into an old man. The door opens even before I ring, and Worth appears.

"Come in."

"Is it me or are those stairs getting steeper?"

"That's definitely you."

I've got a funny feeling there's going to be a lot of that tonight—a lot of "it's you" revelations. Although that's not the primary purpose of our midweek meet-up.

Worth and Fisher have called this meeting to talk about strategy for how to beat Bennett in our annual hotel profits competition. I ignored the new group chat at first. Like I give a shit if Bennett wins the competition? The Avenue is a great hotel. I'm too concerned about everything else going on in my life to worry about it... but the thought *has* crossed my mind that employing Jules as the general manager of The Mayfair might be killing two birds with one stone. But I need a second opinion on that, which is why I'm panting at the top of Worth's steps.

"We need some kind of internal referral system," I hear Fisher say.

"Or some coordinated marketing," Jack says. "We need to work together and figure out what the strengths and weaknesses are, then compensate with each other's hotels."

Is it me or is it weird that we're meeting up in order to defeat one of our best friends at what's supposed to be a friendly game?

I grab a beer and sit down, listening to them discuss various ideas.

There's a pause while Fisher types something into his laptop. The others hush while he does it. It reminds me of being back at business school, when we'd be given a case study to analyze and then have to come up with various solutions—no assistants or employees coming to us with proposals or presentations. We've got our sleeves rolled up and we're in the weeds. Except I'm hanging back. I don't feel as invested as I normally would.

"You okay?" Worth asks.

I nod. "The manager of The Mayfair just resigned."

"Oh no. That sucks," Fisher says.

"Jules wants the job," I say. I know we haven't come here to talk about me, but it *is* hotel related.

"Jules who?" Worth asks.

"My assistant."

Confusion registers on his face.

"She's got lots of hotel experience," I say. "She only came to work as my assistant to try and convince me to hire her to manage The Mayfair. And she's saying she'll pose as my fiancée if I give her the job."

"Sounds good," Jack mumbles, reading over what Fisher has just written.

"You think?" I know he's not listening, but I genuinely want to hear from him. I'm not looking for permission. I just want to know if there's an easy consensus. Does everyone fall on the same side of the argument or is there space for debate?

Maybe I *am* looking for permission. If I don't find a fiancée for the awards ceremony, I won't go. If I don't go, they might rescind the award altogether. I shouldn't care, but I fucking do. I want the badge that says I'm Developer of the Decade. I work hard and built my business from nothing. I want to show my dad and mum that they did the right thing almost twenty years ago by moving us from Slough, just outside London, to New York City. I want to show my dad that all those early mornings meant something. I know they know I'm successful, and I know they're proud, but this is a third party telling them, and the world, that their son came out alright. That I'm a success.

"Sounds like you don't think it's a good idea," Worth says.

I start to give him all the reasons I gave Jules as to why

it's not a good idea. As I talk, Fisher and Jack both turn to listen.

"I don't know why I'm questioning it."

"So why are you?" Worth asks. Damn Worth and his pertinent questions.

"You know how I feel about the separation between me and the people who work for me."

"Yeah, I think we all feel that way," Worth says.

"Right," I agree. "And Jules is... like, I've always been aware that she's low-key hot, right? She's got skin that sort of glows and her hair is always so... and her eyes... Anyway." I shake my head. "I've always been able to keep her in a defined area, where I don't really think of her that way."

"Smart," Worth says.

"And honestly, she makes it easy for me. She dresses kinda dowdy in the office. She pulls her hair back and wears these thick glasses. Do I sound like a dick right now?"

"You always sound like a dick," Fisher says. "Are you concerned you sound like *more* of a dick?"

"It's just weird talking about a woman who works for me this way. It's uncomfortable."

"You're amongst friends. Feel free to be as dickish as you like," Worth says.

"We promise to hold it against you forever," Fisher says.

I roll my eyes but don't laugh, because I know he's not joking. He'll make me pay for this conversation, I have no doubt.

"When she proposed this swap—she would act as my fiancée if I made her manager of The Mayfair—I dismissed it..." I trail off. I'd dismissed it, so why am I considering it now?

"You dismissed it because ..."

"Because she works for me and I don't want her to feel any obligation. I don't want to abuse my power."

Lots of nodding around the table.

"Good reasons. What else?"

"And because I don't want to put someone in charge of my hotel who's not capable."

More nodding.

"Is she capable?"

I'd taken a look at her résumé. She has lots of experience but never secured the top job. It's not so surprising. She's young, she's a woman. There aren't many top jobs to go about. "I think she's young, but she's got a fire in her belly, and yes, I think she could do the job. She's the best assistant I've ever had, and I know it's not the same skill set, but she *cares*. That's half the battle."

"Sounds like ability isn't something you need to worry about," Worth says. "What else?"

I shrug. "I think we've covered the most important points: I'm her boss, she's attractive, she wants a job."

"Let's be real," Fisher says. "You've got your hands full at the moment. If you gave her the job at The Mayfair, you'd be solving a big problem. And you can find another assistant—put Jules in charge of that."

"And then she's offering to solve the fiancée issue," Worth says. "Yes, you're her boss, but she's not going to be your assistant anymore. When's the last time you spoke to your current guy at The Mayfair? From where I'm sitting, you need to thank this woman who solved all these problems for you, instead of just wondering whether she's actually the solution."

Guess I just got the permission I wasn't looking for.

"If you're really concerned," Worth continues, "hire her on a provisional basis. Give her three months to make her mark at The Mayfair. Then fire her if she's not doing the job."

I push my hands through my hair. That's the perfect solution. "Right, and I might put her in this group chat so I don't have to deal with you lot trying—and failing—to beat Bennett and The Avenue."

"I think you're a fucking mole," Fisher says. "Coming here tonight to distract us from trying to beat Bennett."

I shrug. "It worked, didn't it? Anyway, the first thing we need to do is the unofficial referrals. Then we're making the most of what business comes through our doors."

"There needs to be a strict roster though," Worth says. "Otherwise one place might end up with all the referrals."

"Realistically, if walk-ins come up to the desk for a room when we're full, they're going to want to go to the nearest hotel."

"And nobody's going to want to go to Boston," Worth says. "I should have bought a hotel here. Maybe I will."

I laugh out loud and can feel the tension release from my body. The decision is made. I'm going to give Jules what she wants to get what I want.

It's a win-win. I hope.

TEN

Jules

I've compromised on my outfit today. I'm not wearing a trash bag, and I'm not wearing heels so sharp they could cut steak. I have a black pencil skirt with a kitten heel, a little makeup, and my hair down. Leo agreed to think about me being manager of The Mayfair in return for being his fake fiancée. And I'm hoping his answer is yes. If not, it's back to my Hillary suits and recruitment websites. I'll have to start applying for shift manger roles. I won't be able to go back to The Mayfair.

I've only just sat down at my desk when the outer office door opens and Leo appears. He sighs when he sees me. That can't be a good sign.

"Come into my office," he says.

That's even worse. He didn't even say good morning.

Without saying a word, I follow him and sit in the chair opposite his desk.

"I've been thinking about everything." His tone is somber and my heart falls into my stomach. Leo is charming, and cutthroat at times, but I don't think I've ever seen him somber. "I've given a lot of thought to what I need from a fiancée—a fake fiancée. And from a manager of The Mayfair. And... I have a proposition for you."

My heart leaps up like a meerkat checking its surroundings. I'm tempted to launch myself across the desk and tell him whatever it is, I agree, but I manage to hold myself back.

"I'm prepared to give you a trial as manager of The Mayfair—" I know there's a condition about to follow, but I want to let off confetti bombs and hug the shit out of him. "It will be a fair trial. You don't have previous experience"—I start to interrupt him, but he silences me with a raised eyebrow and continues—"as a general manager. I appreciate you have a lot of other experience. And you also have ambition and drive, both of which go a long way."

"I won't let you down," I say. "You're going to give me that job permanently when my trial is over."

"That is my hope and expectation. As you correctly point out, I have neither the time nor inclination to begin a search for a replacement for Louis."

I nod. "And I will find you another assistant."

"I know you will." He smirks at me. "But you're right, your first job is to find me an assistant who's at least as good at your job as you are."

I suck in a breath through my teeth and shake my head. "Not sure that's achievable."

The corner of his mouth twitches and I do my best not to smile. Grinning at each other is not our MO. We are brusque and professional. That's how it should stay.

"Then we come to the matter of our engagement."

I nod, setting my mouth in a thin line, so he knows I mean business.

He slides some papers over to my side of the desk. "This is an NDA, which I require you to sign."

I click the top of my pen and flick over to the last of five pages, sign it, and slide it back to him.

"You haven't read it," he says.

"I really want this job," I reply.

"You need to be aware of your obligations in terms of what I need you to keep confidential."

"I'm aware."

He closes his eyes in a long, irritated blink, like he's trying to compose himself or he'll launch across the desk and strangle me.

I slide the NDA back to my side of the desk and start to read.

It all seems perfectly reasonable. Apparently everything he tells me in relation to the engagement is confidential. I'm not allowed to tell anyone that it's not real.

"So I can't tell my mom?"

He shakes his head.

"My *mom*?"

"Jules, we all know that your mother won't knowingly let the cat out of the bag. But her friends will no doubt find out you're engaged and congratulate her. She'll feel awkward or just not as excited as they'll expect, and then doubt and suspicion will follow. Lies, deceit, revealing secrets. It's a line of dominoes that only requires a touch of a finger to fall."

I can't argue with anything he's saying, but the thought of lying to my mom fills me up to my neck with molasses.

"Does she *have* to know? Maybe I can just skirt over the entire thing?"

"Are you close with your mother?" Leo asks. I've never seen him so serious. He's like a shark—all cold and dead in the eyes. I guess that's how the rich get rich—they see the endgame and are laser-focused on the kill.

"Yes, I'm close with my mom."

"You wouldn't forget to tell her if you'd met the love of your life and you were getting married, then?"

I sigh. "No, but—"

"This needs to be authentic. I appreciate that it's an unusual request. If anyone were to find out that this was an arranged engagement... I have no wish to be the subject of ridicule."

I don't know if it's the Brit in him, but he has these oddly Bridgertonian turns of phrase, and I'm one hundred percent here for it. It's adorable. I realize I'm smiling and wince. I'm not supposed to be finding any part of Leo Hart adorable. These little language quirks are strange and old-fashioned and probably mean he can't fuck. But he has BDE, that's for damn sure.

"I get it," I say. My mom won't like that I lied to her, but I hope she understands when I'm able to explain everything eventually. *If* I'm ever able to explain everything. Maybe I should take a second pass over this NDA.

"I want to go through what I'll need from you in terms of the engagement," he says.

Beyond wearing a ring and looking like I'm in love with him the night of the awards, I don't see how there's much to discuss.

"I want to do a formal announcement." He sounds awkward as he says it, like he's conflicted.

"What kind of formal announcement?"

"A notice in *The Times*."

My eye widen in shock. "*The New York Times*?" I ask.

He fixes me with a stare. "No, the *El Dorado Times*. We

want to make sure the good people of Kansas know we're making it official."

I can't help it—I laugh. I've never gotten to see this side of him before. At least, not at the office.

"So you want to announce in *The Times* that we're getting married. And we barely know each other."

"If I were actually getting married, I'd make an announcement. It will be suspicious if I don't."

"Why would you, though?" I ask.

He goes to speak and then stops himself. His silence isn't aggressive, just contemplative.

"Maybe because I'd want to shout from the rooftops that I was in love. Maybe I'd just want the attention and free publicity."

I laugh again, and he raises his eyebrows in a silent gesture that says, *I know this is ridiculous.* And if he does, why is he so set on having a pretend girlfriend? Not a girlfriend, but a fiancée.

"You've thought this through, and this is definitely the route you want to take?" I ask.

"Are you getting cold feet?" he asks. "I haven't even bought the ring."

A sonorous chime rings deep in my belly and I try my best to push it away. I know it's not wedding bells. Maybe they're the bells of doom?

"L. O. L," I reply sarcastically. "I've agreed to be your fiancée. I just want to make sure you've explored all your options. You haven't really explained why it's so important to you."

"And I won't. Is that a problem for you?" He sounds like one of those uptight, arrogant assholes from *Bridgerton* again. One minute he's all charm and jokes, and the next, he's looking at me like he's plotting my murder. "All you need to know is that it's important to me and I need for it to be believable. More than believable."

"So, I can't tell a soul it's an arrangement. And you want to make an announcement."

"Right."

It's more than I expected or wanted. And I think it's more complicated than he's considered. Engagements don't happen out of the blue.

"And we're not living together, never been seen out together, have no pictures on each other's social media because...?" I'm not trying to be difficult, but for a clever dude, he hasn't really thought this through.

He pulls in a breath and sighs resignedly. "You're right. This is more complicated than I first thought."

Shit, I don't want him to go off the idea. If he decides he doesn't want a fake fiancée, then he's got no incentive to give me a shot at The Mayfair.

"It's fine. I can deal with all that."

"How?"

How indeed. "Well, you have various invitations in your inbox. Not only for business stuff, but social gatherings. Like the opening of The Vault—a new restaurant in SoHo. We could do that together." I'm scrambling, digging myself a mammoth hole I'm not sure there's a way out of. But I really want this job. "I'm sure there are some other events between now and the awards ceremony where we can make appearances."

"I don't have social media," he says. "Other than my official Instagram, which is business focused."

"So it makes sense I wouldn't be on there." I've seen that Insta page. There's nothing personal on it.

"What about *your* social media?" he asks.

"I don't really post," I reply. "Not regularly, anyway.

But I could throw up a couple of pictures of us at these events we'll go to." My friends will want to know immediately who he is. "I'll tell my friends you're really private, so we've kept our relationship quiet. Totally believable."

He narrows his eyes but doesn't disagree.

"And then we'll say we're apartment hunting, and when we find something we both like, we'll move in together," I say.

"No," he says. "That's not going to work. Where do you live?"

"New Jersey."

He laughs, and I want to deliver a short, sharp kick to his shin. New Jersey's nothing to laugh about. It's got good transport nearby and living there means Sophia and I can afford a place with two bathrooms.

"There's no way you'd continue to commute if we were going to live together eventually. And also, we work in fucking real estate. If we were apartment hunting, everyone would know."

I wince. He's probably right. I start to say, "I'll call your broker and go out on some viewings."

But I don't get the whole sentence out because at the same time, Leo says, "You'll move into my apartment."

Now *I* laugh. When he doesn't so much as smirk, I realize he's serious.

"You want me to move? Like, out of my apartment and in with you?" There's no way. I agreed to go to an awards dinner. This arrangement is spiraling.

"Temporarily," he says. "Like you say, if we were really engaged, we'd be living together."

"No way. There's no need. We can say you're old-fashioned—"

"I'm not," he cuts me off. "This has to be believable."

He's not wrong, but I didn't agree to upend my entire life. "Who's going to know? I'm going to be working at The Mayfair, so it's not like we have to arrive to work together."

"I don't want there to be any chance of anyone discovering this isn't real. You moving in is a deal breaker for me."

Deal breaker? So it's this or I don't get my chance at managing The Mayfair? That doesn't seem fair. But what choice do I have? "For how long?"

"We have a month until the awards ceremony."

A month? It's all I can do to keep seated and not race out of the office, pack up my shit, and start searching LinkedIn for other jobs. There's no way I can live with him for a month.

Can I?

For the job I've always wanted? To make my mom proud? To show her girls like her and me can do anything we set our minds to, just like she always told me?

I remember the last time my dad left. I was old enough to understand that we didn't have much money and it was going to be difficult financially for us. Looking back, she must have been terrified that she wasn't going to be able to make ends meet. But she did what she always did—she made it work. And that's what I have to do now.

"A month," I say. "And we break up right after the awards ceremony?"

"Maybe you go back to your place because you need some space. But the engagement's still on for a couple of weeks."

"But wouldn't I have sublet my apartment?" I'm trying to find flaws in the plan, because I want to know what I'm getting myself into from the get-go.

Leo looks puzzled. "I don't know how to tell you this,

but I'm rich as fuck. Why would you need to sublet your apartment?"

"Okay," I say. "I'll move in over the weekend. You have a separate bedroom, right?"

"I have four guest bedrooms. You're welcome to any of them. Or all of them."

"Because, like, there's not going to be a reason to share a bed, is there?"

"I can't think of one," he says.

He's not getting it. I'm not talking about sharing a bed. I'm trying to say to him that sex isn't part of the deal. He hasn't given me any reason to think that *he* thinks it is, but I need to be sure before I move my stuff into his place.

"Because this is a strictly professional relationship. There's no... like the engagement isn't, you know... you don't have any physical expectations."

His eyes grow saucer-wide and his mouth drops open. "No," he says hurriedly. "I'm not expecting anything physical from you."

It's not that I'm disappointed—I'm definitely not. Leo Hart is exactly the kind of guy I don't want to date, or get engaged to, but he was a little too effusive in his reply.

Maybe he sees my conflicted feelings, because he adds, "Not because you're not attractive, it's just—"

I cut him off with a groan. "No, don't say anything more. It will only get more awkward. Let's leave it at we're going to pretend to be engaged until just after the awards ceremony, but we're not going to have sex."

"Ever," he says, relief spilling out of him. "Guaranteed."

"Perfect," I say, my tone a little tighter than normal.

ELEVEN

Jules

I know this is all for show and it's not like I expected anything else, but moving myself into my fiancé's apartment without my fiancé feels a little weird. Since I stepped through the front door, I've felt like I'm somewhere I shouldn't be. All of a sudden, the fact that we met before I interviewed to be his assistant feels like a big deal. Maybe it's because being in his apartment feels like he's showing me his secrets while I'm keeping secrets of my own.

I'm already firm friends with the receptionists at Leo's building. I've explained I'm moving in and that I'm his girlfriend. Thankfully, they didn't roll their eyes and comment, "Not another one." I don't know if Leo has lived with someone before. Maybe he's lived with a harem of women.

The truth is, I don't need to know. I shouldn't care. I just need to focus on me and the next month. The Mayfair isn't going to know what hit it.

I tip the moving guys I hired on Leo's dime to haul the dozen boxes I filled, then shut the door. I haven't been in the apartment with Leo yet. He just handed me his keys, I arranged copies, and now here I am. Not exactly how moving in with a new guy would normally go, I imagine, but there's nothing normal about our situation.

Everything of mine from New Jersey is piled in the entranceway. It's difficult to get through to the living space, but I need to choose a bedroom before I start moving any boxes.

The first thing that comes into view is Leo's huge TV screen. I eye-roll hard. No doubt he likes his sports and his porn big. Giant television aside, the apartment is a little more low-key than I expected. It's big and it's in a great location, so it must be worth a fortune, but it's not fancy. There's no expensive art on the walls and there's almost not enough furniture to fill the place. What's here doesn't precisely *fit*. Some of it looks a little small, like it wasn't purchased for this space specifically.

Which, come to think of it, is a little surprising. Leo knows every interior designer in New York City, and I've heard him on the phone to people talking about design concepts for his build-outs—most recently New River. He's got very clear ideas about what he wants for the interiors of the place.

But his own home doesn't look like it's ever met an IKEA catalogue, let alone an interior designer. I poke my head through the door on the far side of the living space. It's a formal dining room that doesn't look like it's been touched. The next door is an office, which again, doesn't look like it's been used.

Did I pass the bedrooms? I double back and realize there are six doors off the entrance hall currently obscured by my boxes. Leo didn't say anything about any part of the apartment being off-limits and I don't want to pry—scratch that, I absolutely want to pry—but I won't go hunting for his bedroom.

The first door I open is a bedroom. This one definitely looks like it's something a designer has done. Unlike the main living space, this room is coordinated without being matchy, in light blues, silver, and white. The sheer number of pillows on the bed tells me Leo had nothing to do with this room. I make my way over to the window and the eastern view seals the deal. I can see the whole city.

"Hello," a male voice calls. It sounds like Leo. Shit, I'd wanted to have all my stuff in my room by the time he got back.

I race outside to find him surveying the boxes and suitcases. "Hey, sorry, I'll have this all cleared. I was just trying to figure out which bedroom I should take."

"It's not a problem," he says. "Need a hand?" His tone has changed a little from how he usually sounds in the office. It's warmer. More open. It's not like he's cold at work —he's not. He's always friendly and nice, but it feels... different somehow. This is the voice of the man I met at the not-costume party all those years ago.

"Oh I'm good." I'm not good. Hanging out in my boss' apartment like we're old friends when in reality we barely know each other is beyond weird.

"Have you decided?" he asks, nodding to the blue-and-white room. "It's my favorite after the primary."

"It's really pretty."

He chuckles. "Pretty. Okay, let's go with that. Not the vibe I was going for."

"You had someone do the design?"

"Of this room and all the bedrooms. Then, I just... gave up. I had too much to do and I just needed it to be functional. What I actually needed was for the designer to make all the decisions, but I think she was too scared to execute in case she made a mistake. I guess she saw it as an audition. But I've lived with it like this for eighteen months now. I'm used to it, even though it pisses me off that it looks a bit like a student flat."

I laugh, half at his accent and the way he says "student flat," and partly because the design of the place—or lack thereof—bothers him. It's kinda unexpected. "I'm pretty sure there aren't many students who could afford something like this, so you can rest easy on that score."

"Maybe." He shrugs and picks up a box. "Shall I take it in?"

"Sure," I reply, grabbing a suitcase. "Ever had a roommate before?"

"Not since... a while. My friend Fisher and I lived together in our twenties." He sets the box down and I realize I didn't even see it, but there's a walk in closet that leads through to an attached bath.

"You've never lived with a girlfriend?" I ask as we both grab a box from the corridor.

He takes a couple of beats before he answers. "Not really," he says.

That's not exactly a no, but if he'd said yes, I'd have been more surprised. It was clear the first night I met him that he wasn't looking for just one woman to commit to. Hell, he wasn't even looking for just one woman to flirt with. Not that I'm still bitter about it. I'm just pissed I fell for it.

We work together to bring all my stuff into my new room. I've counted. Two suitcases and nine boxes. Well, I didn't want to be going back to New Jersey all the time. I'm going to look at my stay here as a vacation. It will certainly be a break from my commute, that's for sure.

"This is the last one," he says, carrying the final box into the bedroom. "Where do you want it?" It's the smallest box there is, only a little bigger than a shoebox.

"Oh, actually, I'll take that." It's all the stuff from my bedside drawer—an eye mask, Tylenol, aromatherapy roller-balls, and my emergency stash of magnesium.

He hands me the box and our fingers brush.

"Ooops," I say, and then wish I hadn't acknowledged it. All of a sudden I can feel him everywhere. I'm acutely aware that I'm moving into the apartment of a man who's incredibly attractive.

The corner of his mouth lifts a little, but he doesn't say anything. He stares at me for a second, as if he wants to ask a question. "I'm going to order in some food. What do you want?"

"You don't have any food? Your kitchen is huge."

"I have some stuff. A housekeeper comes in to stock the basics, but I usually just order in."

"What basics?" I ask him.

He frowns but turns. I abandon my cardboard box village and follow him out of the bedroom.

"I don't know, like milk and coffee and stuff."

"Your kitchen is that huge and you just have milk and coffee?"

"I should know what's in my kitchen, I guess. But I don't."

"I guess there's no need if you never cook. Can I poke around?" I ask.

He shrugs, but now he follows *me* as I pad into the kitchen. It's so... atmospheric. The countertops are a busy gray marble floated on bronze cabinets. I tap one of the doors: it's metal. Never seen that before.

"This is a proper chef's kitchen."

"Well, it would be weird if a place of this size didn't have a decent kitchen. The people who buy it after me will never cook, but the kitchen will be an important part of their purchase."

I look up to take in his expression because I'm not sure if he's joking. His grin travels down my body like a live wire. I look away. He's exactly that same charming, sexy guy I should have run away from as soon as he introduced himself at the party. Here I am living with him, pretending I'm about to be his wife.

"Did you develop this place?" I ask, trying to keep things about business.

He shakes his head. "I'd never live in one of my developments. If anyone found out, which everyone would, I'd have people banging on the door in the middle of the night to fix their AC."

I laugh. "You think?" I pull open a drawer to find a beautiful set of saucepans tucked inside like they've never been touched.

"Believe me. On my second Manhattan development, I had my unit picked out as soon as we finalized the architect's plans. I couldn't wait to get moved in. I kind of resented the fact I had to sell all the units in my first development. They were all a thousand times nicer than the place I was sharing with Fisher. And then I moved in and I didn't get a moment's peace. People would knock on my door if their doors squeaked when they opened. It was hell."

I can't help but laugh. Leo seems unflappable most of the time, but I can imagine his patience getting tested when people were knocking down his door. "Why didn't you take a unit in your first development?"

"I didn't want to cut into my margins. I was... my finances weren't... I didn't have the money, basically."

I look up from where I'm taking in the vast array of kitchen utensils, half of which I couldn't assign a use to. "I always assumed you came from money, like everyone else in New York real estate."

He chuckles. "Nope."

I like that he wasn't born with money and had to start at the bottom. It makes him... I try to distract myself before I can mentally finish the sentence.

There are plenty of ingredients beyond milk in the fridge. I could whip something up easily. "Are you rich enough now to have a pantry?" I ask.

"If you promise not to judge me." He waits expectantly for my reply.

"I know you don't want to hear this, but I'm not a great liar. I don't make a habit of making promises I can't deliver, and I can't promise not to judge you when I don't know what's in your pantry. Do you collect the panties of the women you sleep with? Are they displayed there behind glass or something?"

I stop and close my eyes. What am I doing? Leo is my boss, not actually my boyfriend or even friend. I can't expect him to put up with hearing my inside voice.

"Sorry, I was trying to be funny."

"It's an interesting theory," he says, without missing a beat. "But I save my panty collection for my office."

I manage to meet his gaze, and he's grinning at me. "The pantry is here." He opens a set of kitchen doors that look like cabinets, but they reveal a walk-in pantry. Which is full.

"Jesus Christ on a bike. You have enough ingredients here to open your own deli."

"Nah, a lot of these containers are empty, waiting to be filled. But there's pasta, flour, tins of beans and... stuff."

"That's for sure. There's plenty of *stuff*." I survey the

shelves, taking in the expensive ingredients, running my finger over the labels of all the different pastas and cans of tomatoes. "Would you mind if I cooked? It's like... I'm a TV chef or something. I have everything I could want in this kitchen."

"Knock yourself out." He leans against the counter and watches as I ransack his kitchen. I feel his eyes on me like a tangible string, pulling my attention to him. I should be focused on this magnificent kitchen, but Leo takes up ninety-eight point seven percent of my attention.

"I've never seen anything like it," I say.

"Are you a good cook?"

I start to laugh, because I'm bordering on giddy for his pantry, yet cooking isn't my thing. "I wouldn't say I'm one of those people who loves to cook. But I make a great mac and cheese from scratch if you want to taste it. If you want some fancy three-star restaurant to deliver instead, I understand."

He shrugs. "Mac and cheese is the best. How can I turn down an offer like that? You need a hand?"

I don't need a hand. The last thing I need is a hand. What I need is for him to go away. Far away. And leave me. I don't want some montage of us in the kitchen being cute together playing in my head all night.

"I'll grab the flour," he says and heads to the pantry.

I reach for a couple of pans. We need to get this over and done with, then I can eat and go to bed.

He comes out with some pasta and flour.

"Good start. I need to know how to turn on the stove."

I start to fill the large saucepan with water and he comes up behind me and turns off the faucet.

"What?" I ask.

"Can I?" he says, taking the pan handle from me and tipping out the inch and a half of water I have in there.

Then he does something weird with the tap and refills the pan with boiling-hot water.

"Boiling water. Straight from the tap?"

"You haven't worked in property development long. No kitchen is without one of these now."

"Good to know," I reply. "It might take a decade to reach Jersey." I watch as he sets the pan on the stove and fiddles with the controls. He might order out a lot but he seems to know his way around this kitchen perfectly well. It's cute. And I hate that it's cute.

He pours the pasta into the bubbling water and then turns and scoops some flour into the smaller pan, then grabs some butter and milk from the refrigerator.

"Shall I grate some cheese?" he asks.

"What the actual fuck?" I ask. "This 'comfortable in the kitchen' thing," I say, waving my hand in his direction. "It doesn't fit your brand."

"My brand?"

"Exactly."

"You're making a bechamel and dried pasta. This isn't Le Bernardin."

I grin at him, because I just can't help it. He's funny and knows what a bechamel is. I mean, who wouldn't smile?

"Right," I say, "but it's not exactly a skill set I would have thought you were blessed with."

"Because it's not on-brand?" he asks, flattening out his accent to mimic mine.

"Exactly," I say.

"What would be on-brand?" he asks, resuming his position, leaning against the kitchen counter to watch me add butter to the saucepan and pull out a whisk from the drawer beneath the stove.

"You ordering all your food from Le Bernardin. It's not a bad thing. You can afford it."

"You're going to lose your mind when you see my stash of ramen noodles."

I laugh. "Nothing wrong with ramen. Do you have them in England?"

"Oh god, no. It's a bloody wasteland over there. We live in caves, don't have cars, no running water."

"Okay, okay, so you have ramen."

He chuckles, and I have to suppress my pleasure at him poking fun at me. Talking to him is so easy. That's how it was the first night we met, too. I was giddy from talking to him after only a few minutes. I was floating when he asked for my number. Then I came down to earth with a thump when I saw him with that other girl.

I have so many different contrasting snapshots of Leo. It's confusing.

As I'm stirring the bechamel, he goes to the refrigerator and pulls out a block of cheese. "One thing we don't have in England is American cheese, and the British people are grateful. It's disgusting unless it's on a burger."

"You'll get no arguments from me on that one. What have you got there?"

"Cornish cheddar." He laughs, and I'm not sure why. "This is very on-brand, as you'd say."

I narrow my eyes, glancing between my pan and him.

"I get it sent over from the UK."

I start to laugh. "That's actually hilarious and totally spoiled. But it's not on-brand."

He shreds the cheddar next to me where I'm stirring and it feels like we've known each other for ages. There's no awkward silences or moments where I say the wrong thing —which is unusual.

"I'm afraid to ask," he says, abandoning the pile of shredded cheese and pulling something out of an overhead cabinet. "But what exactly is my brand, according to you?"

I wince. I can't be honest with him. I can't say *asshole.* "You know, lots of money, fast car, ladies' man."

"That's what you think of your boss?" He looks a little shocked, like he's almost… hurt. It gives him a layer of vulnerability I'm not used to seeing, apart from that first night we met. I wonder if he even remembers that party. Or me. I've probably just melted into a thousand other encounters he's had with random women at parties. To me, our conversation, our connection, our chemistry felt… different. He was joking around, talking about destiny, but part of me wanted to believe he was being genuine—that things could be different from how they actually are.

"We actually met before. Way back."

"We did?" His eyes grow wide, and I can tell he's concerned that something happened between us.

"Don't worry. I haven't seen you naked."

He fixes me with a stare.

I glance at the pan. I'm starting to regret this little burst of bravery.

"When did we meet?" he asks. "At The Mayfair?"

I should fill him in. It's not fair to tell him we've met and then not tell him the circumstances. It's just embarrassing—and I don't just mean about the costume. He was coming on to me, and then moved on to the next woman the second I was out of sight. It was a long time ago, but it still doesn't make me feel good.

"No, not at The Mayfair," I say. "It was a few years ago."

I glance across at him to find him wearing his trademark smirk. "Are you going to tell me more?"

I shrug. "It doesn't matter. It was fleeting."

He chokes out a laugh. "Jules. What are you hiding? Is it really that bad?"

"I'll tell you another time," I say. I shouldn't have said anything. The problem is, I need to remember that we've met before, because At Home Leo Hart seems chill and sweet, and the fact that he can find his way around the kitchen is low-key adorable. But he's a womanizer. A player. I need to remember that.

He doesn't speak. When I glance away from my pan, I realize he's pouring alcohol into two shot glasses.

"If you're not going to talk, we should have a toast," he says. "To our engagement." There's no frustration in his voice. He accepts my lack of disclosure like it's nothing. Maybe it's not, to him.

He offers me a shot glass and our gazes lock. Heat trickles through me, long and languid, like a sensual slow dance.

I'm in trouble.

"On a school night?" I ask, and he sets down the glass he was offering me. I sound more scandalized than I feel. But I know I shouldn't be drinking within a two-mile radius of this man. I don't trust him and I don't trust myself.

"It's a shot of tequila. I'm not suggesting we down the bottle, hop into my very expensive sports car, and take on New York City nightlife. But if you would rather not, that's totally fine. I'll take both."

The sauce is done. I turn to him.

"I'll take a shot of tequila." It might calm the nerves that have started to bubble under my skin.

He's holding his shot, waiting for me. I pick up the one still on the counter.

I raise my glass. "To pretending to be Mrs. Hart."

He groans. "Oh god, you wouldn't change your name, would you?"

I blink, trying to process what he's saying. "You wouldn't want me to?"

"No! Keep your own bloody name. I don't get the name-change thing. It's so old-fashioned. Why should a woman change her name just because she's getting married?"

I swear to god, I just felt a tug in my ovaries. "Oh, you're a feminist now?"

He shrugs and clicks his glass to mine. "Why not?"

Being here in his apartment has shifted everything. He's no longer my boss, who I roll my eyes at when he leaves the room. No, now he's the Leo Hart who loves comic books and makes me laugh. He's the guy who gave me his number who I was actually going to call. And here, now, standing with Leo in the kitchen, I understand why I've hated him so much since that night at the party.

It's because I liked him so much. And because for the short time we spent together at the party, I had allowed myself to hope I'd found something—someone—special.

"Let's not drink to our engagement," he says. "Within the walls of this apartment, we should be honest. Let's drink to being roommates." He eyes me from under eyelashes that wouldn't look out of place on the cover of *Vogue*. I take a breath, trying to give off vibes that say his intense stare doesn't do anything to me. "And to becoming friends," he says.

A shiver passes down my spine.

Friends? With Leo Hart?

Maybe I can drink to that.

TWELVE

Leo

Jules is much better company than I expected. I thought she'd scuttle into her room as soon as I got home, and I wasn't about to coax her out, but cooking with her? Chatting? Having a to-and-fro? It's fun. And... not what I expected.

"That's really nice tequila," she says. "Get that imported too?"

"Ha, but no. I got it from Costco," I lie.

"You did not," she says. I like the fact that she calls me out. Most people, especially most people who work for me, would never dare. "I bet you've never been to Costco in your life."

I chuckle at all her assumptions. She's trying to put me in a very defined box and that never works. Not for anyone, in my experience. "You'd be surprised."

She mixes the pasta into the sauce and I pull out an oven dish. "Thanks," she says, a note of surprise in her voice. Clearly an oven dish is "off-brand" as far as she's concerned.

She pours in the mac and cheese and my stomach rumbles. Proper comfort food. There's nothing like it.

"So surprise me," she says.

I frown, confused. What's she wanting? Me to dress up in a Spiderman costume for dinner? Or maybe Wolverine.

"You said I'd be surprised. You a Costco regular?" She sprinkles some grated cheese onto the top of the dish and slides it into the oven.

"Oh, right. Honestly? Not recently. But as a kid I would go with my dad all the time. He had a bakery in Brooklyn and we'd go a lot."

A grin explodes on her face. She's really fucking beautiful. I've always been vaguely aware that if you stripped off the thick-framed glasses and made her smile, Jules would be pretty, but I don't think I realized just how gorgeous she is. Maybe I'm just a sucker for a girl in sweatpants who can cook mac and cheese.

I pick up the tequila bottle and pour out two more shots.

"So that's why you know your way around a kitchen? It's in the family. You said before that you didn't come from money."

"Not at all."

She looks at me for a long beat and I swallow under her gaze. It's like she's seeing right through to the heart of me. Like she's been looking at me through fog until now and it's finally cleared. "That's nice, I think."

"It's nice that I grew up poor?" I ask on a laugh.

"I think it makes you more... interesting," she says.

"Less on-brand?"

She laughs. "Yeah, maybe."

I pick up both shot glasses and hand her one. She looks a little panicked.

"You don't have to have another," I reassure her.

"That's the problem," she replies. "I want one."

I freeze. Does she have a drinking problem? Have I just enabled her addiction or something? Shit.

She laughs. "You look worried. Don't worry, I won't start playing air guitar and flashing you my boobs if I have another. It's just, you know, even though I'm not your assistant anymore, you're still my boss."

"That's another thing to drink to," I reply. "You have another job. If you don't want the shot, don't take the shot, but can we agree on one thing?"

Her eyes widen slightly and I really want to know what she thinks I'm going to suggest. Her imagination is likely far more potent than the reality. "This is my apartment and my home. I don't want to be a boss here. As soon as I step outside those doors, the only time I'm not... I'm always someone's boss or a developer, someone people want something from. When I'm here... When I'm with my friends, I'm just Leo. And I'd like to be just Leo when you're around, if that's okay?"

Her eyes soften. I can tell she's not going to try to negotiate with me.

She takes the shot glass from the counter and raises it. "Just Leo."

Our gazes lock, and I'm sure she's holding herself back from saying something else. But I want to hear it. She's funny and interesting and I want her to feel comfortable around me.

She tips back the shot and, when she recovers, says, "We need a salad."

I smile. Maybe I'll hear what she really wanted to say

later. "I have nothing salad-like in the apartment. Want me to order something?"

"I'm afraid I only eat salad from Le Bernardin."

"Well, I get my salads from the deli on the corner of 73rd and Amsterdam."

She laughs. "Any salad will be just fine."

I place an order with Door Dash and then dig about, finding cutlery and placemats. "I don't use the dining room much. But maybe we should. The view from that room is great."

"The views from all the rooms are great."

I don't know why I care, but I'm pleased she likes it. "I can't argue. It was a big reason why I bought the place. We came to the US when I was fifteen and I always dreamed of having an apartment with amazing views."

"What made you move from the UK?"

I pull out plates and napkins and together we take everything into the dining room. "My dad worked his whole life in a bakery in Slough, until one day he announced he'd bought a bakery in Brooklyn. My mum cried for weeks. She didn't want to come. Didn't want to leave her friends and family." I shake my head. My dad was an arsehole for not talking to her about it before he went and did it. "It turned out fine. Her best friend ended up moving to Spain shortly after and she made friends here."

"What about you? Did you mind moving countries?"

"Honestly, I didn't have an opinion. My parents made the decisions. I just went along with it. But when we arrived, I knew I'd found the place I was meant to be." I set the plates onto the dining table and look out across the city. "I felt excited. Like my future was going to be... different. I'd grown up in a neighborhood where everything was the same, and looking back, it probably had been for generations. Everyone had a house with a front garden and a back garden. The grass was mown by the dads on Saturdays while the mums did the shopping. Sundays were about washing the car and a roast dinner and then the week started again. I never questioned it until we came to America. In Brooklyn, where we lived, on the way to the park you could see the Manhattan skyline, and I sort of knew that the city was waiting for me."

I glance over at Jules to find her looking at me, the reflection from the lights bouncing off the windows and lighting up her face, picking up strands of her dark brown hair and making them kinda glow. She's gorgeous.

"Sounds like the beginning of a fairy tale," she says wistfully.

I chuckle. "Met a few trolls along the way, but yeah. I feel so lucky we moved here." The door buzzer goes and we both head back toward the kitchen. I collect the salad from the courier and she takes the mac and cheese from the oven and brings it over to the table.

"What about you? Do you feel lucky to be in Manhattan?" I pick up a bottle of wine and a couple of glasses on my way back to the dining room, then set about opening the bottle while she dishes out our food.

She sighs. I like the way she thinks before she talks. It strikes me that I don't have many personal conversations with women. I have professional conversations, and some of them seem like they're personal. I can laugh and joke and do whatever it takes to get the job done. And then in my social life, I'm not looking to share information about myself with a woman. When things are just physical, I'm not interested in where and how she grew up.

It's been like that my whole life, with only one exception. Looking back, even with Nadia this summer, it was mainly about the sex. Every time I tried to connect with her, she'd get naked and I'd get distracted.

"It's hard," she says eventually as she takes a seat. I sit opposite her. "My mom has worked in hotels her entire life. She's had a grueling time of it, and she wanted something better for me."

Her words hit me at my core. I get it. That's why she's here, pretending to be my fiancée. She wants a better life for herself and to make her mum happy. Fuck. We're so similar.

"And she got her wish," I say. "You're going to manage The Mayfair."

"Temporarily," she corrects.

"I've discovered tonight that I don't know you that well. But from what I do know of you, I don't imagine you're going to let this opportunity pass you by."

Her gaze falls on her plate, and I detect a slight blush across her cheeks. "You're right." Then she full-on laughs. "You're *totally* right. You'll have to have security lift me from the building if you want to fire me."

I won't need to. I have a feeling she's going to be exactly what that hotel needs.

"I have something for you," I say, and I quickly go and grab the Cartier bag that's been sitting on the coffee table. "I just got something off the peg," I say, setting the bag down next to the mac and cheese. "That's okay, isn't it?"

She places her palm on her heart. "You didn't have my engagement ring designed and made to order? I'm offended."

I roll my eyes. "I just mean, do you think people will be suspicious?"

"It depends on the ring, I suppose."

I lift my chin in the direction of the bag, inviting her to take a look and make a judgment for herself. She sets down her fork and takes the bag. "I just went online—" I start, but don't get very far because she takes out the ring box, opens it, and screams.

"What?!"

"What?" I echo. I didn't check the box. Did they fill it with joke shop spiders or something?

"*This* is the ring you're expecting me to wear?" She turns the box to me. It looks like the ring I saw online and called up about.

"Do you hate it?"

She splutters, "No, I don't hate it! How could anyone hate it?"

"So why are you screaming like you've just seen a dead body?"

She glances between me and the ring, once, then twice. "It's just *gorgeous*. I'm worried I'm going to lose it."

"It's covered on my insurance. You're not going to lose it," I say.

She's still staring at it like it might bite her.

"Are you going to put it on?" I ask.

She pulls it out of the box and slides it on her finger. "It fits perfectly."

It looks good on her. Appropriate.

"Don't tell me how much it cost."

I chuckle. "I won't if you promise not to get too attached to it."

She sighs. "I can't promise that. But I *can* promise that I won't cause you physical pain when you ask for it back."

"Good compromise," I say, taking a mouthful of mac and cheese. I groan. "This is so good."

"It's homemade mac and cheese," she says. "Of course it's good." She grins at me and forks up a mouthful of pasta.

Her eyes flutter closed, and I can't take my gaze off her. "It's good."

I nod, and we continue to eat in happy silence, the ring glinting on her finger, just like we're an engaged couple having dinner together. And it's easier to believe than I thought possible. The woman opposite me is funny, ambitious, beautiful, and great company, and I've enjoyed tonight more than I thought I would. I've just got to make sure I don't step over the line. I can't fuck this up. For either of us.

THIRTEEN

Jules

I'm officially the manager of The Mayfair. I've used up a chunk of my savings to dress the part in black trousers and a gray silk shirt. Oversized pantsuits were okay for Hart Developments, but this is *the* job. Everything has to be perfect. The only person who doesn't get a uniform at The Mayfair is the manager. Still, these clothes *feel* like a uniform. Or maybe a costume—like it's not quite me. Like it's the grown-up version of me.

I check my hair and makeup in the mirror. My hair's in a low bun, less severe than I'm used to. And I'm wearing my contacts. I'm ready.

My plan is to be on the ground, walking the floor as the manager. I know I've worked in the hotel, but I'm sure I'll see things in a different light as the manager here. But I also really want to get to grips with what all the layers of deputy managers and shift manager do, and work out which of them don't need to be here. It will take cost out of the operation, which I desperately need to do if I want to prove myself to Leo.

A knock on my office door catches me off guard.

"A flower delivery for you," Joan says. Joan is the assistant to the management team. I've known her a very long time.

"Flowers?" I ask and pull the card from where it's tucked in between the stems. The arrangement is luxurious, an abundance of light and dark pink roses in a vase.

I open the card and, even though I know they can only be from Leo, seeing his name on the little slip of paper makes my heart lift in my chest. He's playing the part of the doting fiancé whose almost-wife just started a new job. I get it. But why do I like it so much?

The card reads, "Are roses on-brand? Good luck. Love, Just Leo."

I hate him for sending me such an adorable message. I need him to be more on-brand than this. More of the Player Leo I know lurks under this sweet, sincere exterior. Basically, I need him to display far more asshole tendencies than he's doing at the moment. Because if he keeps going the way he is, I'm going to forget what an obvious asshole he is and I'll start to like him. Really like him.

Or maybe if he's less of an asshole, I won't find myself attracted to him anymore? Maybe that's the way my freaky brain and damaged heart work.

Frankly, I don't get much say on his level of asshole-ness, so I have to go with the flow and just make sure that whoever he is, asshole or not, I keep any feelings for Leo Hart at bay.

I barely saw him yesterday. He had to travel upstate to see a potential development and I spent the day trying to organize my room.

He came home after I'd gone to bed—which was, admittedly, pathetically early. But I wanted to arrive at the hotel early. I got here at seven. I don't hate not having to commute from New Jersey. It was just as well that Leo wasn't around on Sunday. I went to bed on Saturday after mac and cheese and three tequilas, my mind spinning and my heart racing, like I'd just come back from the best date ever. I welcomed Sunday without him. I got to recover and regroup. To remind myself that I'm not dating Leo. I'm not really living with him. We're not roommates and we're certainly not lovers. Even if he isn't an asshole, he's my boss. Like he said, I'm determined not to get fired.

"Shall I leave them on your desk?" Joan asks.

"Sure," I say. "That would be great. If you need me, I have my radio, or I'll be around reception or events." The hotel staff need to see me around—to understand, however subtly, that a change in management means other changes are coming, too.

"Good luck," Joan says. "And remember, you didn't get this job to extend your circle of friends." She winks at me and places the flowers on my desk.

I pause when I hit the lobby to take it all in. I know I don't own this place, but right now, I feel like I do. This is the moment I dreamt of my entire childhood and most of my twenties. I need to appreciate it for what it is and for what it represents: years of hard work and determination.

Raised voices over at the reception desk catch my attention, so I go over to investigate. A couple is talking to Malika, one of our front desk agents, and things seem to be getting heated. I slip behind the desk and listen to their conversation. It's clearly a problem over room allocation. Malika has been in her job for at least three years, and from what I've seen, she's good at it.

"Is there anything I can do to help?" I interrupt, focusing on Malika.

"Mr. and Mrs. Pearson aren't happy with their room assignment," Malika says, her voice lowered.

I turn to the elderly couple, who are almost certainly tourists from the Midwest, and smile. "I'm very sorry to hear that. What exactly is your concern?"

"They want a lower floor," Malika says.

At the same time, Mr. Pearson says, "My wife needs a window that opens. She feels claustrophobic with the windows closed at night. We requested a window that opens when we booked."

"Mr. and Mrs. Pearson, can I get you a tea or a coffee while we sort this out for you?" I round the reception desk and guide them over to the lobby lounge.

"I'd love a coffee," Mrs. Pearson says. "I'm just sorry to create a fuss," she says, "but I won't sleep. I just know I won't."

"Please don't concern yourself. We'll straighten this out." I gesture over one of the lounge waiters. I don't recognize him. "Coffee for the Pearsons, please, and put it on my tab." I turn back to the guests. "I'll be back with you shortly."

I nod and turn back to the reception desk. I hope Malika has found a solution already.

"Occupancy is high today?" I ask as I approach her.

"Yeah," she says, clearly relieved to have some distance from the Pearsons.

I glance over at Ali, the shift manager.

"We're running at seventy-seven percent," Ali says.

We have rooms available, but the need for a low-floor room shrinks the available pool of solutions to a shallow puddle. "Nothing's open on the first floor?" I ask.

Malika sort of winces, and Ali approaches. "Everything on the first and second floors has already been allocated," he says. There's a bit of an edge to Ali's tone that makes me glad he didn't try to "help" with the Pearsons.

"Okay, let's see if we can switch something out. We can't have Mrs. Pearson up all night, can we?"

"But it wasn't on their notes," Ali says. "The rooms have been allocated. We don't change them after they've been allocated."

"What would you do if Taylor Swift checked in and wanted a first-floor room?" I ask.

"I'd ask her why she wasn't at the Four Seasons." He smirks.

It's funny, but at the same time, if he thinks poorly of this hotel and is prepared to say so in front of me and another staff member, his attitude is likely showing through to guests, too.

"What would you do if it were your mom?" I ask him.

He almost rolls his eyes and starts tapping away on the keyboard. "I'd move this room—ten-twelve—to a higher floor, since they're not checking in until this afternoon," he says, pointing at the screen. "It gives them an upgrade and leaves space for the Pearsons."

Well, that wasn't hard.

"Okay, that sounds like a good solution." I'm not quite sure why it wasn't offered in the first place. "Malika, can you show the Pearsons to their room personally?"

Ali stands next to me, his mouth pressed into a disapproving line. It feels like he was deliberately obstructing a good check-in experience. Why would he act like that in front of his boss?

"Thanks, Ali. It's so great you were able to solve that issue."

He gives me a tight smile, and I head over to the concierge desk to leave things to cool down a little.

I've always thought Ali was one of the highlights of The Mayfair staff. He's so popular and always the life of any social gathering where we're all together—the annual holiday party or a break-room birthday celebration. But I suppose I always saw him through the lens of being one of his co-workers. I hope he doesn't make life difficult for me. I already have enough fires to put out. I don't need to find new flames.

I cross the lobby and introduce myself to the two new members of the concierge team before heading back to my office. I've been churning over an introductory email to all staff, and Ali's reaction this morning has just given me an idea.

I open the door to my office to the scent of roses. They really do look incredible. I'm not making an announcement at the hotel about my engagement to Leo. No one needs to know, and I don't need anyone thinking my new role here is nepotism. Maybe some of them will find out, but even if they do, most of them won't know Leo owns the place. All any of the staff care about is who their overall manager is. And that's me. For now.

I sit at my desk and begin to type an email. I introduce myself, explaining my and my mother's experiences in hospitality, how I've worked at The Mayfair in various roles, that I'm passionate about keeping the hotel in the top tier of New York hotels. More like I'm committed to *getting* us into the top tier, but there's no point in saying that.

Finally, I announce that I will be leaving locked ballot boxes throughout the staff areas, and they should feel free to anonymously drop in the three changes they'd like to see in the hotel or the area in which they work. I reassure everyone that I'm the only person who will see anything posted in these boxes.

I know from experience that the people on the ground often know where problems are and how to solve them, but they don't have a voice or are afraid to speak out. Even today, I got the feeling that Malika was uncomfortable providing the obvious solution to the Pearsons' issue because she thought Ali would disapprove. No staff member should ever be concerned about doing what's right to please our guests.

I suspect Ali is a block to a better experience on reception. But before I make changes, I want to give people a chance to have their voices heard.

FOURTEEN

Leo

There are certain points in a development that feel like victories—points I celebrate and allow myself to get excited over. New River just had first-fix electrics and plumbing installed, and the lobby and show apartment are nearly ready. I can finally see how incredible the finished project is going to be.

"Can you open the roof?" I ask my driver. I've already wound down the windows, but I need to feel as New York as it's possible to feel right now. I can't get enough of this awesome city and I want to experience it all. I wanna put my head out of the window, like a dog, and take in the scent of hot dog stands and overspilling garbage and the late September sun that I can see only if I look up to the sky. I want to hear beeping car horns and the shrieks of an unhappy restaurant owner yelling at someone in the street, or the construction workers calling to one another, taking up the road.

I owe everything I have to this city and my parents for bringing me here. There's nothing I don't love about it.

We pull up outside my building and I can't wait to get inside. The phenomenal views from my apartment are calling me; I want to look out onto the skyline and give thanks.

I burst into the apartment and immediately hear Bach's cello suites. I smile. Jules. Who knew that I'd actually look forward to coming home to a roommate?

The door slams behind me and I toe off my shoes before heading into the living space. The music turns off. Jules has heard I'm back.

"Hey," I call.

She pokes her head out of her bedroom. She's chewing. She swallows. "Hey." She comes out and leans against the doorjamb. "How are you? You look mighty happy."

She's holding a half-eaten apple in her hand. I grab her wrist and hold it up, then take a bite of her apple.

"Help yourself," she says, smiling at me as I chew.

This time it's my turn to swallow. "Jules, today is a good day!"

She follows me as I head to the windows of the apartment.

"New York Fucking City," I exclaim. "So great they named it twice." The low sun has turned the skyline dusky orange. It's fucking beautiful. "New York is the love of my fucking life."

She stands beside me, looking out over the city. "You win the lottery or something?" she asks.

"Sure did. Look at my life!"

She laughs. "Yeah, well, when you put it like that. But what happened today? You're not always so... chipper."

I chuckle and my eyes slide to hers. Her hair is on top of

her head in a messy bun with strands poking out all over. "Oh, I didn't even ask—how was your first day?"

She sighs. "I thought it was good, and then you arrive punching the air and doing your little New-York's-so-great dance."

"There's no dance."

"If I wasn't here, I bet there'd be a dance." She looks at me, beaming, and all I can think about is how I'd like to dance with her right this second.

But I'm not dancing with women. I'm having sex with women. That's as far as it goes. I'm not getting embroiled again. Not after making such a terrible mistake with Nadia.

"I just had my first walk around New River and it's great. The views are great. The space is great. It's... lovely."

"That's amazing, Leo. New River is going to be spectacular. I'd love to see it."

"Well, good, because you will see it. I'm having a cocktail party there in a week or so. We're launching the sales center. Did you get the email from Aesha?"

"I did. How's she working out for you?"

"She smiles more than you did when you were my assistant."

Jules laughs and it's like my joy cup is being topped up. She's dazzling when she smiles. "That wouldn't be difficult. But is she a good assistant?"

"She seems fine. You trained her well."

"Of course I did. I don't want to have to go back to that job. Anyway, she's a quick learner."

"Was it really so bad?" As soon as I've asked, I wish I hadn't. There's something in me that doesn't want to hear how bad working for me is. Not from her.

"No, of course it wasn't, but being back in the hotel

today... it's where I belong." She turns and takes a seat on one end of the sectional.

I grin at her. She's so relaxed, so comfortable. It's nice. I'm pleased she's here.

"Thanks for the flowers, by the way."

"My pleasure. How did it go?"

"It was interesting," she says. I pause, wanting her to expand a little bit. I go and get a glass of water from the kitchen. "It sounds kinda douche-y," she calls over to me. "But I see things differently now. I always knew there were areas to improve and things I'd do differently, but today, I saw some things I wasn't expecting to see. It was... disappointing."

"You want to elaborate?"

She laughs. "You don't give two shits about The Mayfair."

"I give *half* a shit about The Mayfair, but I definitely give *two* shits about your day, which happens to have taken place at The Mayfair."

She looks at me for a second, then two, then says, "Goddammit, Leo. Stay on-brand for all our sakes, will you?"

"If only I knew what that entailed."

"I'm going to hold fire before I tell you what happened today," she continues. "I want to do some more digging, figure more stuff out. Then I'll either find solutions or come up with a plan to solve the problems that may or may not require your input."

"How very cryptic," I reply.

"Not cryptic. But you're Just Leo here, right? Not my boss."

She has a point. "Fair enough." I join her on the sofa. "So tell me about when we met before. Was it a work context?"

She shakes her head. Maybe I'm imagining it, but all of a sudden she doesn't seem to be able to look me in the eye. Is she worried I'll be able to place her? Surely not. If I was going to figure out we'd met before, I'd have done it by now. She's been working for me for months.

"Give me a clue."

A grin twitches at the corners of her mouth. "My hair was a different color."

I squint. "What color?" She shrugs. Why is she being so reticent about this? Did I embarrass myself? Did she? I really hope we haven't slept together. "Why won't you tell me?"

"You want the whole list of reasons, or just my top three?"

"Absolutely. If there's a list, give me a list."

She stares out over Manhattan for a few seconds. "I think I can sum it up by saying I'm embarrassed."

What on earth could she be embarrassed about?

"Did we meet in Manhattan?"

She nods.

"If not in work, then at a bar?"

She nods again.

That doesn't really narrow it down. Manhattan has over ten thousand bars. And I'm pretty sure I've been to most of them over the last couple of years. "You're a tease," I say.

"Honestly, I'm not." Her expression is all worry. Despite the fact I want to know where we met, I don't want her to stress about it.

She stands. "I should go. I'm meeting Sophia for a cocktail. I need to change."

I can't help but stare at her as she walks past me on the sofa. *Have* I seen her before? And just then, as she turns her head back to look at me, I see something. There's a glimmer of recognition.

"Hey," I say.

She stops and turns to face me. I stand so we're just a couple of feet apart. And then I see it—can't possibly *unsee* it. And I realize why I haven't recognized her before now. "You're Mystique."

She rolls her eyes and goes to leave, but I grab her arm.

"Hey, wait a minute."

She stills, and I drop my hand.

"You never called me."

She lets out a cynical laugh. "Nope. But I'm sure one of the other girls you gave your number to that night did."

"What?"

"I have to go."

"Just wait a minute. What are you talking about?"

She puts her hands on her hips. "Yeah, I went to the no-costume party in a costume."

"It was a great costume." She'd looked absolutely phenomenal. I remember being mesmerized by her beautiful eyes and trying my best to keep my eyes above her neck. She was fire. And I loved the fact she'd followed the comic book version of the character and not just done the obvious route with the movie version. But it was more than just her costume that had me interested that night. I felt a connection to her that I hadn't felt in a long time. She seemed so... down-to-earth. Despite the fact she was blue, she wasn't trying too hard. She was being one hundred percent herself. As much as I love New York, that's rare.

Her smile that night is still etched in my brain. I've thought about that woman more than once since that night.

And now here she is, right in front of me.

She nods her head in agreement. "Yeah. And I had to go."

"Yeah, you were playing wingman to your friend. But I gave you my number because you wouldn't give me yours. But you never called because..."

"Because I could see you were a..."

I lift my eyebrows, waiting for her to finish her sentence.

"So that's our history," she says. "No big secret."

"But why are you embarrassed?"

"You mean other than the fact that I was dressed as a bright blue mutant at a very non-costume party? Oh, and that you gave your number to another girl *minutes* after you thought I'd left?"

Had I given my number out to someone else? I remember being gutted Mystique never reappeared. I thought I'd left right after. "I didn't give my number to anyone else," I say, searching my brain. The night had lost all its shine after she left. I remember leaving a little deflated, disappointed that Mystique had left but excited about having met her. I know I didn't leave with anyone that night. I remember my head being full of... a bright blue mutant.

She rolls her eyes at me. "I went to the restroom and came out and watched you hand your phone to a woman who typed in—her number presumably. Then she handed it back to—"

"Oh my god!" I interrupt, finally putting the pieces of the puzzle together. "You mean Jean!"

"Her name was Jean? As in Grey?" She rolls her eyes. "Don't tell me, your baby sister, right?" she says sarcastically, anticipating a lie from me. She really has some trust issues.

"No, not my baby sister. My hair stylist. She'd moved

from the salon where she'd been cutting my hair for years to set up on her own. She wanted me to switch."

"Of course she did."

I shrug. "I can't make you believe me." What could I do to convince her? I don't know if I have any actual evidence. I know I shouldn't have to prove that I'm telling the truth, and Jules' distrust doesn't make me bristle; instead, it just helps me see that something's broken inside her.

I pull out my phone. "She messaged me that Monday. What date was the party?" I glance up at her.

"Twelfth of April, two years ago."

I go to search and then look back to Jules. How did she have that date so close to mind?

"What?" she asks. "I remember dates."

I find Jean's thread of messages and scroll back to the fourteenth of April. "Here," I say, offering her my phone.

"Riiight," she says sarcastically. But she takes my phone and scrolls through, skimming the messages, then hands it back to me. Some of the edge has gone out of her voice when she says, "Maybe you're right."

"I'm serious. I remember wondering how long it would take you to message me, and then you never did."

She looks at me for a beat, then finally says, "Just think, if I'd have called you, we'd probably be married right now."

I can't help but smile at her. I can see clearly she wears a veneer of *I don't care*, but now that I know her a bit more, I can tell how fragile that veneer is.

"I was disappointed you didn't call," I say. "And we're not married yet, but we're heading in the right direction, judging by your left ring finger."

She lets out a laugh, and I can feel pride push against my chest. "Thank god I misunderstood. I might have called and you'd be a fake fiancée down." Our eyes catch. She looks away first. "But I didn't and here we are. And yes, I got the list from Aesha. I'll make sure I'm fiancée material on Friday night."

Part of me wants to steer the conversation back to that night at the party. I want her to know that I really liked her and was hoping she'd call. But what good would it do? We're trying to be friends. Anything more would lead to mess and complications.

"Good. I'm glad Aesha's on it. If you need anything to wear, I have an account at Bergdorf's."

"What does that mean?"

"What do you think it means? It means if you need anything, go to Bergdorf's and put it on my account." She starts to laugh, and I turn to watch. I can't not. "What?" I ask.

"I should just go and buy whatever I want?"

I shrug. "If you need something. If you were actually my fiancée, that's what I'd say, isn't it?"

"I have no idea. I've never been a billionaire's fiancée before. Or anyone's for that matter. The idea of someone paying for my clothes—or anything—it's... a lot. Unusual to say the least."

"You don't have to go."

She starts to laugh again. "I promise only to buy the bare minimum of what a fiancée of yours might need."

I get a flash of her in a changing room, undressing in front of a mirror. I turn back to the view of the city.

Messy and complicated, I remind myself. And I'm not up for either.

FIFTEEN

Leo

Jules has just messaged that she'll arrive outside of New River in about two minutes, so I call the lift to go meet her. It will be good to have a few moments alone to compose ourselves as a couple. This is a high-profile event and we need to look like the newly engaged pair I want the world to believe we are.

Thinking about it, we probably should have started off a little slower—maybe had dinner out in public together. I'm used to Jules the assistant: grumpy, efficient, chastising. And I'm used to Jules the roommate: effortlessly cool, funny, and a master at mac and cheese with a little bit of vulnerability simmering below the surface. But who will Jules the fiancée be?

My heart starts to pound in my chest as the lift descends and I realize I can't wait to find out.

The doors open and she's on the other side of them.

When she realizes it's me standing in front of her, she breaks out into the biggest smile. "Hi!"

"Hi," I say, slightly breathless. Slightly dazzled.

"Are you okay?" she asks. "Are you leaving?"

I shake my head and hold the doors open so she can walk in. "I came down to meet you. So you wouldn't get lost."

"That's nice," she says as she steps in and the doors close. "Is everything going to plan?"

"I think so. My realtors have done all the party aspects. My team just had to have everything ready on time."

"You look handsome," she says.

"*You* look stunning." Her dress comes to mid-thigh, one-shouldered and red with ruffles everywhere. It's not too sexy, but just sexy enough. Her lipstick matches her dress and somehow it makes her lips look bigger and more tempting.

"Thanks," she says. "Bergdorf's did okay, right?"

"I'm not sure Bergdorf's can take the credit."

She smiles again. I want to press the emergency stop button and see if her lips are as soft as they look. But I don't. I just return her smile and wonder what she's thinking.

We reach the twentieth floor and the lift doors open. "Oh," she says. "It's all done. I was expecting a construction site."

"Just the lobby and this floor. Just to give people a taste of how everything will look."

"You're so smart," she says, not a trace of sarcasm in her voice.

I start out of the lift toward the door of one of two planned penthouses.

"Leo," she whisper-shouts.

I turn back, and her eyes widen like she's expecting me to remember something I've forgotten.

"You should hold my hand," she says.

I take in a breath and nod. She's right. I should. Except...

I glance over at the waiters and waitresses pouring glasses of champagne and organizing trays of canapes. I turn back to Jules, who's standing right in front of me. She reaches for my bow tie, giving it a little tug. "Very cute."

"Cute? Don't you mean commanding, powerful, with a little danger mixed in?"

She wrinkles her nose. "So, *so* cute."

I chuckle and shake my head. When she's finished, I scoop up her hand and lead her through the penthouse entrance and into the main living area.

"So this is the penthouse to New River," I announce. I hope she's impressed. Construction and the realtors have worked their asses off to get this ready for tonight's launch.

"Do I get a tour?" she says, squeezing my hand.

"Sure, let's start with the kitchen and see if it meets your high standards."

"Tell me about the kind of buyer you expect to want a place like this," she says.

"Well, it's a five-million-dollar apartment, so I'm hoping they have some money behind them, but they can be young and self-made. This kind of place doesn't require your parents to be rich. It's aimed at someone who would have bought downtown ten years ago but is just priced out. They're making money downtown though. I see our target buyers as young professionals who want to stay in Manhattan, who don't have kids, or maybe older people who've moved upstate, want a *pied-à-terre* in town, but don't want to pay Upper East Side prices."

"Makes sense." I watch her as she traces her fingers along the countertops of the kitchen, opening cabinets, peering into the oven. "It's nice," she says. "Modern with a twist."

"Right. That was the look we were going for. And the finishes are good, right?"

"Better than you'd normally see in the area?" she asks.

"Right. The area is up and coming and this is one of the first new-construction residential blocks. People need an incentive to come here. They want a good price for good space and finishes."

"I'm sold," she says. "When do we move in? You can carry me over the threshold."

Our eyes lock and I can't help but picture that—her heels kicking in the air as I carry her inside. "We'll have to find another place. I told you, I'm not living in my own development again."

"Oh yes, that's right. Does Bergdorf's sell houses? Maybe I can pop out on my lunch break tomorrow and pick one up."

I grin at her and we just stand there, facing each other and smiling like idiots. If I hadn't had my ass handed to me by Nadia over the summer, if everything was different, I would have to kiss Jules right now.

Aesha interrupts. "Leo," she calls, appearing just a second later. "Sorry, I didn't mean to interrupt, but Tyler Groves is here and I thought you'd want to say hi."

"Thanks, Aesha." She's right, I do want to say hi. He's a dick, but he's also one of the top agents in the city. I've known him since my bread delivery days. His father set up in competition with Caroline's, and I remember Caroline being really cut up about it.

Jules slides her hand into mine and we head out. I glance down at the ring on her left hand and heat fills my chest. It's a sense of possessiveness I'm not used to. I like seeing her wear the ring I bought her—a not-so-subtle message to the rest of the world that this woman is mine.

"Tyler," I call as he spots me across the living space. His hair is slicked back and he has that year-round perma-tan. Some things never change. I drop Jules' hand only long enough to shake Tyler's. "Good to see you." We greet each other and shake hands and his eyes slide to Jules.

"This is Jules Moore. My fiancée."

"Whoa, congratulations," he says, eyeing Jules up and down. "I didn't know."

He and Jules shake hands before Aesha calls me away to meet someone else. She asked me for names of people I wanted to make sure I spoke to tonight, and I gave her five. She said she'd make sure I saw them all, and so far, she's being true to her word. She's a good assistant. Jules did well recruiting her, not that I'm surprised.

I greet Andrew Feinstein, who is looking to invest in my next project in Harlem. I show him around and talk to him in more depth, but wherever we go, I'm aways aware of Jules. It's like she's my energy source or something, and I need to stay tethered to her in some way to avoid depleting my tank.

"Thanks for coming tonight," I say. "I thought it would be a useful comparison to the development we're talking about doing together. It's similar, but with important differences."

He nods, his gaze skirting the room. "It's interesting. I haven't been up in this area for a while."

I'm so fucking lucky to get Andrew here tonight. He's the kind of money man who doesn't leave his desk, and I knew the idea of developing in this area didn't sit comfortably for him. It was too risky. Being here will make all the difference.

My gaze catches on Jules. She's laughing at something Tyler's saying to her. I want her next to me. "Let me introduce you to my fiancée," I say.

"You're engaged?" he asks, a note of shock in his voice.

"It's recent. We haven't actually done any kind of formal announcement yet." I lift my chin in her direction. "She's the one in the red."

"I should have brought my wife," he says. "Maybe the four of us can go out to dinner?"

"Absolutely. Let me get her so you can meet." Andrew could meet her at dinner, but it's a useful excuse to get her away from Tyler.

I stride towards Jules and hear her talking to Tyler.

She laughs. "He's actually very kind and thoughtful."

He mutters something low and a little too close to her. She noticeably moves her body away from him. What's that asshole saying? I bet he's hitting on her.

Someone I don't recognize stops me and shakes my hand, congratulating me on the development. I smile and thank them, but I'm listening to the conversation Jules is having with Tyler.

"No," she says, a little more forcefully. "I don't think that at all. He's a good man."

She looks up as I join the two of them, her eyes filled with relief and gratitude. Instantly I want to punch Tyler in the mouth. Jules is tough. She doesn't need saving, so why is she so pleased to see me?

I slide my arm around Jules' waist. "Excuse me, Tyler, I'm going to whisk my fiancée away."

I don't give him time to respond, guiding Jules away from him, my hand on the small of her back.

I lower my lips to her ear as we walk. "Are you okay?" I ask.

"That guy's a dick."

"Couldn't agree more. Was he rude to you? Inappropriate? I can have him kicked out. Hell, I can kick him out myself."

She shakes her head. "No, he wasn't rude to me. I mean, he came on to me, which was—"

"Came on to you?" I growl, glancing back toward where we left that absolute shit stain.

"It was fine. I told him I wasn't interested." Jules tugs at my lapel to get my attention, and I look down into her eyes. "He's not a good guy. He was rude about you. I would have kneed him in the balls if this wasn't your party."

That makes me smile. "You'd have assaulted him because he was rude about me or because he came on to you?"

She slips her hand into mine and a sense of peace settles over me. "He was *really* rude about you."

"Don't sweat it," I say. "He's rude about everyone. I've known him a long time. I don't take it personally."

"You guys are friends?"

I chuckle. "Absolutely not. He wouldn't even talk to me when I was starting out in the business. Now he's always trying to collaborate. I keep him around to torture him." He's not the only one. It's exactly the same with Hammonds.

"He was trying to convince me I shouldn't marry you."

"How ironic," I say. "So when you were talking to him and describing someone as a good man and kind and thoughtful, were you...?" I trail off.

"He doesn't know you at all," she says.

I glance down at her. She's right, he doesn't. But does *she*?

"Andrew," I say, as we arrive back where I started, "let me introduce Jules. Jules, Andrew and I might be working together on another Harlem development."

"It's such a cool building, isn't it?" Jules says, the perfect, devoted fiancée. It's a role that seems to come easily to her. "And just what the area needs."

"Couldn't agree more," Andrew says. "I was just saying to Leo that you and my wife should join us for dinner."

Jules doesn't miss a beat, doesn't throw me a look that says, "Is this on the schedule?" As far as fake fiancées go, I got a good one. "That would be lovely. Is your wife here tonight?"

"She's not, she's working. Lawyer, big case—you know how it is."

"Jules just started working as manager of The Mayfair," I say. I'm not showing off exactly, but Jules is clever and capable and should get kudos for that.

"Oh nice. That sounds like a lot of work."

As she smiles, she practically radiates positivity. "It's a lot of work, but also a lot of fun. My background is in hotels. Worked in them since I was sixteen. I don't really know anything else."

Sixteen? I don't think I knew that about her. Had she mentioned it when she was trying to sell me on the idea of her managing The Mayfair? I wonder if she was polishing mirrors in a fancy hotel while I was delivering bread to the kitchen of the same place. Our paths could have crossed a million times in this city, although I am a little older than her. I slide my hand onto her hip and pull her toward me, wanting her closer, as she and Andrew continue to talk.

I tune back into their conversation just as Andrew says,

"If you're ever looking for another job, let me know. I have plenty of contacts in hospitality." He hands her a card.

She shoots me a smile and thanks him, ensuring him she'll be in touch. It's certainly on-brand for Jules—always keeping me on my toes. But the more I get to know her, the more I know I'm going to work hard not to lose her. She's too valuable... an employee.

SIXTEEN

Leo

It's official: Jules Moore is trying to kill me. I'm doing my best not to stare at her legs while she sits next to me in the limo, but she's hot AF tonight. I've managed to avoid her most of the week. I needed to take a step back after our evening together. She'd just been so... perfect in her role as my fiancée, so dazzling, so entirely attractive. Luckily, I've been busy at work and so has she. I was only in one night, when she happened to be out. So here we are. Dressed up and ready to go to the opening of Vault in SoHo.

"The woman says I can resell it and get more than I paid—or *you* paid for it, so long as I don't ruin it," she says.

"What?" I missed everything she just said as I've been running through all the reasons I shouldn't find Jules attractive. It's not a short list.

"My bag. It's Chanel and cost a fortune. But it's what everyone with money wears, so I thought it would be appropriate. I just don't want you to think I'm not thinking about the money. I know it's expensive, but if I can resell it and get more than you paid for it, I'm actually making you money."

"You don't need to return the bag," I say, distracted.

"It was ten and a half thousand dollars, Leo," she counters.

"Keep it. If we manage to pull this off, it's worth far more to me than ten thousand dollars."

"And a half. Don't forget the half. It represents five hundred dollars. Anyway, I'm not keeping the bag. Changing the subject, are we expecting to meet anyone at this restaurant? Do you know the owner or something?"

"Not expecting to meet anyone, but Manhattan's a small place." In a city of over a million people, it should be easy to be anonymous, but gossip spreads quickly in this town. You never know who's watching and whispering. My profile's higher than ever in the business community. Even if I don't know someone personally, they always know someone I know. "I would normally say no to this kind of thing."

"Yeah, you rarely say yes to anything. It always surprised me about you when I was your assistant."

"I like what I like. I have my favorite restaurants and bars. I have a small circle of friends who I trust... Everything else is just noise."

She doesn't answer right away. I turn from the window to find her staring at me. Our eyes lock.

"Is your family still in Brooklyn?"

"Moved down to Florida, although they have a place up here. Heading south started off as something they did in the winter and now... my dad's golf handicap is seven."

"That sounds like he's really bad at golf."

I chuckle. "It means he's really *good* at golf. Much to my mother's annoyance. Last time I was down there, she told me she won't miss my father when he's dead because he's never around anyway."

"Wow," she replies, and I try not to focus on her pout as she speaks.

"Yeah, she's brutal. But she also loves him. She's a pretty good golfer too. She just doesn't want to do it every day."

"It's nice that they're still together."

"It doesn't sound like it, but they were made for each other."

"They must be very proud of you."

She looks at me with a softness I'm not used to. "They're proud of me *and* my brother."

"Oooh a brother," she says.

A lick of jealousy crawls up my throat. "He's married," I reply. "Happily."

She laughs. "I wasn't asking for his number. You've just never mentioned him before."

"We're not close. He's quite a bit younger than me. Went to college in state. My parents had a bit more money by that point. Met his high school sweetheart, settled down in Long Island. He has a good life." I can feel her heavy gaze turn assessing. "What about you? Any siblings whose numbers I need?"

She grins. "Only child, I'm afraid."

I nod. "And are your parents still together?"

"Absolutely not. My father..." She pulls in a breath like she's steeling herself for something. "He wasn't around much when I was growing up. He'd blow in and out of town. Not very reliable, to put it generously."

Shit, that doesn't sound good. "Sounds like a bit of an asshole."

She shrugs and I want her to say more. Maybe now isn't the time.

"New York is full of assholes. Hell, if the hotel manager thing doesn't work out for me, I might try and develop a spray to keep them at bay."

She deflects with humor. Noted. I'm going to go with it.

"I think they did that already? It's called pepper spray."

She smiles just as the car rolls to a stop outside the restaurant.

"Stay put and I'll come around and open your door," I say.

There are a couple of photographers outside, probably trying to grab a shot of some celebrity. Most of the journalists will be inside.

I open the car door and extend my hand. When she takes it, heat courses through me. She looks fucking fantastic and feels even better.

"So tonight is about letting the public see how happily engaged we are?" she whispers in my ear as she stands. "We're not aiming to talk to anyone in particular?"

"No, let's just focus on enjoying ourselves. You know, like an engaged couple."

"That won't be a problem," she says, her tone warm and relaxed like we really are engaged and she's looking forward to an evening out with the lucky bastard who's her fiancé.

She's right. Being with her feels good. She's funny and smart and a lot goes on beneath her surface. More and more I just want to strip down and dive in—literally and figuratively.

Once we're inside, we're shown to a courtyard at the back of the restaurant, where people are enjoying drinks and canapes. There are a few high tables nestled among three olive trees growing out here.

"This is so pretty," she says. "And although cobblestones would have looked nicer, no woman in New York wants to go to dinner somewhere with cobbled floors. The tiles really work. And the electric blue keeps it modern."

"You sound like an interior designer."

"I've just worked in hospitality a long time. I've seen a few things. This is smart," she says, slipping her hand into mine. "It's a real selling point of a restaurant in New York to have a space like this, but not everyone can get a table out here tonight. Better to serve canapes and drinks without worrying about seating anyone, then serve dinner inside." Her gaze continues to roam around the space as if she's trying to memorize every little detail. "I'd love to do something like this at The Mayfair with the roof deck. These tiles are such a clever choice."

"Isn't that a staff area?"

Her eyebrows lift. "Exactly. A total waste of lucrative space. You know better than anyone that fresh air is at a premium in New York, and there's nowhere better to take it in than a rooftop. It could be a great bar space."

I grin at her. She was right—I'm not going to regret hiring her. She's so sharp.

"You're probably right," I say. "Just don't ask me for more investment."

"Honey, you just bought me a Chanel bag. It was ten and a half thousand dollars and I didn't even kiss you. Maybe I should marry you for real and get some capital investment for my hotel."

I chuckle, scanning the outdoor space again as I do. My gaze catches on something. *Someone*. I freeze. I've not seen her in a decade, but I'd know Caroline Hammond at a mile away. I know her laugh at ten miles away. It still echoes in my ears. My heart begins to rev like a race car engine on the starting line.

"Are you okay?" Jules asks, tugging on my hand.

"Sure," I say, pulling in a breath and trying to block out the boom, boom, boom in my ears.

"You don't look okay."

"I just saw someone I was hoping to avoid..." Until the awards ceremony.

"Do I need to kill someone?"

I blink and try to focus on Jules. "What?"

"Oh wow, I offer to murder someone and you don't turn me down flat. I need to know who we're talking about."

"It's nothing." The hostess has started to guide people inside for dinner. My mind spins ahead. If I can get to our table without running into Caroline, maybe our paths won't cross. I'm not prepared to see her. I'm not in the right headspace.

"Well, it's obviously something," Jules says, sweeping her hand over my shoulder and stepping in close. My hand naturally rests at her waist. To the rest of the world, we look like a couple who can't keep their hands off each other.

"I didn't expect photographers inside the venue," I say, nodding toward a man with a camera. She can probably tell it's bullshit, but it's some kind of response.

We're interrupted by a hostess offering to show us to our table. Jules and I follow her hand in hand.

We're seated in the corner of the room, where I take the seat facing the wall. It's a nice, secluded spot. I don't turn to see what's going on to the side or behind me. The last thing I want is Caroline Hammond coming over to say hello like she's a long-lost friend. I need to encounter her for the first time at the awards. I'll be ready for her then.

Instead, I keep my attention on Jules.

"Do you want to share some apps?" Jules asks from across the table. She knows something's off, but I appreciate her not pushing me to reveal what.

"Sure." Her mouth is pulled into a smile. She looks worried. "I'm fine," I say.

She reaches across the table and links her fingers into mine. I can't tell if it's for show or because she's trying to provide comfort. Whatever the reason, I like it. Too much.

Our waitress comes over and we order, after I promise that Jules can have a taste of my potatoes.

"Why don't I just get the kitchen to do you a separate order of potatoes?" I ask.

"Because it's launch night and the chefs and waitstaff have got enough to do. I bet it's chaos in the kitchen. I'd put money on someone getting killed by the end of the night." She pauses and narrows her eyes. "Or at least punched."

"What a happy thought. Behind the scenes in hospitality sounds brutal."

Her eyes widen. "It's like the Hunger Games, but worse, because you never get out. And the odds are *never* in your favor."

I can't help but laugh.

"And he's back," she says, grinning at me. "I thought I lost you for a minute back there."

"Sorry, I just—"

"You don't need to explain," she says brightly.

I should tell her. After all, the awards are coming up soon and she should know before then. If she was my real fiancée, I would have told her. "I just saw a woman from my past."

She looks at me, her eyebrows raised like she's waiting for a punchline.

"We were engaged for a minute there. I haven't seen her in a long time."

She swallows down the bread she was chewing. "You had a *real* fiancée? And she's here tonight?"

"It didn't last long." Her father had her enrolled at Berkeley ten days after she told him about the engagement. And then two weeks after that, she ended it. Officially. "I was eighteen, but yes, I asked to marry her. I was... I thought we were in love." Looking back, Caroline was clearly never in love with me, but I was so besotted by her. I worshipped her. She seemed wise and sophisticated, and the fact that she'd picked me... I'd felt like the luckiest guy in New York.

"But you weren't in love?" Jules asks.

"Can anyone be in love at eighteen?"

"Why not?" she says. "Is there an age threshold I don't know about—you know, beyond the age of consent and stuff?"

"I was a very different man back then."

She wrinkles her nose. "Really? I'm not sure I believe that."

"I was still working for my dad, doing bread deliveries around the city starting at four in the morning. I had nothing." *I was nothing,* I don't add.

"But what you have doesn't make you who you are," she replies simply. "I imagine you are much the man you are now. Handsome. Kind. Hardworking. Not the slightest bit interested in owning a hotel."

I grin at her. "Maybe you're right on that last bit."

"And this woman you were engaged to, what happened? Did she break your heart?"

"And soul and spirit."

"Whoa. Dramatic much?" She laughs and the corners of my lips twitch despite the unanticipated stress of the evening. "What in the hell happened? Did she knock you out and sell one of your kidneys?" She narrows her eyes like she's actually waiting for me to confirm she's right.

I sit back. "Fuck. You heard about it?"

Her jaw goes slack and she covers her mouth with her hand.

I roll my eyes. "No, she didn't sell my kidney. Are you for real?"

She starts to laugh. Tears are forming in her eyes. "You see? It's not as bad as it could have been."

I can't argue with that.

"And she didn't run off with your dad and become your stepmom, because your parents are still happily married, so... how bad could it be?"

"Holy shit, Jules, what's in that brain of yours? I'm seriously concerned."

"My mom thought I should write crime novels because my imagination is so much worse than the reality of the world." She sighs as our apps are delivered. "But actually, I think I'm always expecting the worst, or trying to imagine what the worst-case scenario might be. Because..."

"Because?"

She shrugs, taking something involving an aubergine from one of the three plates in the middle of the table. "God, I love eggplant, don't you?"

More deflection.

"Not a fan particularly, so knock yourself out."

"Not a fan of eggplant? How is that possible?"

"Tell me about you always looking for the worst outcome."

"I used to think everyone did it, until my roommate, Sophia, told me I was freaking her out. I'm just always one step ahead, trying to foretell the catastrophe that's about to happen. Then I try to plan for that, strategize. If I go into a situation with a plan for the worst-case scenario, I know I'm going to be okay."

She says it in the light, breezy way she has, but what she's saying is dark. It's really sad.

"Why?" I ask.

She looks me right in the eye and moans. "God, it's such good eggplant. With the parm." She makes a chef's kiss with her fingers, but I don't respond.

I want an answer.

There's a couple of beats of silence before she says, "I think because lots of bad things happened when I was a kid. I think I'm wired to expect the worst." Her words feel like they're winding around my lungs, making it hard to breathe.

"What kind of bad things?"

She rolls her eyes. "I still have my kidneys, if that's what you're thinking."

"That's not what I'm thinking." I don't want her to joke her way out of this. I want to hear about it.

"I guess now I'm the one being dramatic. It's not *that* bad in the list of bad things that can happen to a kid. But my dad was an asshole, always coming and going, like I said. Even when I was really little, I don't remember him being with us for long. I remember our neighbors in the next apartment would babysit me when my mom went to work in the mornings. I didn't understand until years later that she took the job in the hotel because it finished at three, which meant she could pick me up from the bus and make me dinner and put me to bed."

Her voice cracks on the last word. She swallows and pulls her shoulders back.

"Anyway, my dad would breeze into town like he'd been at work for the day, like I saw him that morning, even when he'd been gone for months at a time. When he'd arrive on our stoop, I'd be so happy to see him. He always brought me a toy or a book or something that was what I'd always wanted. I'd start to imagine the three of us as a family, hitting the beach, playing cards, moving to the country and picking apples from an orchard behind our house. We'd have all kinds of contests—tickling contests, copycat contests, smiling contests... I'd always be the happiest I'd ever been. And then he'd just disappear. He'd go out for milk or to get a paper or something, and he wouldn't come back." She pauses, and I know she's picturing those times in her head. "I'd cry and cry and grieve him every time."

Fuck.

This time, it's me who reaches for her hand across the table, but she pulls it away and shakes her head.

I get it. She doesn't want to lose it here. Maybe not ever, but definitely not in public.

"He sounds like a fucking *ass*hole," I say, my voice tight, fists bunched. What a dick of dicks to do that to a little kid. "Do you see him now?"

She shakes her head again and I can see the tears welling in her eyes, despite her best efforts to keep them at bay. "No. I have no interest in seeing him. My mom is my family. And my aunt."

"Shit, I'm so sorry," I say. I want to make it better for her, but I don't know how. We could leave. We don't have to be here. Maybe some deflection is what she needs. "But at least you have your kidneys."

She bursts into laughter, dabbing her napkin at the corner of her eyes, where tears had been threatening to fall. "Exactly," she says. "Could have been a lot worse."

Our appetizers are replaced with our entrees and there's no aubergine to distract Jules now.

"So you still haven't told me the story with your fiancée," she says.

She spilled her heart out to me. It's only fair that I tell

her why she's sitting opposite me with a huge diamond ring on her finger.

"You thought you were in love with her and she with you. And you proposed."

"And then her dad found out and shipped her off to college on the other side of the country. She was due to go to NYU and ended up at Berkeley."

"And that was it?" she asks.

Don't I wish. "I told my dad I was leaving the bakery so I could follow her out west. It caused loads of rows. My mum told me I was throwing my life away. My dad didn't speak to me for weeks. Anyway, two weeks later, I road-tripped to California. I'd told Caroline I was coming. I figured I'd get a job locally and she'd continue in college... apparently she didn't see things the same way."

"I'm taking it things didn't end happily ever after."

"No. She laughed and said she never expected me to actually follow her." I haven't told anyone this for years. In fact, I think only Bennett knows the whole story even now. But there's something about Jules that makes me want to be my whole self with her. I don't need to water things down. I have no doubt she's on my team. Whatever I tell her won't change what she thinks of me.

"But you told her you were coming to California."

I shrug. "I guess she was seeing how far she could push me."

"So she was—what, taunting you? Testing you?"

"She was trying to aggravate her father. I was caught in the crossfire. I just wish it hadn't taken me so long to see it. Looking back with twenty-twenty hindsight, it was obvious."

"There were signs?"

"My family saw it. Everyone but me apparently. We

rarely spent any time with her friends. And she never wanted to hang out with mine. But I was in love. I just wanted to be with her. I happily dropped my friends like a burning log. She didn't, which was fine. But there were evenings when she went out with her girlfriends, except the group that appeared on social media involved plenty of guys. And I was making a lot of the effort. But what did I know? I was eighteen and she was a total princess. I assumed that was how things were supposed to be. And I was happy to do it, you know. I just wanted her to be happy."

She nods. "Because you were in love."

"Right." I pause, wondering if I thought I was in love with Nadia this summer, but no, I hadn't even been close. She'd just been around. I think I'd gone along with what she wanted because the sex was good.

"So when you turned up in California, she broke off the engagement?"

"If you mean laughed in my face, then yes, she broke off the engagement."

"What do you mean, laughed?"

"She said, 'Oh, you really would do anything for me, wouldn't you?' Then she told me she'd just been trying to piss off her dad the entire time we were together. I think the last thing she said to me was, 'You didn't think I was actually going to marry you, did you?' Then she reminded me of her last name." Thoughts of her, of that day, churn in my gut, and I get the urge to run. To bail out of this restaurant, to tell *Property International* I'm not going to accept the award. I don't want to see Caroline Hammond again. Not ever.

"Sounds like a keeper," Jules says, and I can't help but laugh.

"Right."

"And she's going to be at the awards."

I freeze. I hadn't said anything about the awards. "How did you guess?"

She pulls in a breath. "I never understood the whole 'I need a fiancée for business reasons' thing. But if she's going to be there, it all makes sense."

"Her father is the Hammond at the head of Hammonds. Caroline's husband is taking over, and they're sponsoring the awards to show how strong the company still is, I guess."

"Urgh," Jules says. "That's so pathetic. So she's not even taking over. Her husband is. Does she do anything beyond have her nails done and go to the spa?"

"The family has a lot of money. She doesn't need to work."

"You have a lot of money. You don't have to work, but you work harder than anyone I've ever known."

"You always beat me to the office."

She winces.

"What?"

"I used to go in early to work on my plans for The Mayfair."

"So? You were still working."

"Yeah, I work hard," she admits. "But I bet Caroline Hammond doesn't. And so you want a fiancée on your arm when you meet her because, why? You're a self-made billionaire, you're handsome as all holy fuck. Any woman in American would want to marry you. What could you possibly have to prove to her?"

I push my hand back into my hair. "Yeah. I just..."

She looks at me, her gaze dipping to my mouth and then back up to my eyes. "What?"

"We never had much money growing up," I say. "We

had a roof over our heads and food on the table, but we never had anything spare. I was happy, don't get me wrong. I never felt like... I never felt small in the way Caroline managed to make me feel. And you're right, I have the money, but I want her to know that I share a life with someone who made the right choice."

"No," Jules says. "You want to prove to her that she didn't crush your soul. That she didn't break you." She pauses. "And in order to be able to prove that, you need to lie, because there's still a part of you that's a little bit broken."

I blink, and blink again. I wonder if I just imagined what Jules just said.

"I think it's just... I don't want any chinks in my armor when I see her. I don't want her to be able to point to anything in my life and say, 'I did better than you.'"

"I vote for my theory," she says. "Either way, I'm right there by your side. And I'm going to Bergdorf's this week to buy something that will make her look like she's wearing the housekeeping uniform from The Mayfair."

She sounds like she's coaching me back into the boxing ring. The corner of my mouth turns up. Right here, right now, Jules Moore might be my favorite person on the planet.

"Whatever you wear, you'll outshine her."

"What about the pantsuit I wore when I was your assistant?"

"Oh, your asshole-repelling outfit?" I shrug. "Never worked on me."

"It kinda did," she says. "It's not like you ever made a pass at me."

"Because you *worked* for me, not because I didn't find you attractive."

She shrugs. She clearly thinks I'm lying. "If you say so."

"I say so. I have a strict policy of not dating women I work with. So yes, I tuned out that side of you."

She starts to laugh. "You tuned me out?" She wrinkles her nose and brings up her shoulders as if she's hugging a teddy bear or something. "You say the *cutest* things to me."

"What are fiancés for?" I ask. There's no way I'm getting out of this hole. The only thing I can do is stop digging.

The fact is, I'm tuned all the way into Jules Moore, no matter how she's dressed.

SEVENTEEN

Leo

Despite having to share air with Caroline Hammond, I had a great night tonight. I follow Jules out of the restaurant, enjoying the sight of her as I do. As soon as we get outside, she stops and turns so suddenly, I almost run into her.

"Can I suggest something?" she asks, her eyes full of mischief.

"What?" I ask.

"Promise you'll say yes?"

Her smile is infectious and I can't help but grin back. God only knows what she's up to. But right now, I don't care. I want to be carried along by her enthusiasm. "Okay, I promise."

She grabs my arm and squeezes me, like I just told her the manager job at The Mayfair is hers permanently. "Tell your driver to meet us in a couple of blocks. Let's walk for as long as these shoes will let me. I love these late summer nights. We haven't got many left."

I chuckle. She gets an unrestricted promise from me and walking home is what she asks for?

Just as I press send on a text to my driver, asking him to follow us in the car, a boom of thunder sounds above us.

Jules' eyes widen and she bursts out laughing. "Looks like we're getting wet."

I expect her to change her mind about the walk, but she just slides her hand into mine and we begin to stroll. It's late, but New York doesn't want to sleep tonight. There are people everywhere and the traffic is rush-hour heavy. Quarter-sized drops splat onto the pavement as we head west. I peek up at the sky, wondering how quickly we're likely to be drenched.

"Why don't we just drive with the windows down?" I suggest.

"Because we'll be home too quickly and I'm not ready for tonight to end."

Something pulls in my gut. I'm not sure if it's because Jules just called my place home or because she wants tonight to continue some more. Maybe it's because I feel the same way.

"We can do a circuit of the park," I suggest.

She grins and her eyelashes flutter away the rain. "You promise we can keep the windows down?"

I nod and put a hand out to my driver, who's just behind us.

As soon as we slide into the car, Jules lets down her window and glances as me. "Come on," she says. "We need New York turned up to full volume tonight." It's exactly how I felt when New River's first fix was complete. This is a city of so many possibilities. We just have to open our arms.

I stare at her, completely unable to reconcile the

grumpy assistant she was in my office with the fresh, light, complex woman sitting next to me.

"A promise is a promise," she says, reaching across me to hit the button that lowers the window. Our faces are so close now; she looks up at me, smiling, and all I can think about is how beautiful she is. I catch her wrist and I let the window down myself, but I don't release her or take my eyes from her.

The light must change because the car jolts and Jules gets pushed even closer to me, her arms on my chest, her lips an inch from mine.

"I'm going to kiss you," I warn, giving her plenty of time to object.

When she doesn't, I cup the back of her head and press my lips to hers.

The scent of New York ebbs away as we kiss, the chatter of tourists on Broadway being accosted by street sellers turns to whispers, competing music from bars and restaurants and the inevitable honk of impatient New York drivers all fade into the distance. All I can think about is how she's the calm in this storm—the light in this darkness, the sun to my frozen heart.

I slide my hand up Jules' thigh and pull her onto my lap, our lips never parting. She tastes of honey and heat and evening jasmine. Her fingertips skim my cheekbones as my hand travels up her skirt. Not all the way, because that's not how I want this to go. Not in the back of a car like this. But enough so I feel more of her, am surrounded by her.

Tonight, things have shifted between us, although maybe it's not just tonight. Maybe this has been threatening for a while, like the storm waiting to break over the city. The more I get to know Jules, the more I want to know. The more every inexplicable thing about her becomes not only understandable, but compelling, the more I'm drawn in. I feel like I *get* her. And she gets me.

The car is stopped for a while and I glance out the window. We're outside my building. We break our kiss and Jules goes to slip out of the car, but I grab her hand as she exits. I don't want to let her go.

The big drops of rain have all merged together on the pavement, and the humidity has shifted up a gear. I'm not sure if that's the entire city or just this stretch of sidewalk, where Jules and I are building heat.

We cross the pavement, ignoring the rain, and I press Jules up against the wall of my building. I kiss her again, relishing the way she gasps underneath me. My body begins to throb. I want this woman. I want her in the rain. On my lap. In my bed. I growl, deepening our kiss, frustrated by the lack of privacy on the street.

"Take me upstairs," she whispers as I work kisses down her neck. "Please, Leo."

The *please* is all it takes to make me shift gears. There's no more holding back.

I march us across my building lobby, her hand tucked firmly in mine, and straight into a waiting lift. Our kisses are increasingly frantic, desperate and wanting. Her hands slide up my shirt, pressing against my stomach.

What happened tonight? Should we think this through?

Jules slides her hand over my dick. Thoughts about anything other than her hand and what it's doing to me dissolve. She wants this just as much as I do.

There will be consequences. We both know it. But right now, I can't think of anything besides sliding into Jules and feeling her tighten around me.

The elevator doors open, and we fall out. My mind is a blur of feeling and need. Our kisses are frantic and passionate. Her teeth graze my neck. My fingers pull at her dress. I want everything now and I want it to last all night.

The apartment is only lit by the city outside and somehow getting to those lights seems like where we're meant to be. I want to fuck her with the city spread out below us.

I press her against the window, working my tongue down her neck, along her collarbone. She spins and lifts up her hair, revealing her zip.

I tremor with anticipation.

I've been waiting for this for two years.

I take the zip between my finger and thumb and begin to pull it down, tantalizingly slowly. As I reveal her soft skin, I trail my fingers over it, looking for... more of her. I want to know every bloody thing about her—body and mind.

Her breaths grow shallower the lower I go. I can tell she's nearly as worked up as I am.

"I'm going to fuck you with the whole city watching," I growl as I finish undoing her zip.

Her breath hitches, and she releases her hair, covering the skin I just revealed. Then she throws me a glance over her shoulder, shimmies, and her dress falls to the floor. I take a half step back to appreciate her ass in all its glory. Just as I reach for her, she turns back to the window, opens the pocket doors to my roof terrace and steps out.

She's wearing panties and high heels and I follow her, like she has me on a leash.

The rain is still falling and it's so hot, steam practically billows out as soon as it hits the stone floor.

"It's a beautiful night," she says, holding up her palms to catch the drops.

I pull my tie off and strip naked as she watches. We

don't stop grinning at each other. Her gaze catches on my cock, rigid and rearing for her.

She licks her lips, and I groan.

I don't know where to start.

I take a step forward and skirt my fingers up the sides of her soft, hot body. She presses her fingers into my chest. We're body to body, skin to skin, and it feels like we're where we should have been a long time ago.

"I feel like I took a pill and now everything is... *more*," she says. "Like all my senses are amplified."

I nod, unable to take my eyes from hers. She's so beautiful and fascinating and—

She leans forward and places a kiss on my chest. The world stops for a second as I relish the feel of her lips on me. Still holding her, I step us forward toward the stone balustrade and turn her around.

"Look at the lights," I say, pushing my hand down between her legs.

"You have the best views," she says on a sigh. "We can see everything, but no one can see us."

"Would you care if they could?"

There's a beat where she considers it before she says, "Yeah. This should be just you and me."

It wasn't the answer I thought I wanted. It's better. The idea of her and me hits me in the solar plexus and radiates out. Just her and me. We.

I slide my fingers along her folds. She's so wet it's dizzying. My cock pulses into her back, wanting more of her.

"Do you have a condom?" she asks.

I take her wrists and place her hands on the top rail. "Don't move."

I go grab some condoms—because I know one won't be enough. I want to fuck this woman at least fifty times tonight. She's going to be coming so often on my cock, she's not going to be able to walk tomorrow.

As I return to the terrace, she's looking at me from over her shoulder, her hands exactly where I left them. Jules has turned me into a neandertal. The fact that she did as I instructed her to sends a rush of blood to my cock and makes my balls tighten.

"Please, Leo." She twists her hips, impatient for me.

I hook my fingers under her hip bones and pull her back slightly. Her long dark hair falls to either side of her back, revealing more skin for the rain to wet. I trail my hand down it, forcing myself to take my time with her, prolonging these few moments before...

I roll on the condom and round my hands over her smooth, plump arse.

I look up and take a breath, letting the rain fall on my face.

She gasps as I press into her, just an inch.

"More," she whimpers. "More, please, Leo."

My jaw tightens. She can't be begging for my cock. This beautiful woman up against my city can't possibly want me as much as I want her. It's doesn't feel real.

Slowly, agonizingly, I push into her.

The city disappears and all I can do is feel. *Her*. She's clenched around me, her breathing ragged, her body weak. Already. I fold over her, my front to her back, my hands covering hers on the stone, my breath on her neck, still. I need time to adjust to her before I can move. She's just so much.

Is it the rain? The city around us? The gravity of this evening?

Why does everything feel so intense?

I don't need to ask myself the question. I know the answer.

It's her.

"Leo?" she asks.

I grunt from behind and start to slide in and out of her. Slowly, unable to focus on anything but the grip of her around me.

"Leo?" she asks again, and I detect a note of panic in her tone.

"You feel so good," I whisper to her.

"I don't think I can—"

I know without asking, without having had her before, that she needs me to reassure her. "You're perfect."

"But... I'm so full—"

And then I realize what's she's trying to tell me. I haven't learned how she works. Not yet. But I get that she's close. Something primal booms in my chest—pride that I can get her there so fast.

"Let go, Jules," I say.

She shudders beneath me, and I hook my arm around her waist to keep her from falling.

"So quickly, baby? You're going to be exhausted by the time we're done." I wonder if we'll ever be done. This feels so good, so right, so bloody destined.

I pick up my rhythm and my fingers dip to her clit. Her hands ball into fists against the concrete and she starts to whimper, punctuated by "*Please*" and "*Leo*" and "*More.*"

My orgasm rachets up and I'm not going to be able to hold it off for much longer. I'm not ready for this to be over. But I don't get a choice. The woman beneath me has me helpless.

I slide my fingers over her slick, throbbing clit and she writhes underneath me, twisting her hips one way and the other, grinding against my hand, changing the angle of my cock.

My jaw clenches. Fuck. She's so sexy. How was I able to see past her for three months while she worked from me?

My movements become jagged and I push into her in needy, sharp thrusts, trying to get deeper and deeper and deeper.

"I'm coming, Leo." She says it like she's disappointing me.

Like that could be true, ever.

All I can think is *thank god*. Thank god I get to come. For the first time ever in my life, I have to fight the urge to pull out, rip off the condom, and come inside her. I want to be closer to her. I want to own her, mark her. I want her to be full of me.

Shit. What's the matter with me?

A rumble of thunder passes above us, or maybe it's from my chest. I groan as I fuck and fuck and fuck, as she quivers and shakes beneath me.

Her knees buckle, and I only just catch her before she collapses. I don't know if I'll ever have the energy to move. But I don't think I'll ever want to break the spell cast on us this evening.

My breath settles back into a normal pattern and the pulsing in my neck returns to normal. We shift and she turns in my arms.

"That was..."

She wraps her arms around my waist and rests her head on my chest as we stand in satiated silence. Rain continues to fall and it's impossible to get wetter, but it feels good. Like we've stepped out of reality for a while.

Neither of us moves until Jules reaches around me and grabs a sodden cushion from one of the chairs on the terrace. I take off the condom as she drops it at my feet and it lands with a splat. She looks at me, her face wet from the rain, and the corner of her mouth turns up.

She sinks to her knees and grabs my thighs. I gaze down as she glances up at me before taking the crown of my cock in her mouth.

I'm not sure what's hotter: the feel of her mouth on me or the visual of her at me feet, taking my cock inch by inch. She reaches up and takes my hands, putting one under her chin. Another on her head.

I'm as hard as fucking glass as I realize she wants me to set the tone, the rhythm, the pace.

I freeze, all the possibilities scrolling through my head. She swallows around me, bringing me back to the moment.

I increase the pressure in my hands, an indictor to her that I'm taking over. Holding her still, I move slowly at first. Her eyes flutter shut at the realization that I'm now in control. I slide out and then push back in, taking things carefully, wanting to make sure I don't find her limits too quickly.

She opens her knees and her fingers find her clit.

My heart hits my breastbone, it's beating so fast. She really is trying to kill me. But if she comes with my cock in her mouth, I will die a happy man.

She groans and the vibrations connect to my cock, making it buzz as I push into her. I'm not sure how long I'm going to be able to keep being as considerate and gentle. She tips her head back like she wants more of me, like she wants me to fuck her mouth so hard she'll choke.

Something snaps within me and all my most base instincts take over. I *need* to give her what she seems to be craving.

I push into her, pressing against the back of her throat,

the smooth wetness of her tongue. And my hands hold her still so I can get deeper and deeper. My vision drops to her fingers on her clit, then back to my cock sliding into her mouth, and I cry out, "Jules. Fuck."

My legs weaken and I anchor myself to the ground. She's going to have to come to me. I tighten my grip and guide her deeper onto me, pulling her forward, my cock disappearing into her mouth.

Her eyes open and I see the flicker of vulnerability I've noticed before. She's worried. Worried that she's going to let me down. She's about to come again.

The thought of her being so turned on right now drops me down the well of my climax. I fall and fall and fall. I don't even try to be polite and pull out. I erupt in her mouth, coming, coming, coming on her tongue, down her throat, across her lips.

I step back and try to catch my breath, but seeing her on her knees, her legs spread, her fingers circling her clit, keeps me weak. Her tongue sweeps over her mouth, taking in the drops of come smeared on her skin. The action gives me the strength to scoop her off the floor and take her inside.

I take her straight to my shower. I set her on the built-in bench and turn on the handheld spray. Neither of us speaks as I get to work, warming her, trailing the water up and down each limb, soaking her damp hair. I take the shampoo, wash her hair, then rinse it. Then I soap her entire body. I use a sponge and work fastidiously to clean her. She's spent and exhausted, and I move her limbs like she's a doll. I work down her body, over her shoulders, down her back, her breasts, stopping to drop kisses intermittently, wanting to resuscitate her, to care for her.

I help her to her feet and I work down over her hips, between her thighs, over her arse, down her legs and finally her feet. I wash myself quickly, and after wrapping a towel around my waist, I bundle her in a huge white towel and carry her to my bedroom.

I set her on the stool opposite a full-length mirror and kneel at her feet to pat her dry. She goes to help and I shake my head. "Let me," I say.

She doesn't put up a fight. I like the fact that she lets me care for her. Doing this unlocks something in me I didn't know was hiding.

I comb her hair, then grab a white t-shirt of mine and help her into it. Then I find a hair dryer in the bottom of my closet and proceed to dry her hair. The long, dark, silky strands change as they dry, becoming softer. I can't stop touching her. I'm behind her and she's watching me in the mirror. Every now and then we lock eyes and there's an intimacy between us I've never experienced before.

When her hair is finally dry, I lift her into my bed, discard my towel and climb in next to her.

My housekeeper always keeps my nightstand stocked with a water bottle, which I grab and twist open.

"Thank you," she says as I hand it to her. "For the shower too. No one's ever... done that."

I don't tell her that I've never done it before, never even considered it. But for her it's different. I want her to be warm and safe and comfortable. "You were cold and wet and tired and... I wanted to."

She nods. "I know, but... thank you."

A smile threatens at the corners of my mouth. She slides her leg over mine, and I exhale at her touch. Like without it I'm not quite whole.

She sits up, pulls my t-shirt over her head and the sight of her hard, deep red nipples has the blood rushing to my cock.

She lies back down and we're facing each other on our sides, our legs tangled. She presses her fingers along my jaw, down my neck and along my collarbones. The heat of her hands melts me. I need more of her, but I want to go at her pace.

Her hands slide lower, across the ridges of my chest. "I like this," she says, and I'm not sure what she means, but I'm happy she likes anything. "The hair," she adds, as if she knows what I'm thinking.

She dips lower and circles the base of my cock with her fingers. "And this." She laughs. "I like this a lot."

I growl and flip her to her back. "Oh yeah?" I ask. "You like my cock?"

Her eyes grow dark and serious and she nods. "And you," she whispers. "I like you."

I drop a kiss to her mouth. "I like you too."

She spreads her legs and wraps them around my waist. She turns her head, and then reaches for a condom packet lying on the bedside table. "I also *really* like your cock."

I chuckle, sit back, and roll on the condom.

EIGHTEEN

Jules

The staff is going to be pissed. Or at least some of them will be. But I can't let the potential of The Mayfair's rooftop go to waste.

"Does this need to go as well?" Jimmy calls from the other side of the roof terrace, pointing to a small table that up until ten minutes ago had been covered in ashtrays.

"Yes," I reply. "Absolutely everything."

I pull out the metal tape measure I found in Louis' desk and wince. Just moving my arm makes my body ache. What in the hell did we do last night to make my goddamn arms hurt?

The answer is *everything*. Absolutely everything. I can still feel Leo all over my body.

I roll my lips back to stop myself from smiling.

I place the toe of my stiletto on the end of the tape measure and pull. I have no idea what Louis needed to measure, but he wasn't doing anything else, so he must have been measuring something. I just hope it wasn't his dick.

I start at the far end of the roof terrace. My guestimate is sixty by fifty yards. I keep pulling out the metal tape, which seems to go on forever.

I wonder how Leo's feeling this morning. Neither of us got much sleep last night. I crawled out of bed at five, showered, and left around six. He didn't stir. I wasn't sure if he was deliberately avoiding a conversation about the night before, so I didn't wake him.

There will be plenty of time to talk, although my vote would be to skip right past conversation and put the entire episode behind us. That, or get naked again. Naked is definitely the more complicated of the two options, but I have evidence in my aching muscles that it would also be the more *fun* option.

"Should I start sweeping?" Bill, one of our maintenance team, asks, pulling me away from thoughts about Leo.

"Yes, please. The surveyor is coming at two." At least it's cloudy, so he won't be cooked up here as he does... whatever he's going to do. We'll need shade up here if this is going to be a guest space. Umbrellas or a pergola. It's just before twelve, so we've got time to clear the rest of the chairs and sweep up. The surveyor is going to tell me how much weight the roof can take, and any safety renovations needed before I engage an architect and a designer. I need to know the structural costs before I get excited about anything else. I'd really like to cover the place in decking. We also need to put electricity up here. At the very least we'll need music and refrigeration, but I'm not opposed to a full bar. Maybe even a grill.

My phone rings and my heart splutters, as I immediately assume it's going to be Leo.

But of course it isn't. It's just Joan.

"Are you up on the roof?" she asks.

"Yeah, just getting things ready before the surveyor gets here."

"Well, you might want to come down here—"

She stops short. I pull the phone from my ear to check if she's been cut off.

"Jules?"

"Oh, you're back," I reply. "I lost you—"

"Leo Hart is on his way up to the roof."

"Leo is here?" Joan is one of the few people who actually knows Leo is the hotel owner. It's not a secret, per se—people just don't care. Joan found out because she was so pissed off with Louis, she wanted to know who to write to over his head.

What the actual fuck? Why's he dropping in today of all days? He can't want to have The Talk about last night while I'm at work. He's too professional for that. Unless he's throwing me out and calling off the fake engagement. Will last night go down in history as the mistake that blew up my whole life, just as things are falling into place?

"Shit," I say. "Can you stop him?" I'm not mentally prepared to see Leo at all, but definitely not here and now. I wanted to present the roof terrace development idea as a no-brainer, so he'd have to invest. But he's caught me on the fly.

"He's gone already. Bruce is bringing him up."

I groan and head toward the exit, hoping I can be halfway down the stairs as they come up and we can double back. That's another cost I'll need to factor in: renovating the stairs and access so guests don't come through staff-only parts of the hotel.

I'm about five yards away from the exit when Leo appears at the door with a shit-eating grin all over his face. Bruce is nowhere to be seen.

"Jules, Jules, Jules. This roof terrace thing is an addiction, isn't it?"

"You're hilarious. What are you doing here?"

He shoves a brown paper bag at me and nods toward the group of chairs Jimmy hasn't cleared yet.

I peer inside the bag. It's a sandwich. "You brought me lunch?"

"I did. Thought you might be hungry this morning after..." He grins another shit-eating grin and it's like he's set fire to my cheeks. "After skipping breakfast this morning." He sits, looking me over like I'm a painting in a museum, like he's trying to take in every hue and stroke.

I'm not embarrassed because we had sex. More like... I feel like he's seen too much of me, too much of what's below the surface. But it was just... it was the kind of sex where I feel like he knows me better afterwards. Soul-baring sex. But now that he's seen me that way, I'm not sure what his reaction might be.

I perch on a raised concrete wall by the railings and pull out the sandwich. I take a bite, staring at him right back. It feels like his presence here is some kind of dare, and I never back down from one of those. After I swallow, I say, "I didn't skip breakfast. I ate yogurt with fruit. Some of us like a head start on our day." I take another bite. The sandwich is good. Chicken salad—exactly what I'd usually order for myself.

"You didn't run off?" he asks, his voice a little quieter than before.

"I came to work. I have a lot to do at this place you've been running into the ground."

He nods and crosses the space between us to sit down next to me. He's just far enough away that I'd have to reach out to touch him. "Right. Good."

"You're not going to make me have The Talk here, are you?" I ask.

"The Talk?"

"Yeah, you know, where you tell me how you were drunk and upset about Caroline Hammond or whatever, and last night was—"

"Fucking epic. Wanna do it again?" He smiles but it's less shit-eating and more... hopeful. I've seen Leo Hart work a room. He knows how to turn on the charm. But when he's being awkward and a bit goofy? That's when I like him best.

I can't help but laugh and my nerves drift away. He doesn't regret last night. Neither do I. The idea warms my muscles and relaxes me, like my entire body was gripping on to something I can now release.

"So why are you here?" I ask, avoiding his question.

"I told you, I brought you lunch." He rolls back his shoulders, his white shirt sleeves clinging to his arm muscles. I wonder if he's feeling the effects of last night, too. "I didn't even know this was up here. It's got railings and everything." He pulls a bottle of water out of the bag and twists open the cap. He takes a sip. I watch as his Adam's apple bobs under his warm skin. I want to press my lips to his heat.

My eyes flicker up to his. I've been caught staring.

He offers me the bottle.

I don't want water. I want to make out with him, right here and right now. But I settle for the drink. Our fingers brush as I take the bottle from his hands. There's something about the way he's looking at me that sends my heart into free fall in my chest, a stone kicked off the edge of a bottomless well.

I smile and put my lips to the bottle, just like his were a minute ago. I taste him there. My mouth begins to buzz.

My radio bleeping interrupts our little staring contest. I turn the volume down. If anyone wants me, Joan knows where to find me.

"It's a great size," I say. "Incredible views. And you're going to invest in it."

His eyes widen. "Am I?"

I scrunch up my nose. Maybe I shouldn't have put it so aggressively. "It should be guest space. You'll see when I show you the plans. Just keep an open mind."

"I'll listen to anything you say," he says. His gaze drops to my lips, then flit back to my eyes. Desire stirs inside me. I want to slide onto his lap and kiss him for the rest of the day. From the look in his eye, I'm starting to think he wants that, too.

"What time are you back tonight?" he asks. "I have a work thing. Drinks, but—"

"I'm out with Sophia. When I told her about the engagement..." I trail off. I tried to tell her with No Big Deal energy, but it didn't work. We kind of danced around the subject of Leo and how he needed a fake fiancée and now he has a real fiancée. She knows, but she hasn't asked me directly and I'm grateful. After congratulating me, she started asking about the logistics of subletting my room. I told her that since my fiancé is a billionaire, I'd be happy to pay rent until the end of the year. What she doesn't know, but might suspect, is that I'll be back in that room well before the year's end.

"You're celebrating," he says.

As soon as the word is out of his mouth, I put my hands over my face. "Oh god. I hope tonight isn't an impromptu bachelorette party."

"Relax," he says. "You're just going out with your friend."

"I hate not being able to speak freely to her. And I really hate lying to my mom. She hasn't even met you and I've agreed to marry you. She's going to think I've lost my mind."

"I can meet her if you want me to," he says.

I start to laugh. I can't help myself. "So you can start lying to her, too? I can see us getting married for real, just because it's easier than lying to everyone all the time."

"I can get us booked on a flight to Vegas tonight. Oh, but I have that work thing and you're on your bachelorette."

"It will have to wait 'til the weekend," I deadpan. "Oh but tomorrow's Saturday. Gosh darn it, I have plans. Maybe next weekend?"

His phone goes off, but his eyes are on me as he pulls it out of his pocket. I can't place the expression in his eyes. Is it lust? An appreciation of my humor? Something else? He glances down at his phone and silences it.

My radio, his phone—it's like the world is trying to pull us back to reality, but we want to stay right here.

"You've ditched the pantsuit," he says, gaze trailing down my body.

His phone buzzes again and this time it gets his attention. "Shit, I have to go," he says. We both stand. He glances down at my ring and lifts up my hand. "Looks good," he says. He presses a kiss to my knuckles and starts for the door.

"Thanks for lunch," I say.

"Have fun tonight," he calls over his shoulder.

Just before he reaches the door, it busts open. "Dollface!"

The shock of hearing my old nickname doesn't have time to fully register before the man standing in the doorway starts making his way across the roof terrace. He's smaller than I remember, with slicked-back, thinning hair that accentuates the lines on his forehead. But even ten years after I last saw him, there's no mistaking those twinkling blue eyes and that broad smile.

"*Dad?*"

"Come and give your pa a hug." He beckons me over.

I glance at Leo, then back at my father, walking forward like I'm attached to a string. "What are you doing here?"

"Saw you got a new job!" he says, flinging his arms around me. I can't bring myself to hug him back, but he doesn't seem to notice. I detect the scent of alcohol on his skin and realize that's his signature scent. As I child, I didn't associate it with alcohol, but as an adult there's no mistaking it. Has he just come from a boozy lunch? Or has he always had a drink by this time? "I wanted to come and give my congratulations." He doesn't sound drunk. Maybe he had a drink to settle his nerves before coming to see me. If I'd have known he was coming, I probably would have done the same thing.

I know Leo needs to go, but he's lingering by the door. It feels like he's a tether to get me out of here. I step back and out of my father's embrace. "What do you mean, you saw I got a new job? How?"

"In the paper. And you're engaged. And the manager of this place!" He holds his arms out like I'm in charge of the entire island of Manhattan. "You've done well, Dollface. And you look good. Turned out real well. Always knew you would."

I feel myself warm under his inspection, even though I know I shouldn't care at all about his approval. "In the paper?"

I see Leo wince out of the corner of my eye. He didn't mention we'd been in the paper, but I knew an announcement in *The Times* was part of the plan.

"*The Times*. I came back into town and it caught my eye. Now I'm back for some daddy-daughter time. Thought you might give your old man a job so we can see a lot more of each other."

My entire body relaxes. I've been tensing every muscle since he burst through the door, but now I understand why he's here. He hasn't dropped by to offer his congratulations. He doesn't want to hang out with the daughter that he hasn't seen in a decade. He's here because he wants something from me.

I shake my head. "I'm only the temporary manager," I say. My gaze flicks to Leo. I'm about to lie and I need him to back me up, no questions asked. "I don't get to make any hiring or firing decisions. I'm not allowed. It's in my contract." My mom used to work in housekeeping here. She'd kill me with her bare hands if I gave my father a job in the same hotel where she worked. "And anyway, what kind of job would you want?"

He shrugs, the disappointment across his face pulling at something inside me. "I can turn my hand to most things. I like the idea of standing outside in a top hat, opening car doors and getting nice tips."

He wants to be a doorman? The guys on the door at The Mayfair have been doing the job thirty years minimum. It's not about opening a car door. It's about knowing whose door you're opening, knowing who's a regular, remembering their kid's birthday or their favorite restaurant. Our doormen are the first encounter a guest has at this hotel. That encounter can't involve my dad.

I shake my head and try to find the right words. My tongue feels like carpet, my jaw heavy. I don't know what to say. How does he think it's okay to ask me to put my job on the line for him after everything? This can't be happening.

"I'm just as happy helping out wherever. You tell me what you need and I'll give it my best shot."

What *I* need? How about a dad who doesn't disappear for weeks and months and *years* on end?

"Thought you'd want to help out your old man," he says, his voice a little softer. He looks out onto the city and scoops up my hand, bringing it to his chest. "You remember when we used to climb out onto the roof of that apartment in... where was it?" He glances at me.

"Jersey City." It was the last apartment where he visited me and Mom. We only went up to the roof once. When my mom found out, she lost her mind. When Dad suggested it again—our little secret, he said—I refused, knowing my mom wouldn't approve. Looking back, it wasn't the best decision my father ever made from a safety perspective. There were no railings and I had to climb out of a window to get on the rooftop, but I caught a glimpse of the freaking Empire State Building. It was one of the best days of the summer for me.

"We ate beef jerky and played Fleetwood Mac until it rained," he says.

I can't help but smile. "I remember."

"Not quite the views from this rooftop, but not bad."

"I'm Leo." Leo steps forward and holds out his hand to shake my father's. "I'm Jules' boss." He dips his hand into his jacket pocket and pulls out a business card. "Why don't you come see me and I can figure out if I have a job for you? Call that number and my assistant will set something up."

I feel my pulse start to throb in my neck. No! He can't give my father a job. He doesn't understand how this will turn out. My father won't turn up. Or will turn up and—god knows where he got the handfuls of cash he used to turn up with after a period of being gone. Did he rob banks in that time? Steal from his employers? I won't let him take advantage of Leo.

Dad can't have read the announcement in *The Times* very well, because he doesn't put together that Leo is my fiancé. Long may it stay that way.

He reads the business card and I catch Leo's eye. I shake my head. "Don't do this," I mouth.

"It's okay," he mouths back.

"Dad, you have to go," I say. "I'm working."

"Okay, okay. I know when it's time to leave a party. Speaking of party, is there a nice cozy bar in this hotel?"

"It's not open," I lie. "Please, Dad, you need to go."

"I'll walk you out," Leo says. "This place is a maze. Don't want you getting lost."

"Dollface, I'll call you," Dad says from halfway down the stairs. He pauses and turns back to me. I don't have his number, and he doesn't have mine. "We'll go for coffee," he says.

"Sure," I say. That will never happen.

"I'm busy this weekend, but what about next week?"

"Maybe. Before work?" I ask, expecting the early hour will put him off.

"Sure thing, doll."

I wasn't expecting him to say yes to that. The next thing I know, he's coming back up the stairs at a jog. He holds out his phone and I realize he's asking for my number. I enter my details. What am I doing? Should I just shut him down and get Leo to throw him out?

Thoughts of that afternoon on the rooftop in Jersey City fill my head. I wanted him to be that dad all the time. The exciting one. The fun one. The one who was *there*.

I hand him back his phone. "You have my number," I say. "If you message me, I can give you a date for coffee."

"And if you call my assistant, we can arrange a meeting," Leo says.

I exhale. The balls are all in his court. As much as I've agreed to coffee, I understand there's a ninety percent chance I won't see him for another decade after today.

But then... there's that one-in-ten chance he might call. We might have coffee. I might rebuild some kind of relationship with him. I didn't realize it until now, but something buried deep within me hopes that's still possible.

NINETEEN

Jules

I'm starting to think the double tequila shot before I came out this evening was a bad idea. But after seeing my dad, I needed something to help me chill out before meeting Sophia. Part of me wanted to cancel tonight and run back to my mom. But I don't want to let Sophia down.

"Shots!" Sophia calls. I know I should say no, but alcohol makes it easier to lie to my friends that I'm engaged and not tell them I saw my dad today. Both topics feel equally forbidden.

Sophia still hasn't straight-up asked me if the engagement is real. She's asked me some more questions, almost daring me to be honest with her. I explained that we'd shared a kiss and he'd decided he didn't want a fake fiancée anymore. She's going along with it. It's all I can ask.

"Only one more," I say.

"You're going to need them, trust me." She winks at me and nods towards Natasha, one of our old school friends. She lives in Ohio now but happened to be in town.

"Why am I going to need them?" I ask.

"Because," Natasha says. She digs around in her bag and pulls out a plastic tiara. "This." She squeals. Part of me dies inside.

"No," I groan.

"Yes!" Sophia takes the tiara and places it on my head.

The headpiece has a short veil in front, prickly and stiff. I feel about as comfortable wearing it as I would a real wedding tiara.

"It actually suits you, which spoils the effect a little," Sophia says.

"You mean it would be better if it made me look terrible?" I ask. Sophia isn't the kind of friend to set anyone up for a fall, so it's a weird thing to say.

"More... I think it would be better if it didn't look like it could have been a deliberate choice."

I laugh and reach up to pull it off, but both Sophia and Natasha stop me. I don't know if it's the booze or the way it's just good to see my friends again, but I relent and let the wonky tiara be.

"So how did you meet him?" Natasha asks. "I feel so out of it in Ohio. I didn't even know you were dating."

"I live with her and I didn't know," Sophia says. "I thought you hated your boss."

"He's your *boss*?" Natasha asks.

I've been a little vague with Sophia about my change in employment and relationship status. Of course, she knew why I took the assistant job, but I've just told her my role at the hotel is temporary.

"What's with the sudden change of heart?" Sophia asks. "I don't get it."

I shrug. "I've always thought he was hot," I say. Again, it's kind of true.

"Thinking someone is hot is a far cry from marrying them," Natasha says.

"True. What can I say? I found out he's... different to how I thought he was." Now *that* is one hundred percent true. Yes, Leo is a flirt who's had more than his fair share of women, but he's kind and sweet and humble. I like him. I keep replaying the way he guided my dad away from me earlier. I need to talk to him about not employing my father, but he would have known seeing my dad again would be difficult. He made it easier without being asked.

Leo's a good man. I like chatting with him, I like cooking with him. I like feeling his hand at the small of my back and his tongue between my legs. I press my fingers to my temples. I need to think straight and stop focusing on all the reasons I like Leo. I'm not his real fiancée.

"Do you remember that costume party you dragged me to a few years ago?" I ask Sophia.

"The one that *wasn't* a costume party?"

I nod. "And that guy from the party that I got chatting with?"

"The one you really liked who ended up being a dick?" We'd talked about it for weeks afterward. Sophia wanted me to text him, find out where he lived and then send him weird things in the mail. I think we'd both been drinking pretty heavily at that point.

"Right," I say. "I didn't tell you because I know you would have thought I was crazy, but that's Leo. My boss. My fiancé. He's the guy from the party."

"Shut the fuck up," Sophia says, grabbing my shoulders. "Are you serious? Why didn't you tell me when you realized?"

"I thought you'd tell me to tell him to shove his job up his ass, and I really wanted the job."

She releases me and slumps back onto the bench. "Yeah, I probably would have told you that."

"And he didn't recognize me, being human color and all. I just tried to pretend I hadn't met him before. That he wasn't the guy from the party."

"I'm so confused," Natasha says. "Can we double back?"

We fill in Natasha about the details of my first encounter with Leo. She listens with rapt attention.

"And kismet wouldn't be shaken off," she says, slowly shaking her head.

"You can't dodge destiny," Sophia says. "You and him haven't come out of nowhere at all. You've been simmering for two years!"

I try not to groan. It all sounds so cheesy. It was a coincidence.

"If you're fated to be together, then the sex must be off the charts. Tell us everything!" Sophia says, and my heart leapfrogs into my feet. "I always think sex with rich, powerful, good-looking men must be a complete letdown because they've no reason to try."

I nod, thinking back to last night. In no way was it a letdown. Things had been simmering between us for a while, but the boil? I wasn't expecting it. I wasn't expecting to feel the things he made me feel. I wasn't expecting to feel so comfortable with him, like I could be every version of myself, bare in every sense, and he'd worship every part of me.

"You're saying it's bad?" Natasha asks.

I shake my head. "He has no business being so good in bed," I say. "Maybe that's why I said yes."

We dissolve into laughter and another round of shots

gets delivered to the table. It feels good to laugh. Every smile makes my dad feel a little further away.

"Now that I know how good the sex can be, I don't want to go back," I add. I hope memories of last night will fade, because if they don't, I'll never be able to settle for anything less.

"Does he have any single friends?" Sophia asks.

"I'm not sure Jamie would like you asking that question," I reply.

She sighs. "Yeah, well, we're on a break. We never see each other and it's not like we're working on changing things so we do. We're in this weird limbo, which is fine if we were twenty, but I'm about to hit thirty."

"God, Sophia, that's shit," I say. "But a break? What does that mean?"

"That we're delaying the inevitable breakup, I suppose." She nods and tips back her shot. She winces. "You're right. It's shit. And what's worse, I can feel us both inching toward the exit and neither of us is trying to stop the other."

I squeeze her hand. We're going to need a lot of alcohol.

"You deserve someone amazing," I say.

She nods. "You too."

I don't say anything and Natasha looks between us like she's missing something.

"I don't think men learn to fuck by talking about it in front of the game," Natasha says out of nowhere. She adopts a deep voice, before going on to say, "'Yo, dude, I discovered my girl's G-spot last night. You gotta try this thing with a finger.' So just because Leo is perfect, doesn't mean his friends are. But it might be worth a try."

Sophia and I both laugh at Natasha who's clearly a little tipsy already.

I haven't met Leo's friends, but I'm guessing they don't

have conversations like that. I feel a pang of longing and wonder what he's doing right now—whether he's with his friends. I wonder what they're like, whether I'll like them as much as I like him, and whether they'll like me.

"You're probably right," Sophia replies. "I just live in hope that I can find someone half decent in this town." She turns to me, her expression serious. "I know that we're joking around, but I'm honestly really happy for you." Her voice breaks. "I'll miss you, that's all."

I put my arm around her, my stomach tightening at the idea that I'm upsetting her for nothing because it's all a lie. "Hey, I'm not emigrating. I'll just be over the river and across the street."

She nods, pasting on a fake smile that doesn't quite hide the disappointment in her eyes. "Let's have some fun tonight." She pulls out her phone. "Let's get a picture. You can send it to Leo to let him know you're having fun."

I hope the wince I feel isn't translated into my expression in the photo. Leo and I have never texted unless it's purposeful—directions to New River, timing for dinner, that kind of thing. I don't know how I feel about sending him a text just because.

Natasha gets up and comes to stand on the other side of me, so I'm in the middle. Sophia holds out the phone, and before I know it, we're striking poses and taking selfies like we're seventeen again.

Sophia flips through the options. "This one is definitely the best."

My phone bleeps immediately and I bring up the photo.

I look ridiculous in the fake bridal tiara. What the hell was I thinking?

"Send it to him. You look hot."

I shake my head. "No, I'll show him later," I say.

"You have to send it!" Sophia says.

Natasha pulls the phone from my hand. "Why wouldn't you send it? You look hot as fuck."

"My point exactly," Sophia says.

I glance up and they're both looking at me. What do I do? If I refuse to send my fiancé a picture of me dressed up in a fake tiara, they're going to think there's something wrong with me. If I send it, Leo will think there's something wrong with me. This is a lose-lose situation.

"Go on," Sophia says.

I relent, bringing up my chat with Leo and dropping the picture before turning my phone facedown on the table.

We order another round of shots. Sophia tells us about her first post-Jamie date with a guy who's an actor—not a famous one. He's trying to "make it" and Sophia can't decide whether he's worth all the time she spends analyzing him. My vote is *hard no*, but I'm not going to say that at the moment. She's still too into him. My phone vibrates and I feel it in my thighs. I know without checking that it's Leo.

I wait until Sophia and Natasha are elbow-deep analyzing this new guy's refusal to see Sophia more than once a week. If they were sleeping together, a once-a-week thing would mean he was trying to keep it casual, but they're not having sex yet. Whatever game he's playing, it's not worth Sophia's time. She needs to look for someone who cares about her. Someone who's thoughtful.

Someone who comes down in the elevator twenty floors so you don't have to ride up on your own. Someone who brings you lunch because you left before breakfast. Someone who deflects your dad's attention away from you when it's too much to handle.

While they're both busy, I slide my phone off the table and take a look.

Hot

It's all Leo writes, but afterward, he sends a picture of a half-eaten bowl of mac and cheese.

I smile to myself when the three dots on-screen tell me he's typing. I suck in a breath, waiting for his follow-up.

Doesn't taste as good as you.

My blush starts at my toes and ends at the tips of my ears.

TWENTY

Jules

I have a thousand busy construction workers in my brain, trying to force their way out using pneumatic drills and pickaxes. I'm wearing my eye mask, but it still feels like someone's poking needles of light into my eyeballs.

Someone needs to make it stop.

I pull the pillow from under my head and put it over my face, but inexplicably the fabric smells of Leo. Like smelling salts to a weak and wailing woman, it actually perks me up. I throw the pillow off and peel up one corner of the eye mask.

"Good morning, beautiful," Leo says from the bottom of my bed. Jesus Christ, why is he in my bedroom? Did we... I can't remember even getting home last night.

"Why are you—?" I glance at the inexplicable artwork behind him. That's not the usual view I wake up to. I look left and right, then I pull the eye mask off completely and sit bolt upright. "This isn't my room."

Leo chuckles. He's in a towel, his hair still damp from

the shower. He looks so clean and fresh and so unlike how I feel, which is like someone threw me in a dumpster and shut the lid. "This is my room."

"Why am I in your room?"

He shrugs. "You came in just after midnight. I'd already gone to bed, but you decided there was no time like the present to uh... thank me. Then you closed your eyes and sort of fell onto the bed."

I cover my mouth with my hand. "Oh my god. I slept here?"

"It's no big deal," he says.

"Did we... did I... I mean, did anything—"

"You fell asleep. I went back to sleep. The only thing either of us did was sleep. You weren't capable of remaining upright, so once you timbered into bed, we were both out cold."

I bite down on my bottom lip. "I'm a mess." Having sex with your boss is one thing but passing out disheveled and incoherent is quite another.

"It was funny. And no big deal. Don't sweat it."

He heads back into his bathroom and I half roll, half crawl out of his bed. I'm still dressed in my outfit from last night. I clutch the top of my head. At least I'm not still wearing my bridal tiara. I immediately spot it on the nightstand and groan. I didn't fall asleep wearing that, did I?

Leo reappears in soft gray joggers and a white t-shirt. I have an urge for a toothbrush and a Silkwood shower. "I'm going for coffee. No need to ask whether you want one. I'll bring you two."

I laugh and immediately regret it when it feels like my skull and my brain just suffered a high-speed collision. I hold the sides of my head with my palms.

"Anything else or shall I just bring you back an assortment of carbs?"

I nod. "Sounds perfect. I'm going to try for a shower."

He laughs, but it's not at my expense—more of an *I feel your pain, my friend* kind of laugh. I smile slightly.

"See you in a bit."

"You're not ordering in?" I ask.

"I'll run there and cab it back."

I groan. The idea of fresh air, let alone exercise, makes me want to hurl. "Good for you," I manage to croak.

As I pass him to head for a shower, he stops me and lifts my chin. "You're a very cute drunk, you know that?"

If I felt ten percent better than I did, I'd grab his t-shirt and snuggle into it, thank him for trying to make me feel better. But I don't. Not to mention, I still feel a little awkward for passing out in his bedroom.

"Cute is not what I'm feeling right now."

"You're always cute." He presses a kiss to my forehead like he's my boyfriend or something, then heads to the door. "If you think of anything you want while I'm gone, text me," he calls over his shoulder.

I trudge to the shower, putting one foot only slightly in front of the other. Eventually, I'll baby-step all the way across the apartment. If I don't pick up speed, I won't make it to my bedroom before he's back.

But I do reach my bedroom. And I make it in and out of the shower before I hear the front door open. I pull on a t-shirt and some leggings and plod toward the kitchen.

"You were quick," I say.

He turns to face me from the counter where he's pulling cups out of a paper bag. It hits me like a brick how good-looking he is. His chest seems wider than normal and his arms seem stronger—more muscular than I've seen them looking before. I can't have had him in focus before my shower.

"You said before that I came into your room to thank you for something. What was I thanking you for?" I ask him.

He narrows his eyes and then hands me a coffee cup. "Oh, last night?" He shrugs. "Not sure. You passed out before I understood entirely."

"Must have been for dealing with my dad." My gaze hits the floor. I'm so embarrassed he had to see that. Of all the days to get two unexpected visitors. "It was really nice of you to escort him out, but you can't give him a job. You know that, right?" I shake my head. "I don't know why I'm saying that. It's not like he's actually going to call and set up a meeting."

"He already did. A week on Friday. One thirty."

"He called?" He must really want that job. "You're seeing him the day after the awards ceremony? Will you be working that day?" Before Leo can answer, I groan. "He won't turn up. But on the off chance he does, will you please not give him a job?"

"You don't think he'll show?"

I shake my head. "No way." He hadn't even messaged me. I shouldn't be surprised, and I'm not. It's just...

"When's the last time you saw him?" Leo asks.

"I was a teenager. He turned up after being gone six months. He'd never left for that long before. It was the first time my mom didn't let him swan in to pick up where he'd left off." I shrug. "I was proud of her. He always brought a lot of stress when he came back. It felt like we finally got off this endless merry-go-round of him coming and going."

"You deserve better than that. You deserved it then, and you especially deserve it now."

I smile and take a sip of coffee. When I look back at

him, he's still got his eyes on me, but I don't want to talk about my dad. "Sorry about crashing in your bed," I say.

"Anytime."

"You could have carried me back to my bed. Although, thank god you didn't, I might have barfed on you. I haven't been that drunk in forever. I think it was the tequila before I left here that tipped me over the edge. I thought it was liquid courage, but it was just liquid alcohol."

He laughs and then hands me a pastry on a plate. He's very civilized. It must be his British genes.

"Wanna watch a movie?" he asks.

"Sure. Is this what you'd normally do on a Saturday?"

"Nope," he says as we head toward the couches. "But there's not much normal about today."

We get situated and Leo pulls up a list of movies to scroll through. I pull out my phone from where I've slipped it into my waistband and check my messages. There's nothing from either Sophia or Natasha. They're probably still asleep.

"What do you like?" he asks.

"Something quiet and peaceful with no explosions or flashing lights. Basically anything you'll hate."

He chuckles. "What about a TV box set binge?"

"Like...?"

"*Killing Eve*?"

"I don't think I have the stomach for murder. I need gentle."

"That British baking show?"

"I *love* that. Are you sure *you* have the stomach for it?"

"I know it's off-brand, but I'm completely invested. I've only watched the first series though."

I sit up straighter, completely charmed. "Me too!"

He shoots me a smile. "We're made for each other. Who knew?"

My stomach flips as Leo hits play.

We're two episodes in when he hands me a second pastry, and I don't turn him down. "I want to eat everything in New York City right now. A hangover and a binge of British baking isn't a recipe for calorie control."

He laughs and settles deeper into the couch. I wonder what he'd be doing right now if he wasn't here with me, helping me nurse my hangover. Before I can ask him, my phone beeps. It's Natasha.

Just coming to life. My head is about to explode, but had a great night celebrating with you. Tell Leo hi and thank him for me. What a swoon-meister.

So not only did *I* want to thank Leo last night, but Natasha wants to thank him this morning. For being a swoon-meister—whatever that is. Maybe it's an Ohio thing.

As I reread the message from Natasha, I get another one, this time from Sophia.

Hope you're feeling better than I am. Say thanks to Leo. Hope to meet him soon.

That's it. I've got to know what we're all so thankful for.

"Leo, why did I come into your room last night to thank you?"

He shrugs. "Can't remember."

I'm not buying it. It wasn't about my dad if my friends are grateful, too.

"But Natasha and Sophia messaged and asked me to thank you. What's going on?"

He groans and stays focused on the screen. "Such bad luck on the technical. I think he's going home. Joanne's got this series in the bag. I'm calling it."

"Leo," I say. "Please tell me. Even if I did something really embarrassing, I want to know."

His eye slice to mine. "Why would you have done something embarrassing?"

"You're obviously avoiding telling me why we're all so grateful to you," I say. "Probably because you want to spare my feelings. I can handle whatever it is."

"It's nothing. I just... picked up your tab last night, that's all. It's no big deal."

My heart clenches in my chest. "You paid for our dinner and drinks last night? How?"

He narrows his eyes. "With a credit card," he says, like I'm a simpleton.

"I mean, how did you even know where we were?"

He shrugs. "I recognized the restaurant from the picture you sent."

"So, you just decided to—"

"It's really not a big deal. I called them and gave them my card number. It's nothing."

But it wasn't nothing. Just like him dealing with my dad yesterday wasn't nothing. It was a big deal. A really big deal. Not just because of the money—the money doesn't mean much to Leo. His thoughtfulness and kindness, though? His generosity and humility? Those are the kinds of things a boyfriend—or a real fiancé—brings to the table. At least if they're one of the good ones.

"That was really nice of you, Leo." My voice is a little shaky. We're not joking around, teasing each other. He did something really nice and I'm grateful from the bottom of my heart.

He must catch the difference in my tone, because he pulls his gaze from the TV and regards me. "It's fine. It wasn't anything."

We stare at each other for a beat, then two. He circles his fingers around my ankle and pulls me toward him. "You're worth it. I wanted you to have a nice time. You'd had a rough day."

I want to kiss him. I want him to kiss me. I know he's not the guy I'm going to end up with—I understand a man like Leo can never settle down and commit to a woman. But right now, I don't want to think about commitment or settling down. I just want Leo Hart to kiss me.

It's like he can read my mind, because he shifts over me, pushing me back onto the couch, his breath against my neck.

"You look so sexy right now."

My hair is damp and I'm in a t-shirt and leggings. I'm anything but sexy. "I guess it's all relative," I huff out. "You're used to seeing me in secondhand pantsuits."

"You're always sexy." He places a kiss to my collarbone. Every molecule in my body stands to attention. It's like he has some kind of code to my body that I didn't know existed, and with just a few movements—a sweep of his lips, a press of his fingers—I'm unlocked and all his.

I feel his erection against my leg and I'm instantly wet with longing. How is that possible? I'm hungover to Colorado and back and I still want him. His hands slide up my t-shirt and he finds me braless and groans. "Fuck, Jules." He pushes the t-shirt higher, and I help him take it over my head. He pinches and pulls my nipple between his thumb and forefinger, and it's such painful pleasure that my back arches and I cry out.

He releases me and strips off his t-shirt. The skin on his arms and neck and face is so smooth it looks like it's polished. As he bends over me, I slide my hands over his shoulders and down his front. His chest has a little hair and it makes me giddy—like some kind of biological switch is flicked at the sight of it.

"How's the hangover?" he asks.

"What hangover?"

He chuckles and leans in for a kiss. He grazes his teeth across my jaw and then dips between my lips, as if he's tasting me. It's like he's trying to torture me. I want his tongue, his cock, his fingers—all of him inside me right now.

I scramble for the waist of his joggers and try to push them down, but my hands find his cock and I reach for it. He twists his hips away and shifts so he's lying behind me, one hand around my waist, another down the waistband of my leggings.

"You're not touching me. Not until I've had my turn touching you," he says. He holds me in place as his fingers slip down and between my folds. I want to be better than melting every time he touches me. But I'm not. He strips me of any self-control.

I moan as his fingers circle my clit. I can feel him pressing hard into my ass and I just want him inside of me. "Leo, please," I say.

"You have such beautiful manners," he says, with a twist of his hips. "But you don't get to decide when you touch me, when I touch you, when I slide inside you." His teeth graze my neck and I whimper. I can't help it. I'm so overcome with need for him. I circle my hips against his hand, wanting more, trying to steal sensations from his fingers.

With his free hand, he forces my leggings and underwear down. His erection sits against my ass. Hard. Hot. Pulsing. My body shivers with relief. It will happen soon. *Soon, soon,* a voice inside me chants.

"You feel how hard I am for you?" he whispers in my ear. "What are you doing to me?"

He strips off the rest of my leggings and his joggers so we're both naked. He sits up and guides me to straddle him. His cock is pointing at the ceiling and he rolls on a condom before guiding it to my entrance.

I don't know if I can do this. I don't know if I have the strength to move when he's inside me.

Slowly, I sit and he slides in, stretching me out, filling me deep. My heart is pounding out of my chest and I'm breathless.

I can't move. I'm too full. Right on the edge of a cliff.

His fingers find my nipples again and that's all it takes. I drop my head back as my orgasm spirals through me like it's the first time I've ever come. My legs begin to tremble and my back arches. Leo groans as I come.

"Fuck, Jules. You're so gorgeous."

I take a couple of deep breaths as I float back down to earth. He cups my face with his hand and I lean forward, our foreheads touching. "I'm sorry," I reply. "I don't usually... This isn't normal for me."

"Don't apologize for coming," he says. "Don't apologize. You're not broken. You haven't done anything wrong."

We haven't moved, but I can still feel him deep inside me. Even though I only just came, I start to shift, moving my hips back and forth in tiny movements.

"Don't fucking apologize for being so turned on you lose control. You're safe with me."

My movements become bigger, faster, and he grips my hips, slowing me down. "We're in no rush," he says. "We're going to fuck all day. There's no race to the finish line."

I whimper as he pulls me down firmly, and I bite my bottom lip, reveling in the hardness of him inside me. I don't know if it's the feel of him, the idea that he's going to fuck me all day or that he wants to take his time, but I'm ready for him again. Maybe it's all of it.

He lifts me up slightly and pulls me down again, bigger movements now but all at his pace. All the way he wants it —but it's also the way I want it. He knows what I need.

I press my hands against his chest and our bodies move like they're engineered to work together, his cock pistoning in and out, my hips rocking. Our eyes are locked like we can read each other's minds.

Then all of a sudden, he grips my hips and forces me back and away from him, leaving me empty.

"Fuck," he says, his head rolling back onto the sofa. "I'm so close."

"So quickly?" I arch an eyebrow. "It's like we're kids." I trail a finger down his breastbone and then down the base of his cock. "I like it," I say.

He chuckles. "You do?"

"I mean, it's not like I didn't come first. It's not like I'm not going to come a second time with you."

I kneel up and press him to my entrance.

I moan as he fills me up, like it's the first time I've ever had him inside me. I start to rock my hips and his expression urges me on. My fingers dip to my clit and he glances down, groaning.

A buzz starts in my fingers and soon covers my body. I'm vibrating for him, with him, on him. I grab at his shoulders, wanting to pull him closer as he pushes up harder, deeper. We both explode at the same time, clasped together, our orgasms thundering through us as if we're sharing one huge climax.

TWENTY-ONE

Leo

Monday nights are sacrosanct, spent chewing the fat with my best friends. It's a night dedicated to the five people I trust with my life and who trust me with theirs. As my success has grown, I've realized how important my inner circle truly is. I'm friendly with a lot of people, but friends with just a few.

This Monday, everyone's meeting at my place. Often we're out at a bar or a restaurant, but when someone's got something private they want to discuss, we congregate at one of our apartments. This week, Worth suggested we gather at my place so they can all meet Jules in a low-key way before the awards. He rightly pointed out that introducing my fiancée to my best friends that night would be suspicious.

Jules gave me a hard time when I told her the guys know she's not my real fiancée. I get that it feels inequitable because I've asked her not to tell her friends or family. The difference is, this fake engagement was *their* idea. And I have more than enough secrets of theirs to ensure they definitely won't tell a soul—in particular, Fisher, who has to do everything I tell him, now that I have that shot on my phone of him with the two cucumbers.

I haven't hosted a Monday night since Nadia, and I feel a little weird about it. Luckily, Jules doesn't feel weird at all. She even helped me pick out the snacks we ordered.

"This is basically our engagement party," she says, uncovering a plate of roasted vegetables. "And I get to wear sweats because I'm not trying to impress anyone, because they all know it's fake."

She doesn't need to try to impress anyone. She always looks gorgeous, no matter what she's wearing.

"I don't mean to be a pedant, but you're not wearing sweats," I say.

"Good observation," she says. "The point is, I could if I wanted to."

I chuckle because I can't follow her logic. "You look great," I say. Her hair is down and it hits her waist. I've learned Jules' hair is a barometer for how comfortable she feels. When it's down, she's her most authentic self.

"You okay?" she asks, catching me staring at her.

"I pay you a compliment and you ask me if I'm okay?"

She laughs. "I mean, you seem a little tense."

"I am a little tense."

She takes the cover off another platter. "Why? Aren't these people your best friends?" She pauses, turning to face me. "Are you worried about me being here? I can head down to the gym if that would be easier."

I shake my head. "No, that's not it. It's just..."

"What?" she asks. "You can tell me anything. It's not like I'm your actual fiancée who will hold it against you for the rest of our marriage."

Now isn't the time to unpack that grim view of marriage, but I've heard the stories about her dad, so I get it. "It's a boring story, and it will pass. I'm just a little freaked out."

"I live for a boring story," she says. "I want every detail. Tell me everything." She continues to organize the food and arrange plates and cutlery. I should help, but watching her has induced me into some kind of trance. I can't take my eyes off her.

"Over the summer, I spent a little time with someone. She was kinda pushy about being in my space, but I was more relaxed about it than I'd normally be. She told me she was leaving New York at the end of the summer, so I figured we had a natural end date and she wasn't expecting anything from me, so I just went with it."

"Riiight," Jules says. "You went along with her being pushy. What does that mean exactly?"

"She wanted to spend a lot of time here. At my place. And then she wanted to meet my friends. Hang out. Looking back, she was very blatant about it."

"Blatant about what? Wanting to spend time with you?" Her tone has an irritated edge to it.

I sigh. She clearly thinks I was being a dick. I still feel like such a fool for taking Nadia at face value. "Turns out, it wasn't me she wanted to get to know. She was trying to hack into Bennett's IT system."

"I don't follow." She sets down the last piece of cutlery and looks at me.

"She targeted me as a way to get to Bennett. He owns an IT company doing really cutting-edge stuff. She was a hacker—possibly representing a foreign government—using me to get physically close enough to Bennett to access his systems."

"Wow," she says, crossing her arms and leaning against the counter. "That officially sucks. Did you really like her?"

A tricky question that's impossible to answer truthfully, now that I know what she was trying to do. "I don't know. I think she was, deliberately, very easy company."

"Well, that's how you know you can trust *me*. No one's ever accused me of being easy company."

I chuckle and don't say, *I like you a lot better*.

The buzzer goes. Jules straightens and turns back to the counter. "What about drinks? Should I have made cocktails? I have no idea what I'm doing as a fake fiancée. Will someone please write a book on that?"

I head to the door and meet Worth coming toward me.

"You need to get better about your security," he says, pulling me into a hug.

"I left it open for you." Probably not the best idea in New York City.

"This is Jules," I say.

She's a little stiff and awkward, but why do I find it low-key adorable? It's like she's my actual girlfriend meeting my friends for the first time.

I slip my hand to her back, trying to offer some reassurance, even though she doesn't need it. My friends will make her feel comfortable. "Worth is as good as it gets, so if you don't like him, you're in for a shitty evening."

"If you can put up with *him*," Worth says, nodding in my direction, "I'm going to be like a dream come true."

Jules grins and pulls Worth in for a hug. "So nice to meet you," she says.

"And you. Thank you for doing this for Leo. It's a big ask."

She turns to me, her head tilting in consideration. "Oh, it's not so bad," she says.

"I beg to differ," Worth says. "Leo says you've taken over at The Mayfair. You need to make sure he's not underpaying you."

She laughs. "Oh, I'm all over that, don't you worry."

The door buzzer goes again and this time it's Bennett and Efa. I asked him to bring her, partly because I thought it would be nice for Jules to have a little female company, and I'm pretty sure the two of them will get on. But also... Efa sussed out Nadia quicker than I did. It's not like I don't trust Jules, I do. But... I don't know. I don't one hundred percent trust myself, either.

Fisher and Jack arrive just after Bennett, and Byron sends his last-minute apologies, so we're all here but the vibe is very different than usual. I've turned on ESPN, but no one's even glancing in that direction. Everyone's chatting and picking at the food and talking to Jules like this is a party.

"Does anyone want water?" Jules asks. "I need to stay hydrated."

"Yes, please," Worth says. Turns out, Fisher wants water too. I cross the kitchen and reach for a jug, which I place in Jules' hands just as she's about to ask me where she can find one.

She smiles wide, and I can't help but mirror her. "Just what I was after." Our voices are low, the two of us carving out a private space in the crowded kitchen. It's nice.

"Thought so," I say. "I think I have some lemon too, if you want to be really fancy."

"I know you have lemons, because *I* bought them."

"What is happening to my life that I don't even know what's in my fridge anymore?"

"Me," she says, beaming up at me. "I'm happening to your life."

"Don't I know it." And I don't mind it. Not at all. She's good company, funny and thoughtful and kind. The sex is great. She's—

"You two look good together," Worth says, interrupting my thoughts.

"The light in this apartment makes everyone look good," Jules says. "And the views make your friend bearable."

I can't believe I ever thought she was furious most of the time. I can't remember the last time Jules wasn't smiling or making me laugh or just generally happy. I find myself craving her company when she's not around, wondering what she's doing and when I'll see her next.

"So you're managing The Mayfair?" Fisher asks Jules.

"I am," she replies. "Best job ever."

"It's a shift for that place to have someone at the helm who actually gives a shit, unlike Leo here," Fisher says.

"Hey," I say. "I give a shit."

"No you don't," Jules says, poking me in the ribs.

I'm about to contradict her, but what's the point? I sigh. "You're right, I don't. Not that I wouldn't like for Bennett to lose."

"Bennett to lose what?" Her gaze flits from him to me.

Of course, Fisher is the one to fill her in. "We each own a hotel and hold a yearly competition of sorts. Mainly based on percentage of net revenue increase. But we also look at gross revenue."

"Huh," she says. "You each have a hotel. Is that a coincidence?"

"They bought them so they could bond and compete in equal measure," Efa says. "It's basically a dick-measuring contest. But for billionaires. Some guys simply would buy and trade *Star Wars* memorabilia..."

"Or maybe race muscle cars?" Jules says on a laugh. I'm

not sure if she's laughing at the idea of me in a muscle car or the sheer ridiculousness of the hotel contest. Both maybe. "I can't believe you bought The Mayfair just so you could fit in with your gang." She elbows me.

"That's not it," I say. "It's about..." I can't finish my sentence. Because it is ridiculous. But it's also not. Even though I'm not truly invested in The Mayfair, I wouldn't sell it. Doing so would give up a connection to my best friends.

"It explains why you put up with Louis for so long," she says.

Fisher groans. "I begged him to fire that guy. I knew he was useless."

"He was running the place into the ground," she says, "but keeping net profit relatively stable because of underinvestment."

Bennett laughs. "So what you're saying is that Leo is going to take an absolute bath when it comes to net profit this financial year."

She nods. "Got it in one." What does it say about me that I like how no-holds-barred she is? She doesn't sugarcoat anything. It's refreshing. "It's going to take a while to get us out of the hole Louis got us in."

If anyone can do it, she can.

I turn my attention from Jules and realize my friends are all staring at me. "I get it," I say. "Louis was crap. Should have gotten rid of him earlier."

"How is it having a roommate?" Worth asks, changing the subject completely.

It's like I've been slammed into a brick wall of thoughts about my last roommate, Nadia. It's a stark reminder that for all the jovial banter and relative comfort between us, I really don't know Jules that well. I thought Nadia was a certain type of person and she turned out to be another. I thought Caroline was in love with me and wanted to be with me forever; that turned out to be a lie, too. I have to be careful who I trust.

"Better than the last one," I say. Nadia basically moved in, given the amount of time she spent here.

Jules skims her palm over my back and the muscles in my jaw lock tight. "Can I get you anything?"

I shake my head, and I see her register my shift in attitude. I'm being a dick. She's never done anything to make me the slightest bit suspicious. Things are different with Jules. To start, I know she's using me. We're using each other. I want a fiancée; she wants a job. All our cards are on the table. I think.

I hope.

TWENTY-TWO

Jules

I still don't understand the rules of football. Every couple of years, I google it, or I ask someone to explain, but then I remember I don't give a shit and get on with my life.

It took them awhile, but Leo and his friends are spread out on the sofa, watching and roasting each other and catching up. It's cute, even if they are fully grown men. Even billionaires need to blow off steam and be silly from time to time.

"This happens every Monday, huh?" I ask Efa, who's just come back from the bathroom.

"Every Monday no matter what." She hops up onto a barstool and starts helping herself to the charcuterie board. "It's a real priority for Bennett. He won't miss it unless there's an emergency."

"It's nice, right?" I say. "That they prioritize each other."

"They pretend it's about the sport." Efa laughs.

"It's not about the sport," I say. "I've been here five minutes and I know that."

"They trust each other. And they're so successful, finding people to fully trust can be hard."

"Finding people you can fully trust can be really hard no matter how successful you are."

Efa sighs like I've pressed a button that brought back a memory. "That's very true."

"So congratulations on your engagement," I say. "I hear it happened fast."

"Really fast," Efa says. "I never expected to be engaged so young, but... He says I have an old soul and he's an immature asshole at times, so we meet somewhere in the middle."

"A match made in heaven."

She nods. "What about you? You and Leo seem..." I tense, wondering what she's going to say next. "Like you're having a lot of sex."

My eyes widen and I'm not quite sure what to say. "What do two people having a lot of sex seem like?"

She laughs. "Like you and Leo. So is it a casual thing or...?"

There's clearly no point in denying it. "Did Leo tell Bennett?"

"No, I can just tell by the way you are with each other. You seem connected. Like more than a fake-engaged couple. Do you like him? What's the deal?"

The deal is I *feel* connected to him.

"I don't know if we have a deal, to be honest."

"You've not talked about it?"

I shake my head. How would that conversation go? *"Hey, you're great in bed, wanna make this fake engagement into a real one and see how it goes?"*

"He's not my usual type." I pause. "No, maybe he is my usual type. I'm not sure. I haven't really analyzed the situation."

"Really?" she asks, taking a corn chip. "Then let's start."

Efa is a stranger. I get that she knows Leo and everything, but she doesn't know me. I can't go around analyzing my feelings with someone I just met. I don't even know if I have feelings to analyze.

Well, that's not true. I'm pretty sure I do have feelings to analyze, I'm just not sure I want to think about them.

"When did the sex start?" she asks, just as Bennett comes up behind her and adds a few more things to his plate.

"Jules, please ignore Efa if she's being too intrusive. Don't worry about being rude, just tell her to mind her own business."

She playfully thwacks him on the arm and he chuckles before going back to the game.

"Were you together when you were his assistant?"

"God, no," I reply reflexively. "I kinda hated him when I worked for him."

"I hated Bennett too!" She seems enthusiastic that we have this in common. "Well, I fucked him first, then I hated him." She laughs to herself. "Is Leo an arsehole to work for? He's always so upbeat and charming. I imagine he's a pushover as a boss."

"He's not a pushover. But he's not an asshole. He lets everyone thinks he's relaxed and a bit of an airhead, but nothing could be further from the truth. He knows what he wants and how he wants it. But he's charming about it."

"He sounds like a great boss—kinda how he is outside of work. So why did you hate him?"

I pull in a breath. Efa wants to know everything. "I guess because he's charming and flirty and good-looking and... I imagine not the most faithful guy in the world. Like, he'd be unreliable as a boyfriend. I've been burned by that kind of guy."

Efa hums as she thinks. "And you've found out he's not like that?" She pauses. "I mean, he is charming and flirty and good-looking. There's no doubt about that. But he's not unreliable. And I've never known him to be unfaithful. He's been burned too. Maybe that's made him a little afraid to commit."

My stomach squeezes and twists. "Yeah, he's told me bits and pieces," I say.

"He's such a good man," she adds quickly. "He just hasn't met the right woman yet. Maybe you're who he needs."

I force a small laugh. I don't want her to think I'm some girl who thinks she's the exception—that this time will be different. "We're not *actually* getting married, so it's completely fine. I'm living in the now." I take a chip and load it with dip. I don't want to talk about this. I don't even want to *think* about this. Leo and I haven't discussed anything beyond having sex while we're living together. And why would we? For starters, I still work for him. Then there's the fact that we're not going to be living together forever. We don't need to discuss this stuff because whatever we have between us will come to a natural end when I move out after the awards ceremony. I know Leo's never going to settle down. He's not the asshole I thought he was, but that doesn't mean he's going to anoint me as the Chosen One, either.

"Now's a good place to start," she says. "But don't write off tomorrow. Since I met Leo, it struck me that what he needs is someone in his corner. He's been so afraid of finding someone, but I think deep down, that's what he wants."

I start choking on my chip. "Good to know," I say when I've recovered.

"He's got a really good heart." She glances over at the couch. "They all do. They just need the right women to round off their hard corners."

"Is that what you do for Bennett?"

She smiles. "I think we do it for each other."

I like the idea of the man I'm with making me slightly better, and me being able to do the same for him.

"Are Leo and Bennett the closest?" I ask.

"I'm not sure. Sometimes, from what I can see. But then sometimes Worth and Leo spend a lot of time together. Fisher and Jack are really close. But they all trust each other. They'd do anything for each other."

It's nice to see that side of Leo—the side that's fiercely loyal and a good friend. If Caroline Hammond had never happened, I wonder whether Leo would be less afraid of being in a committed relationship.

"Do you know about his ex?" I ask.

"Caroline? Or Nadia? He only has two from what I know."

I'm interested in both, but I settle on Caroline. "The first one. She seems to have really..."

"Fucked him up? What a bitch, right? Was just using him to irritate her father. Apparently, she got a chunk of change when she got shipped off to California. Her father tried to pay Leo to dump her, and when that didn't work, he paid *her* to dump Leo and sent her west."

My stomach churns at the thought. How can people treat each other like that? "Do you think that was her game plan all along?"

"Probably. But why did she have to string him along for years?"

"Well, if he was as good in bed then as he is now, I think I know why." I laugh, and Efa joins in. "I'm kidding. There's no excuse to behave like that. But it says far more about her than it does about him."

"Maybe she liked him, but not enough to marry?"

"And then he decided never to trust another woman with his heart again," I say out loud. "She ruined him."

"Maybe you're the woman to change that."

I groan. "Women always think they can fix men." My mom always thought if she loved my dad enough, he'd stay with us, or he'd do the right thing by us, but he never did. He always put himself first. "In my experience, people don't fix other people emotionally. If he doesn't want to commit, I'm not going to change that." I'm telling myself what I need to hear. I need to remember who Leo is at his core and why. He's not going to change. Just like my father is never going to change.

"I know he appreciates what you're doing for him," she says after a few minutes. "It's kind of you."

"Not really," I say. "I get a job out of it." My phone buzzes on the countertop and I flip it over to see who's messaging.

"True," she says. "That's how it started. Doesn't mean it has to end that way."

The message alert flashes a number I don't recognize and my heart aches in my chest. I swipe down on the screen. "Sorry, I just want to check this."

It's my dad, asking if we can schedule that coffee.

He messaged me just like he said he would. Maybe him reaching out wasn't all about the job—or maybe the job was the excuse he needed to take the initiative after all these years. Maybe he's picking me. Finally. I hate myself for it, but I can't help but hope. Maybe now that I'm older and things are different—now that I'm not relying on him for anything, now that he doesn't have to worry about being a provider—maybe now things will be different.

Hope splutters into my chest and I turn the phone back onto its face.

"Sorry, what were you saying?"

Efa smiles at me. "God laughs when we make plans. You said yes to being Leo's fake fiancée for the job, but maybe you'll end up being with him for real. I mean, you're *already* with him for real."

"We're not together," I say.

She shrugs dismissively. "You're not pretending to have sex though. That's happening for real."

"Right. But sex is sex. Sex isn't a relationship."

"But you're in his apartment, you're his employee. He may not have thought about it too much either, but this is a big deal for Leo. Don't underestimate what you have together."

What we have together?

"Leo is a really good guy at heart," Efa continues. "He's not one of these narcissistic players who doesn't think about other people's feelings, or see sex as a sport. The reason he doesn't get close to women is because he's afraid of being hurt. You two have built trust. I think this is different."

Different.

I feel something nudge in my chest. I so want what Efa says to be true. I want to be different for Leo, because as I sit here, listening to Efa talk about him—describe him as the good and kind and sensitive guy I've come to know him as—I realize things already are different. For me.

TWENTY-THREE

Jules

Leo's working late tonight and I can't sit still.

Maybe it's because I'm not used to being here on my own. Or maybe it's because I miss him. Either way, it feels uncomfortable to be in this apartment without him. I'm used to his easy smile, the crease between his eyebrows when he's concentrating. I kinda feel empty without him, even though I just saw him this morning.

I'm in dangerous territory. I'm not supposed to get attached to Leo. I know who he is. I know he doesn't commit. And I know I'm not the exception. I get it. Or at least, my brain understands all this. My heart? That's another thing entirely.

I pull out my phone and bring up our message thread. It's no big deal to offer to order food for him, is it? Maybe I should stop pretending that I don't want to be the exception and start acting like I should be.

Before I can overthink anymore, I type out, Going to order sushi. Want some?

I send the message and then re-read it. By accident, I've also given him the opportunity to make some kind of joke about wanting some.

He replies right away.

Sounds good but no, thanks. I don't know when I'll be home.

I know this is his home, but my heart squeezes at the thought that him coming back here, to me, is home.

I miss him.

I read his message again. Something about it doesn't feel right. Maybe I'm an idiot, but it doesn't seem like everything's okay. The vibes are off. I type out another message.

Where are you?

He replies right away.

New River.

Maybe he has a late meeting. It's nearly nine. Why else would he be there now?

I put my hair up in a bun and head to the door. I grab my sneakers from where I've flung them in the hall closet and head out. There's only one way to be sure if Leo's okay. I'll go and check.

Within a few minutes, I'm in a cab heading up to Harlem. I stop for sushi on the way and arrive at the New River building thirty minutes later.

I get out of the cab and suddenly realize Leo might have left in the time it took me to get here. Luckily for me, security is behind the desk and lets me in after I tell them I'm delivering dinner to my boss.

I step into the elevator and change my mind about being here at least five times on the way up.

What's the worst that can happen?

He can look disappointed to see me. He can ask me to go.

The lights are all on when I step out of the elevator

into the penthouse, which looks even bigger than it did the night of the party. It's empty, for starters, but the unobstructed views of the city out the floor-to-ceiling windows are what make the biggest difference. I think it's because I see views across the entire city that it looks so big. Like the entire island of Manhattan is up here in this apartment.

I sweep through but don't see Leo. It's not until my second walk-through that I spot the back of his head over the top of a chair on the terrace. As I walk toward him, I see he's in his suit, one ankle crossed over a knee, his hands joined together in front of him.

Why is he here? He's not working.

I slide open the glass door onto the terrace but he doesn't turn at the sound.

"Hey," I say. "I brought you dinner."

He finally turns in his seat and gives me a half smile. "Oh hey."

I offer him a tray of sushi, which he takes.

He doesn't say anything and neither do I. I just take a seat in the chair next to his. We sit in silence as we eat. The air has a chill to it, and I wonder if there's a blanket I can bring out here.

Or maybe I should head home. Only… something tells me Leo wants me here.

After about twenty minutes, he slides the empty sushi tray onto the table.

"It's the delivery drivers who know the city better than anyone," he says.

"I can see how that would be true," I reply.

"They know the shortcuts, the back entrances, the traffic patterns. Where construction has popped up overnight."

I nod and slide my half-eaten tray on the table next to his.

"Driving deliveries was how I developed my love of New York."

"When you were delivering bread with your father?"

He nods. "Yeah. We'd be up so early, before the streets came to life. People are wrong when they say this is the city that never sleeps. It does—but it's in shifts. Certain areas are quiet at certain times. The early mornings on the Upper East Side are peaceful."

Leo's not here because he wants to look out over the Upper East Side in the dark.

"That's when you met her?"

He nods. "It was a long time ago, so why can't I just move on?" he asks. "Why do I care enough about what she thinks about me that I'm prepared to make someone pretend to be my fiancée?"

"Do you think those old feelings were made worse because of what happened with Nadia this summer?"

"Probably. But I hate that even my subconscious is still so affected by Caroline. Like, why was I taken in by another cold blonde this summer?"

"By the sounds of it, no one could have predicted what she was after with Bennett."

"True, but what was it about *me* that meant I was targeted by her? Why not Worth? Or Fisher or Byron or Jack?"

"Who's to say? It might have been an alphabetical list and she was working backwards."

He looks at me—really looks at me—for the first time tonight. It feels like his hand around my waist, warm and safe.

"You're looking for closure," I say. "That's normal."

"I got closure when she laughed in my face and told me she had no interest continuing our relationship. There was literal closure, Jules. It was a door in my face."

"I think it's normal to want to prove to your enemies that they didn't break you."

"Maybe she *did* break me," he says more quietly.

"I don't think so. She might have just bent you a little, and now you're looking to straighten back out. But no one can do that for you but you."

His eyes slice to mine and we sit there for a few moments, the city in the distance, a backdrop to our whole lives.

"You think someone else could straighten me out? Make me someone who's less driven to succeed by the knowledge of what it's like to feel small? Disposable? Someone who's friendly with a lot of people but who has few actual friends? Someone who carries this anger toward a woman he hasn't seen for fifteen years. Why can't I just put it down?"

"I wish you could see yourself the way I do, Leo. You have a small circle of friends who would bury a body for you. You're lucky. Most people get one of those people in their whole lives. And being a bit suspicious is a smart move. You're a rich, successful guy, and this is a tough city—a tough *world*. Someone's always going to want something from you. I think you've kept your humanity when life could have turned you cynical and cold. You're kind and sensitive and thoughtful and... I'm proud to know you. Yeah, maybe Caroline coming back into town has you shaken up. But maybe she's the closet you never cleared out—something that's been on your to-do list for the longest time. Maybe the awards ceremony is the perfect opportunity to—"

"Purge?" he asks.

I laugh. "Maybe."

Silence echoes out from our terrace.

Maybe I shouldn't have come tonight. Just as I'm about to leave, he reaches out a hand and I take it. He threads his fingers through mine. We sit there together in a quiet that speaks volumes.

"Thank you for dinner."

"You're worth it," I say. He turns his gaze full on me again, and it takes my breath away.

What have I gotten myself into?

"I'm considering not going to the awards ceremony," he says.

I feel like I've been dropped to the ground. "You really don't want to see her."

"It's not that. I just feel like I've given it way too much attention. Like, no offense, but I knew you for five minutes before I brought you on as my fake fiancée and moved you into my apartment."

"Right," I say. I'm getting whiplash right about now. "I can go stay with Sophia tonight." I manage to keep my voice steady as I deliver the words, but it's an effort. Is this why he's up here tonight? Because he wants space? I tug my hand from his. He reaches for me again, but I don't reach back.

"No," he says, his tone sharp. "That's not what I'm saying. I want..." He sighs. He doesn't know what he wants. "I want you to stay."

"The awards are in a couple of days. And then it will be over. I'll be gone."

"I want you to stay. Not for the awards, but because I..." He looks me in the eye. "Because I like you."

My heart lifts in my chest, even as my throat goes tight. "I like you, too."

He pulls me onto his lap and circles my waist with his hands. "I don't want you to go."

This is what I missed when I was back in the apartment. This feeling when I'm with him like I belong. Like I'm someone's priority. I'm sure Leo doesn't mean to make me feel that way, but he does. Like I'm special—the only woman he'll open up to, the only woman he'll bare his soul to. The only woman he'll look at just this way.

He makes me feel like I'm his exception, and I can't decide whether to be moved by the realization, or afraid.

TWENTY-FOUR

Leo

I'm pacing outside the apartment building, waiting for Jules to show. She sent me downstairs about thirty minutes ago to *get some air*. That was right after I asked her for the fiftieth time when she'd be ready. I glance at my watch. Obviously, I wore my most expensive one. It's not my favorite, but it's part of the image I need to project tonight. Paired with a handmade suit, it almost completes the picture. But there's one more thing I need, and she's twenty stories up.

"Hi," Jules says from behind me.

I spin around to find her coming toward me in a black, floor-length, strapless gown. The fabric clings to every curve and it's the sexiest thing I've ever seen, even though the most it reveals is her shoulders.

"You look... incredible," I say.

She grins at me, and I have to fight the urge to cup her face and kiss her into next week. "Thanks. You look pretty great yourself." She tugs on my bow tie.

I half choke on my words like I'm a nerdy thirteen-year-old being introduced to Emily Ratajkowski. "Thanks. Are you ready to go?"

She lifts her chin slightly. "Sure am."

We're only a few blocks away from the Plaza, where the awards will be held. I slip my hand under hers for the drive and we sit in silence. For a second I wonder what will happen with Jules and me after tonight, but I push the thought away. I can't think of stuff like that now. Someone opens the car door as soon as we pull up and I jump out the other side. I should be the one who helps Jules out.

I take her hand and she steps out of the car. She doesn't look like a million bucks. She looks like a billion.

She stands and sweeps her hair over one shoulder. I take her hand. We should be moving into the hotel, but I can't stop looking at her. She's so beautiful.

"I like your hair down like this." I press a kiss to the side of her head.

"I'm beginning to learn that about you," she replies, and I swear it feels like she's reading my mind, seeing every image running through my head: How she looks when she's on all fours, her hair curtaining her either side. How it feels when she's on top of me, leaning back, her hair sweeping over my legs as she comes. How she moans when I gather her hair in my hand and use it to lift her chin to give me more access to her.

All I can think about is Jules, naked, when I see her hair down.

"You should definitely not wear your hair down if you want me to concentrate."

She lifts her eyebrows slightly, like she knew exactly what she was doing tonight when she had her hair styled like this. Like she wanted my mind to be completely full of her when I see Caroline.

I'm content to stand on the red carpet, at the entrance to the hotel ballroom, but apparently Jules isn't.

She starts to walk and tugs on my hand, laughing. "Come on. I'd like a martini."

"I think we should make it a margarita," I reply. "We can make that back home. Do we even need to be here?"

"Not for long," she says.

Already she's got me *not* thinking about the worst parts of this evening more than I thought possible. She's deliberately distracting me, because that's who she is. Always thinking about me. Caring, concerned, committed.

We make our way to the cocktail area.

"What happened to the dinner with your would-be investor in Harlem?" she asks.

I take two full champagne flutes from a tray and hand one to Jules. "Andrew? The guy you met at New River?"

"Yeah, weren't we going to have dinner with him and his wife?"

I nod. "Yeah, trying to find a time in his diary is insane. He's being wined and dined by the whole of New York. I'll ask my new assistant where we are with that."

A breeze of awkwardness passes between us. Tonight was the night that Jules and I have been working toward for the last few weeks. It was all meant to end tonight. I've not thought past the next few hours. We haven't discussed what's next for us. Is she moving out? Do I want her to? What are we doing? Are we sleeping with each other because it's convenient or because—

I can't think about any of this until after tonight. I just need to focus on the here and now.

I scan the room and see various people I know. I raise my glass to the head of one of my go-to brokers just as Jonathan comes up behind us.

"Leo, my friend. The man of the moment. How are you doing?" His eyes flit between me and Jules. I smile as I see him work out whether or not we're together.

"Great to see you, Jonathan. Have you met my fiancée, Jules Moore?"

"Your fiancée?" he asks. "You usually come stag to these kinds of events. No, I've not had the pleasure."

"I couldn't miss a night like this," Jules says without missing a beat. "I don't usually tag along to work events, but I made an exception for the Developer of the Decade." She's smooth and charming and everything I'm not feeling right now.

Just as I'm about to make an excuse and head to the bathroom, Worth appears. "Hey, guys. Jules." He pulls her in for a hug, completing the picture that Jules is part of my inner circle.

As I chat to Worth about who from our group has arrived, which is easily cleared up because I've seen no one, Jonathan continues to talk to Jules. It's only fleeting, but for a second, I wonder if they've met before. I know that finding out Nadia wasn't who she said she was did a number on me, but I wish I could put those fears behind me. Everything I want to put in the past is right here in this room tonight.

"Have you seen her?" Worth asks, his tone hushed.

I shake my head. "I haven't looked."

"I checked the table plan. You're at the table at the front and she's two tables over."

I nod, grateful that Worth's thought to look. Forewarned is forearmed.

A couple of people from my team arrive. As I greet them, I check for Jules out of the corner of my eye. I don't see her, and so I scan the crowd.

Someone slips a hand into mine. "Hey." Jules is beside me. "Sorry. Jonathan sure can talk."

"Is that Jonathan Klein from *Property International*?" Franchesa, from my team, says. "He could actually represent the US in the talking Olympics. I've never met a man with more words."

Bennett arrives with Efa, and I glance at Jules. Is she pleased? Does she like Efa? I do, but she's my mate's girlfriend—as long as she's good to him, I'm happy. Has Jules made a friend in Efa? Why am I even thinking about this? *Because you're living in the future instead of staying in the present*, a voice inside chides. Is there a future where a friendship between Efa and Jules matters to me? Do I want there to be?

Bennett comes over and we hug.

"Thanks for coming," I say.

"Wouldn't miss it."

People start moving toward the ballroom and I brace myself. If Caroline and I are sitting near each other, we're likely to bump into each other sooner rather than later.

Jules squeezes my hand. "Do you know what table we're at?" she asks.

"Four. We're at the front."

We enter the ballroom and Jules glances around. I've been here countless times before, but fresh eyes give it new perspective. It's very classic, old money New York. Crystal chandeliers, Grecian columns, gold leaf detail on the plasterwork. It's so different from the developments I bring to the market. But this version of New York, built on generations of inherited wealth, is fading away.

"I bet these guys don't have a problem booking weddings," she says, and I smile at her understatement.

"Yeah, I don't think the Plaza is too worried about their events calendar."

"Maybe I'll come and manage this place," she says, grinning. I don't bite, offering only an eye roll in response. I see our table and nod toward it. "There we are."

Just as we get to our seats, I see some movement out of the corner of my eye. I don't sit immediately. Instead, I slide my arm around Jules' waist and brace.

I turn slightly and see Caroline's father, Frank, coming toward me. "Leo!" he calls, lumbering toward us at speed. I hold out my free hand to shake his as he gets to us. "The man of the moment!"

"Have you met my fiancée?" I ask him. "Jules Moore."

"Delighted," he says, shaking Jules' hand. "I have to introduce you to my son-in-law and daughter." He turns and cranes his neck, beckoning someone over.

"At least we can get this bit over with before the food and your award," Jules says beside me.

I chuckle. "That's one way of looking at it."

"Grant, let me introduce you to Leo Hart," Frank says. Grant and I shake hands. "Caroline, this is Leo Hart."

She narrows her eyes for a split second, as if she's looking for confirmation that I'm who she thinks I am. She hasn't changed much. She's a little thinner. More polished. Her hair's a little blonder. I'm waiting for the wrecking ball to knock me on my arse, but it doesn't come. I'm tense, but nothing more. Maybe it will come later. Perhaps a knot in my gut will appear over dinner. Maybe a faint whisper of memory will settle over me as I collect my award. At the moment, though, I don't feel anything.

"Leo!" she caws. "So good to see you." She raises her arms slightly, like she's expecting a good-to-see-you hug. I tighten my arm around Jules' waist and offer my hand to shake as I kiss her cheek. "Leo and I are old friends," Caroline says. "Knew each other when we were kids." She smiles and it's full of genuine warmth, like she doesn't even remember how things ended between us.

"Really?" Grant asks. "Such a small world."

Far too fucking small. I could have happily lived without this moment for the rest of my life.

"This is my fiancée, Jules Moore," I say, and Jules shakes everyone's hands.

"We should all get together for dinner," Caroline says. "Catch up. It's been a minute."

"We'd love to," Jules says, a little too quickly. She's probably concerned I might tell them to shove their dinners up their arse. I wouldn't, because I've prepared myself for this moment for far too long. But I'm still grateful that she speaks, because I wouldn't have been able to get the words out. Even though I don't want to be rude, I can't bring myself to pretend away what happened between us. I don't experience a rush of feeling for or about Caroline, but the incredible shitty-ness of what she did washes over me like it happened just yesterday. She's a bitch.

"I've been following your career for a while now," Grant says.

I nod, not sure if he's bullshitting me or not. It doesn't matter. It's not like we're ever going to do business with him.

"You've really done some amazing work. The stuff in Harlem looks incredible. I'd love to get a tour at some point."

"New River is incredible," Frank says. "You should definitely go and see it. It's going to change that part of New York forever. It will bring new life to the place. The finishes are second to none."

"Sales have launched, so if you have buyers, Annabelle Swain's team would love to hear from you," I say.

"I'm sure we have buyers," Grant says. "If we bring enough of them, maybe we'll get to be the agents on your next development."

Grant is a typical agent. Pushy. Underinformed. But it gives me a sense of satisfaction that I don't answer him with a commitment either way. He'll take hope from that, just as Frank always has. It means he'll waste energy and effort trying to win my business when I'll never work with him.

A gong sounds and people start taking their seats. Frank and Grant say goodbye. Caroline reaches for my hand and squeezes. "So good to see you, darling. Glad we've run into each other all these years later."

"She acted like—" Jules whispers as we move to our table. She's practically stuttering over Caroline's audacity.

I chuckle. "Like we were old friends reunited. So very typical of her. She doesn't really get how her actions affect anyone. Or doesn't care."

Why was I so worked up about seeing her? It's not like I want her back.

"Are you okay?" Jules whispers.

I nod. "I am." I squeeze her leg under the table and sit back. It's like something's been released in me that's been bolted in place for years. "Thank you for being here."

She reaches up and pushes her fingertips through my hair, over my ear. "It's my pleasure," she says.

The rest of the members of my team join us at the table. Fisher sends over six bottles of vintage champagne before the awards announcements even begin.

"I think it's shitty that they don't announce your award first," Jules says.

"You do?"

"Yeah, because then you could sit back and relax."

"But would we stay?" I ask. "I'm not sure I could sit through all these awards if I wasn't waiting for mine at the end."

"I thought you've been to these awards before?"

"Only when I've been nominated for Developer of the Year. It's a networking opportunity. I'm rarely in my seat." Realistically, I don't know if I'll attend again. What's the point? I've built a reputation so everyone in New York real estate knows me. I'd prefer to be at home right now. Or at dinner with Jules one-on-one.

"You do a lot of late-night events," she says. Her tone is off. A few weeks ago, I wouldn't have noticed, but I know her better now. What's she thinking?

"Yeah. People tend to be more available in the evenings. It's often easier to get dinner in someone's diary than a meeting."

She nods. "Right. Makes sense." She clears her throat and busies herself smoothing her napkin in her lap. "I've hired a guy to help me move out tomorrow," she says. "I don't want to outstay my welcome. I've taken tomorrow off and I'm working Sunday. So tomorrow morning, I'll have coffee with Dad and then I'll be out of your way by the time you get home."

It takes me a couple of minutes for my brain to process exactly what she's saying. When her words land, the knot in my stomach I was expecting when I saw Caroline earlier finally twists my insides. "You're moving out tomorrow?" I keep my voice low.

"Yeah. That was the plan, right? We have the awards tonight and then, that's it?"

I've been so focused on tonight, I haven't thought about what comes next. What she's saying makes sense. The deal was that Jules would pretend to be my fiancée until tonight. And although lines have been blurred, it's not like we're really engaged.

"I'm just going to the restroom," she says, before I get a chance to answer.

The awards are whizzing by quickly. Ben, sitting next to me, warns me I'm up next, or I wouldn't have noticed that Developer of the Decade was about to be announced. I turn to see where Jules is. She's nowhere in sight.

Jonathan comes onstage and I can feel people's eyes on me. I focus on the stage—and realize that Jules is standing slightly behind him. Why is she onstage? She doesn't know him.

Dread spreads through my brain and down my spine. What is happening? Am I about to be embarrassed in front of the entire industry? Is Jules in on some kind of scheme?

I tune in to what Jonathan is saying. He's going through some of the developments I've brought to market over the last decade. People interrupt with smatterings of applause. I glance across at Caroline, who's grinning up at the stage as if she's enjoying the description of my success.

Jonathan steps to the side and Jules takes his place. I hold my breath, gripping the table, waiting.

"How Leo Hart does business is just as important as how successful he is. He's as popular in the office, with all the people who work for him, as he is with the people he sits across from at the negotiating table. He's a man whose word stands for something. A man of principles and integrity. I'm lucky to be his fiancée, and proud to tell you that the man you're celebrating tonight deserves every honor and then some. Let's all welcome to the stage, Developer of the Decade, easy to like, easy to love, Leo Hart."

Our table is just steps from the stage, so I'm face-to-face

with Jules in a couple of seconds. Our eyes lock as she hands me the award. Yes, she had to say all those things about me, but did she mean it when she said I was easy to love?

Jules turns to leave the stage, but I catch her hand and hold it as I make a short speech, thanking everyone who's helped me get where I am now. It passes in a blur, and before I know it, Jules and I are making our way back to our seats.

I hold her hand tightly in mine for the rest of the evening, not wanting to let her go for a second.

The rest of the night passes quickly. When the ceremony's over, we're told there's an after-hours party in the room next door.

My gaze slices to Jules and it's clear that neither of us wants to go. Bennett, Fisher, and the others all come up and congratulate me, then it's just Jules and me heading to the car. We're in the lobby when Caroline and Grant appear in front of us.

"Darling, wonderful speech," she says. "Let me get your number and we'll arrange that dinner."

My eye twitches, but I dutifully pull out my phone. Before we can exchange numbers, Jules interrupts. "I'll give you my number, Caroline. I'm much easier to get a hold of."

Caroline smiles, and she and Jules swap numbers.

Grant slaps me on the back. "Here's my card. If you ever want a second opinion about anything, just give me a call. I know you haven't worked with Hammonds before, but we have some great international reach. Asia in particular is a strength for us. I just had an investor buy five units in a new development over the phone. He didn't even see renderings."

I nod, pretending I'm interested. I'm not. Not even if

Hammonds was the only brokerage in the city. If that were the case, I'd set up my own fucking brokerage. I glance across at Caroline, giggling with Jules like they're best friends. Grant is so close, I'm slightly concerned he's going to try to crawl up my arsehole.

I need a shower.

"I'll keep it in mind," I say. "Jules, the car is just there. We should go."

"Lovely to see you, darling," Caroline says again to me. "It's wonderful seeing you've made something out of yourself. I always knew you would."

I no longer care if I look rude. I nod, scoop up Jules' hand, and head out to the car.

I'm not just going to have a shower. I'm going to have to burn my suit and shave my head to rid myself of that encounter.

I slide into the car next to Jules and sweep my hands through my hair.

"That went well," Jules says.

I should thank her for making her speech, but I can't bring myself to speak. I can taste Caroline's heavy perfume, feel her fingers on my hand.

"Are you okay?" Jules asks eventually.

"I'm a fool," I say finally. "How could I have ever loved her? How could I have let Nadia get so close? What is the matter with me that I can build a successful business like I'm riding a bike, but I can't read people?"

"That's bullshit," she says, her voice harsh compared to the saccharine-sweetness she poured on for Caroline.

I choke out a laugh. "Not from where I'm sitting."

"Then you need to sit over here. Firstly, running a business like yours isn't easy. You work really hard and you're completely committed. Secondly, you were a teenager when

Caroline Hammond got her talons into you. You were a kid. And Nadia? Who the fuck is she, anyway? Some woman you knew for five minutes who probably had nice tits and gave a great blow job? She wanted something from you and she got it because you weren't focused on *her*—you were focused on your business. She was just white noise."

I laugh at the way Jules puts things. *White noise?*

"You can't give yourself a hard time about either of those women. Yes, they were using you, but everyone uses everyone. That's just life. You needed a fiancée; I wanted a job at The Mayfair. New York City needs more apartments and you want more money. A billionaire wants a hot wife and a hot girl wants billions. That's the way it is. You've just got to make sure you're getting what you need while everyone else is getting what they want. Separate transactional relationships from your friends and family—the ones who would walk through fire or bury a body for you. You have more people like that in your life than most. Those are the people you need to spend your energy on. Everyone else can fuck off."

"I never thought of my relationship with Caroline as transactional."

"That's why it smarts with Caroline—because she took what she wanted from you and didn't give you what you wanted in return. But that's one woman, one time in your life. You're one of the most powerful men in Manhattan. That's not going to happen again."

"How can you be so sure?"

"You're not eighteen anymore," she says. "You're smarter. You're more experienced. And you know when to trust your heart and when to trust your gut."

"Do I?" I ask. I'm not so sure.

"You do. You're talking about *two* instances where

someone has used you in over a decade. But people are actually using you all the time and, importantly, vice versa."

"That's not true," I say. When did Jules get so cynical?

"What about real estate agents? They use you. You think they'd be as nice to you if you weren't the biggest developer in New York City? Of course not. But you need them, too. It's just business. It's a mutually predatory relationship. It's a trade. Just like us."

"Like us?"

"I said yes to being your fiancée because you said I could manage The Mayfair. It's... it was business."

"And now? You move out tomorrow and that's it?"

She holds my gaze.

"That's the end of our arrangement," she says.

What if I want a new arrangement?

"Right." I can't think of anything else to say. I like Jules. Really like her. And I don't think what we have together is any kind of trade. We're not using each other. Are we? Is she? I know she wants the permanent job at the hotel. But that's not why we're sleeping together, is it?

I shake my head. That can't be it, or she wouldn't be moving out. She'd be trying to stay.

One thing I know for certain is that being with Jules doesn't feel like being with Caroline or Nadia. Jules feels like she fits with me in a way I knew I didn't with Caroline —or maybe it was all too long ago to remember. Now, with the awards ceremony behind me, memories of me and Caroline are fading. The hatred and disgust I have for her and myself for falling for her seem further away, like they were part of another life. Another lifetime.

I'm more focused on the *we* of me and Jules, and why she's so keen to move out. Doesn't she want to stay?

"Tonight is the end of our business arrangement," I say. "Tomorrow is a fresh start."

She's staring straight ahead, her expression closed to me. I want to know what she's thinking.

"Let's have lunch tomorrow. Talk about some stuff." I need tonight to sort things out in my brain. Asking Jules to stay living in my guest room doesn't seem like the right thing to do, but if I ask her to share the master? I'm not sure either of us is ready for that.

"I can't tomorrow. I'm meeting my dad for coffee and then he's coming to meet you, remember? I figure I can pretty much drop him off at your door. At least that way I know he'll show."

She smiles at me and slides her hand into mine.

"Dinner, then?" I ask. "Why don't you delay your move-out a couple days? We can have dinner." We need to talk—I'm just not quite sure what about yet. I don't want to give her up simply because our fake engagement is over. I really like her.

She looks at me, her eyes narrowing. "The weekend?"

"It makes more sense."

She sighs as if the thought of dinner with me is a chore. "I suppose." She says the words carefully, like she's arranging them between shards of broken glass. If I didn't know her better, I would say she just wants to move out and get on with her life. But I *do* know her better. Maybe neither of us knows where to go from here. All I'm sure of is that I want to figure it out.

"Hey, careful. Don't get overly excited at the prospect of dinner with me."

She laughs. "I am excited. This is my excited face."

I grin at her, relief shuddering through me at the familiar warmth in her tone. "You're beautiful."

"And excited."

TWENTY-FIVE

Jules

I don't know if it's because of the fresh, crisp air of this October day, but there's a lift in my chest and I can't stop smiling. I feel like I'm about to go on vacation or something. I've spent the morning trying not to replay my conversation with Leo last night. He wants to have dinner. To talk. And I want that too. I like the guy. I *more* than like him. He's not the man I thought he was when I met him. He's a flirt for sure. And he has women asking for his number all the time, I have no doubt. But I don't think he's some kind of unreliable, unfaithful womanizer. He's not the player I thought he was. It's early between us, but we share an undeniable chemistry in and out of the bedroom.

Maybe he was right the first time we met. Maybe he *is* my destiny.

I arrive at the coffee shop where I'm meeting my dad and order. It's just before twelve, so there's no line. I'd like to order for him too, but I wouldn't be able to recite his coffee order for a million dollars.

I can't help but think about my mom's reaction when I tell her Dad has reappeared. I haven't said anything about him turning up on the roof terrace. I know it would upset her, and if he's just going to turn around and disappear again, there's no point. I get the feeling I'll have to have the conversation sometime soon. He texted this morning to confirm our meeting, and he seems determined to get a job here. I know I've told Leo I don't want him to hire my dad—and I don't—but I wonder if he knows someone outside of the Hart company who might have an opening. My dad's obviously motivated about finding work.

I take a seat and check my watch. It's two minutes past twelve. A shiver of anxiety passes down my spine and I try to shrug it off. I don't need to worry. He's going to show. If he wasn't, why would he have texted this morning? He wouldn't have bothered. I swallow and try not to look out the window. I used to spend hours sitting on my windowsill as a child, waiting for an unfamiliar car to pull up outside our house, hoping my father would open the driver's door. Every now and then, that's exactly what happened, and for a few days or weeks, or sometimes even a month or two, we would be a family.

Until he left.

I'd never know when he was going to go. He could be happy as a clam at dinner, and by morning, his car would have disappeared, the suitcase he came with vanished with him. He'd never leave a trace of himself behind. Except that last time, when he left his comics. When I was old enough to analyze these things, I often wondered whether his leaving them behind was a sign. Did he want to leave a piece of himself with me?

"Hey, Dollface!"

I snap my head up to find my father standing over me,

arms outstretched. He's fifteen minutes late, but who's counting?

"Dad," I say, jumping up from my seat. Without thinking, I accept his hug. He pulls me in close. It should feel familiar. A hug from my dad is something I should take for granted. But his arms feel alien, his frame doesn't fit. It feels a little awkward, but at least I can't smell whiskey. I hold on for as long as I can.

Eventually, he pulls back and holds me by the shoulders. "You look great, kid."

I smile. "Thanks. Can I get you a coffee?"

He sits while I get him a double espresso. While I watch the barista make his drink, I wonder whether he always drinks espresso, or only when he might want to be done in a mouthful. He just has to take a gulp and it's gone. Then he's free to leave. Espresso is the coffee for people who don't want to be in one place for very long. It's coffee for my father.

I slide the cup onto the table.

"Thanks, doll," he says.

"You're welcome. You ready to meet Leo?" Between his lateness and the time it took to order his drink, we don't have much time. Twenty minutes or so before we'll have to leave.

"Sure thing," he says in the same upbeat voice he uses when he says "Dollface."

I know Leo's not going to give him a job, but I still want my dad to make a good impression. "He's my boss, Dad. So... you know. You gotta be on your best behavior."

He laughs. "I'm always on my best behavior. Tell me about being manager of The Mayfair," he says. "What's it like being the boss of so many people?"

"It's good," I say. "It's early days, but I'm enjoying getting things in shape. I think it's got an exciting future."

"Miss Boss Lady. Who would have thought it? You were such a funny kid. Always had your head in a book. Your room was always neat as a pin. And so independent." He grins as he shakes his head.

My stomach starts to curdle. I don't want to talk about my childhood. About how I was so independent because my mom was working two jobs to put a roof over our heads.

"So are you back in town to stay? Where have you been living?"

He leans back in his chair, stretching out his legs under the table. "Gotta love New York. Place is always changing and never changes at the same time."

I smile at his description. He's not wrong.

I wait for him to answer. How long is he back for? If he asked for a job at The Mayfair, he must be planning to stay for a reasonable amount of time.

"Do you live in Manhattan?" he asks.

"Jersey," I say.

He nods. "Great place. I'd love to see your setup."

My heart inches higher in my chest at the thought of showing my dad around my apartment. It's not big, but Sophia and I have made it cozy. "I like to decorate for fall," I say.

"You do? That's nice. With the acorns and stuff?"

"Yeah, I like to have a wreath on the door, even though we're in an apartment building. And inside, on the table, there's a centerpiece of mini pumpkins and faux leaves."

"You like interior décor? Doing stuff like that for fun?"

I sigh. "I suppose I do." I've been having some ideas for the hotel lobby that I think will elevate the area. Louis took away the fresh flower arrangements. I want to bring them back, but in a modern, creative way that's more cost effective than having huge numbers of fresh flowers delivered twice a week. I'm thinking I'll pair planted orchids with fresh flowers on the table, then put air plants on the reception desk in striking glass containers so they're a talking point for guests. At the moment the lobby looks bleak. I think we can do better.

"Looks like you get on well with your boss," he says.

I hope the heat in my cheeks doesn't show. "He's a good guy." There's no point telling him about the engagement. It will make things more awkward for him when he meets Leo next. He needs to see him as a potential boss, not a future son-in-law. "He took a chance, giving me the job managing The Mayfair."

"Hopefully he'll do the same for me."

I smile and I hope it looks genuine. "So where are you staying? With a friend or—"

"Oh just here and there," he replies. "For some reason I thought your mom worked at The Mayfair."

"She did. Are you staying in Manhattan?" I ask again. I'm not sure the change of subject was deliberate, but either way, I want to know where he's staying.

"Yeah, don't you worry about me," he says, patting my hand.

I'm not worried exactly. I just... want to know. So far we've talked about me, but I don't know what my dad's being doing with his life since he walked out all those years ago. The way he's dodging my questions is starting to feel deliberate.

"What made you move back here?" I ask. "Did you lose your job?" I don't even know if he got married again. Maybe he's had more children.

"Just haven't seen New York in a while," he says with a

simple shrug. There's not even a rushed addendum about how he's missed me—how a reunion was overdue.

I can feel myself begin to deflate. The little bit of hope that had lodged itself in my heart is working free.

Maybe he sees it in my gaze, because the next thing he says is not what I expect.

"I know we've got a lot to catch up on," he says. "And I want to do that. I want to hear all your news. I want to know about every job, boyfriend, dream you ever had. I'm going to listen to it all. I've missed out on so much... I'd like to get up to speed if you'll let me."

He reaches for my hand and I let him take it across the table. That sliver of hope settles back in my heart. He *does* want to know me. I'm rushing everything, but we have time.

The alarm on my phone bleeps.

"We should leave for your meeting with Leo," I say.

"You're coming too?"

I shake my head. "No, but his office is on my way. I can drop you off."

"Great," he says, slapping his thighs and standing. "Let's go."

Outside, he scoops up my hand and tucks it under his arm. We walk arm in arm, heading north on Madison. He starts pointing to buildings and telling me snippets of history about them or which movies were filmed there. This is the Dad I remember from when I was a kid—the interesting Dad whose every word I clung to. The Dad who knew everything.

"Here we are," I say, stopping outside Leo's building.

"Already?" he asks. "I was just getting started with my tour." He grins at me and I smile.

"I have the annual pass," I say. "So we can pick up

where we left off next time. Are you around over the weekend?"

He nods. "Should be. Got a couple of meetings but apart from that..."

This time I initiate our hug. It's a little less awkward than it was before. Maybe I'm less stiff. Less nervous. "Good luck," I say. "Leo's a good guy."

Maybe I was too quick to ask Leo not to give him a job. Maybe he deserves a shot.

"Thanks, kid." He gives me a wink, turns, and pushes through the revolving door to Leo's office.

I stand and watch as he heads to the reception desk.

Maybe I was wrong about my dad. What if he's changed? Parenthood is tough and it's possible he just couldn't cope with me when I was a child. But it's different now. He's got his life. I've got mine. I don't *need* him for anything. He's got nothing to run from.

TWENTY-SIX

Jules

Leo didn't mention a specific restaurant when he suggested dinner, so I'm in gray joggers and a Taylor Swift tee, researching food delivery options. It will probably be for the last time. I'm going to miss living here. But it's not just the convenience and the view. I'm going to miss Leo.

The sadness of moving out is replaced by a nugget of excitement about what's to come. I really like Leo and I know he likes me. I want us to navigate this next part of whatever we're doing so we can keep liking each other. I can't remember the last time I felt that I wanted *more* with a man. This feels like a fresh start.

A fresh start with Leo—and perhaps a fresh start with my dad too? I'll have to tell Mom that he's back in town. She won't like it, but I also know she won't stand in the way of him being in my life. All those birthdays and Christmases I saw her crying when she thought I wasn't watching... I knew she wanted my father to be with us—she wanted a family. Maybe it's too late for a conventional family, but that doesn't mean that we can't fashion something out of what's left.

My phone buzzes and I see Leo's name as soon as I pick it up.

Running late. Can you order in some sushi?

No problem. How long do you think you'll be?

An hour. Maybe a bit more.

No problem. Looking forward to hearing how it went with my dad.

Three dots that indicate he's typing show up and then disappear. He probably has to focus on his current meeting. And then, while I'm staring, they reappear. And stop again. Is he distracted? Busy?

I follow up with, And sushi with you, as well!

The three dots reappear and then I get a message.

Can't wait for sushi either. Not much to say about your dad. He didn't show.

It feels like the seat just fell out of my chair. I'm in free fall. He must have been there. I showed him to the door.

I start to type out a message asking if Leo is sure, but then I delete it. Of course he's sure.

I walked him to the door of your building.

I press send and try to remember what Dad said before he went in. We talked about how he loved New York, though he didn't say how long he was staying. We walked to Leo's building arm in arm.

Something must be wrong.

I call his number, but he doesn't answer.

I feel nauseous. I clutch at my stomach with my hand. He seemed perfectly well when I left him. It can only have been something big that got in the way of him getting from the building reception up to Leo's floor. Something huge. A heart attack. Or stroke.

I should start calling around hospitals. I don't even know if he has insurance. As I bring up the keypad on my phone, ready to call god knows who, my cell rings again.

It's my dad.

"Hello?" I answer. "Is everything okay? What happened?"

"Hey, Dollface," he answers. "How are you?"

"Forget about me. Where are you? How are you? Are you in the hospital?"

"No, no, no," he says. "I'm in my car." In his car? I can't picture it. I don't know what car he's driving.

"On the way back from the hospital?" I ask.

"No, I haven't been to the hospital."

"Dad!" I say. "Leo said you didn't show for your meeting."

"Ohhh, yeah. That. I was going to call you. I got a message just after I saw you. I had an emergency."

"What kind of emergency?" I ask.

"It's taken me out of town for a couple of days. That's all."

"You're not in New York?"

"I've got a few things to clear up. I might even have a job lined up. You never know. Wish me luck, Dollface."

I hold the phone away from my ear, hoping I'll get more of a clue about what's going on by looking at the screen. It doesn't make sense, but neither does my dad right now.

"So... you're not sick?" I ask.

"Fit as a fiddle," he replies.

"You just ditched the meeting with Leo."

"Like I said, I had an emergency." He clears his throat. "Listen, Dollface, I'm driving. I'll call you another time."

Before I can respond, the phone goes dead.

Suddenly I'm six years old again, sitting on the windowsill, watching the taillights of my dad's silver Honda disappear into traffic.

I put on my sneakers and head out to find a cab that will take me to New Jersey.

TWENTY-SEVEN

Jules

I hold the door to Leo's apartment open so Sophia can follow me in, then I drop the keys on the side table. I don't need those anymore. I can't wait to get moved out and move on with my life. Leo was a diversion. I need to reframe and refocus. I need to get back to celibacy and the career ladder.

When I arrived back at my apartment last night, I didn't need to tell Sophia that it was serious. My puffy eyes and rumpled tissue did the talking for me. I told her about my dad and she didn't say *I told you so* or *what did you expect.* She just gave me a hug and a glass of wine and let me cry through back-to-back episodes of *Bridgerton.*

It wasn't until episode three that I managed to tell her I was moving back in permanently this weekend. I didn't need a conversation with Leo before I moved out. What would be the point? What could we possibly say to each other? We're over. I thought I liked him, and maybe I did, but what's the point of dating? At some point it will end.

Better to stop before we really start, before he can rip my heart out.

"You still haven't told me what exactly happened with you and Leo. It seems... quick to be calling off an engagement and moving out."

I swallow past an unexpected lump in my throat. "It was just a whirlwind. It came to its natural end." She doesn't have to know there was no real beginning.

I turn into my bedroom. Everything is exactly where I left it when I walked out two minutes after my dad hung up on me.

"Do you want to talk about it?"

I shake my head as I pull out one of my suitcases from the closet. The sooner I'm packed up, the better.

"Did it get violent?" she asks quietly.

I gasp and spin around. "God, no. Why would you think that?"

She shrugs. "It's all so sudden. Why aren't you trying to work through it?"

I toss a box from under my dressing table onto my bed and start filling it with the contents of my nightstand. "Because the obstacles are insurmountable."

"Okay," she says, stooping to pick up my hairbrush and drop it into the box. "What kind of obstacles?"

"Big ones," I say vaguely. "I'm going to pack up the bathroom."

I find my toiletry bag and clear the shower shelf of my shampoos and conditioners. Jeez, this shower had good pressure. I'll miss it.

"Big ones?" Sophia appears in the doorway, her hand on her waist like she's not picking up what I'm putting down.

"Like he's afraid of commitment."

She bursts out laughing. "You two were engaged out of nowhere!"

"Doesn't mean he's not afraid of trusting people, letting people in. That's what I mean by commitment," I say.

"Is this mixed up with your dad?"

"No," I snap. "Why would it be?"

"It's just weird that your dad comes back into your life and suddenly you're not engaged, you're moving out of your fiancé's apartment. It seems like the two things are connected."

"Well, they're not," I reply. Okay, maybe they're connected a little bit—but not how Sophia thinks. Dad leaving again simply made me realize what my priorities were, and who I can and can't rely on. Did I think there was a chance we could finally have some kind of healthy relationship? Sure. Was I wrong about that? I was. But sometimes, being wrong about one thing just helps you see everything else with more clarity.

"So, you're just walking away?" she asks. "You liked him enough to agree to marry him, but the relationship isn't worth trying to save?"

I put what's left of my toiletries into a box and head back into the bedroom, all the while thinking of a way to respond to Sophia that isn't a lie, but isn't the truth either.

I collapse on the bed, tears pricking my eyes. I won't let them fall. This situation has gotten so complicated. I'm lying to my best friend and I might be in love with a man I hated a few weeks ago.

Sophia sits down beside me. "Tell me what's going on," she says, picking up my hand.

I lay my head on her shoulder. I know Leo doesn't want me to tell anyone, but I trust Sophia like he trusts his best friends. She'd help me bury a body. She'd certainly tell a few lies for me.

"I'm not sure you'll believe me if I tell you," I say.

"Try me."

I sigh and then tell her the entire story of our fake engagement and the reasons Leo wanted a temporary fiancée. "The awards ceremony was Thursday night," I conclude. "So our time is up."

"Hold on," she says. "I thought you two hooked up."

"We did," I say.

"So that changes things. It's not fake. You're moving out, but are you going to continue to see each other?" she asks.

I shake my head. "We were supposed to talk last night and then—"

"And then your dad did a runner just like he used to when you were a kid."

"I couldn't face Leo after that. I didn't want to talk about anything last night."

"Did he call? Did you tell him what happened with your dad?"

I shake my head. "I texted him I had to go back to Jersey and deal with some stuff."

"So Dad wasn't the only one to bail," she mumbles.

"What?" My voice comes out like a distressed kitten's mewl. "You're saying I'm like my dad?"

"Not exactly. But aren't you bailing before things get complicated—or more complicated—with Leo? It's not *not* what your dad did..."

"Dad wasn't avoiding a hard conversation with me. If he was, he wouldn't have turned up and asked for a job out of nowhere."

"He is the master at deflection and avoidance," Sophia

says. "You need to talk to Leo. You can't run from your feelings, Jules."

I hate the thought that I could be like my dad. He causes so much hurt and pain in what he leaves behind. I don't want to hurt Leo. It's the last thing I want to do. But I can't cope with being hurt either. Not by Leo. I think it would break me. Better to run while I'm still able.

"What's the point in talking about anything? It's not like the guy is going to marry me for real. I'd rather walk away now. We were only ever temporary."

"Things have changed," she challenges. "Maybe he *is* going to marry you. At the very least he deserves a conversation."

I know she's right. I know I should talk to him, but I don't have anything left for more emotional upheaval. "Things haven't changed," I say.

"Things always change when sex is involved."

"Not for Leo," I say. "He's been burned before, and it's made him the way he is. People don't change." I sigh. "I'm not going to be the pathetic woman who convinces herself she can teach an old dog new tricks." I've made the mistake of having hope—of thinking things could be different with my dad. I'm not going to make the same mistake with Leo. "I'm not going to try and fix anyone. I'm not going to hope anyone fixes themselves. I'm done. Can we just get me packed up?" I feel drained from the last twenty-four hours. I don't want to talk about this anymore.

"We can. But I'm going to bring this up again. I want you to be happy."

"I want me to be happy too. But wanting something doesn't make it reality."

She closes the cardboard box and lifts it off my bed. "Admitting you want something, someone? It's the first step,

Jules. I can see how that would be hard for you, after the way your dad constantly raised and dashed your hopes when you were little. You've trained yourself not to want anything from anyone. But I'm not sure that leaves room for much happiness."

The front door of the apartment slams. *Leo.*

"I'm going to take these boxes downstairs," she says. "Talk to him."

I groan. I really am too tightly wound to see him now. I don't trust myself to keep it together.

I work quickly, stuffing clothes and papers from work into boxes. I'm going to regret my bad packing, but I need to get out of here as soon as possible.

I stack the boxes by my bedroom door and check the time. Sophia has been gone for about twenty minutes. What the hell is she doing down there? Of course, she's giving me time to speak to Leo.

I pull my hair out of its ponytail and take a deep, steadying breath. Time to face the music.

I open my bedroom door to the sight of Leo leaning against the wall opposite.

"Hey," I say, trying to sound light. Breezy.

"Hey," he replies, scratching the back of his head. His faded blue t-shirt lifts an inch, revealing that hard, flat stomach I know so well. "You need a hand with anything?"

I shouldn't feel upset. It's not like we were ever going to be a thing.

"No, Sophia and I have it." I transfer my weight from one foot to the other, trying to think of something to say.

"Let me help," he says.

It feels almost worse to have him moving me out. Like he can't wait to get rid of me.

"If it's okay with you, I'd rather do it myself."

He shrugs. "Okay. If that's what you want."

"It is," I say.

He narrows his eyes likes he knows I'm trying to communicate something but he's not sure what. Me neither, honestly.

"I thought we were going to talk. Have sushi."

I nod. "Yeah, sorry about that. I had to... get back to Jersey."

His eyes narrow, like he expects me to elaborate, but what can I say? Sophia's right, I'm running. But I don't know what else to do.

"So do you want to get dinner tonight?" he asks, looking me straight in the eye.

"I think it's best to keep things... to go back to being what we were before," I say. My stomach churns as I speak. It takes everything in me not to take two steps forward and collapse in his arms.

"So, that's it? Destiny is at a standstill?"

It's the first time he's referenced that first night we met since he found out I was Mystique.

"Destiny?" I ask him. "New Yorkers don't believe in stuff like that." I fight to keep my voice steady.

"Well, I'm technically from the UK and you're from Jersey. So..."

I have to look away from him. He looks so hurt. Like he wants me to tell him we can try and make things work. But I can't open myself up to him when I know at some point things will shift and he'll leave. I can't let that happen to me again. I'm too bruised and broken from a lifetime of people leaving.

He sighs and shoves his hands in his pockets. "Well, it's been a blast," he says.

I nod. I can't speak, because my nose is starting to fizz and my stomach feels like it's turning inside out.

"You're the best fake fiancée a guy could ever wish for."

The problem is, it got too real for me.

There's no solution to the sense of loss I'm feeling right now. Accepting his dinner invitation would only prolong the inevitable.

"Glad I could help."

Our eyes lock, like we both want to tell each other we're feeling conflicted. I offer him a small smile that I hope says *I'm sorry*.

"I've really enjoyed having you here," he says, oddly formal all of a sudden.

"I've enjoyed being here. More than I thought I would."

"Really?" he asks, the corner of his mouth twitching.

My stomach flips at the hint of flirtation in his voice. "Well, the kitchen alone makes it worthwhile."

He nods and runs a hand through his hair. "Right."

"And the view." I lift my chin at the wall of windows overlooking Manhattan, but don't actually take my eyes from Leo.

"The view. Of course."

Silence twists between us. I so badly want to stay. But I know I can't.

"I better go and help Sophia," I say.

He stands and pushes his hands into his pockets. "We'll have to catch up about The Mayfair at some point."

"But I still have a three-month trial, right?"

"Right," he replies. "Though I'm sure you have a plan to present for the roof terrace development?"

"Oh, yes. Right. Yeah, I'll follow up with your new assistant and put something in the calendar in a couple weeks."

"Good," he says. "Well, if you don't need my help, I'm going to head to the gym."

I flex my biceps like a complete freak. "Go get 'em," I say and turn, shaking my head at myself and all my awkward.

I disappear into the bedroom, blinking back tears. I fill another box and a couple of bags and head to the elevators. I just want to disappear. From Leo's apartment. From New York. From being my dad's daughter, and all that it entails.

TWENTY-EIGHT

Leo

I don't enjoy running on the streets of New York. There are too many people and too much traffic, but I needed to take the edge off my goodbye conversation with Jules. The gym wasn't enough distance—I had to get out of the building entirely.

I head to the Upper East Side without making a conscious decision to do so. Though I'm on the way to Worth's place, I make a detour. I run up Park and turn left at 79th Street. I slow my run to a walk and look up, taking in the tall brick façade, still the same as it was when I used to deliver bread here to the Hammonds, when I first met Caroline. It's like no time has passed whatsoever. The wrought-iron railings that surround the front entrance still gleam. The windows are still blank, like their panes are all painted white, except I know it's the effect of blinds you can see out of, but not into. For all I know, Caroline might be in there now, looking down at me.

I remember thinking that I needed to have enough

money to buy a house like this for Caroline and me to raise a family in. I never doubted my ability to make that money —to make something of myself—but it was never going to be enough for her. Or her father.

"Leo," a woman's voice calls from behind me. I turn around and come face-to-face with Caroline, beaming at me. She still has the same air about her that she had when I first knew her. It says she's going to be fun and mischievous and a complete handful, but everyone's going to love her anyway. I've never met anyone who upholds such a perfect veneer—never breaking character. She's always smiling. Always "on." She's beautiful—there's no doubt about it.

She's wearing gym gear and carrying a coffee—just like any New Yorker on a Saturday morning. Except from her tan to her blowout, money oozes from every pore. I have no doubt, she turned the head of every man she passed on her way home. "How wonderful to see you," she says. "We've gone so many years and now twice in three days!"

I lean in and air kiss her cheek. She leans her free hand on my upper arm and it feels like liquid metal burning into my muscles. I step back. "I'm just out for a run and was passing. Not seen this place in a while." I always avoid this street whenever coming up to see Worth.

"Do you want to come in for a coffee? Or a glass of water?" She smiles. "You look like you might need to hydrate."

"It's okay, I'm good," I say.

"My dad's inside," she says. "I know he'd love to see you."

I let out a cynical half laugh. I'm sure he would. But not because he likes my company—more because he likes the money I could make him. Hammonds like to use people.

"How things change, right? Another time. I'm on my way to a friend's for coffee."

She goes to speak and then stops herself. Finally, she says, "You know way back, when we first knew each other. My memory isn't great, but I'm sure we both did things we weren't proud of. We were kids, though, right? It's water under the bridge now."

It's less of a question and more of a commentary or maybe a command. It would be on-brand for her to believe she has the ability to decide what's forgotten between us. She flicks her hand up and then tosses her hair over her shoulder in the way she always used to. Younger me was mesmerized by her confidence and ability to take everything in her stride. But now it seems kind of sad. I can't help wondering how much she pushes away—out of sight and out of mind.

I pause, waiting for her to finish her sentence, to offer me some kind of apology. But after a few long moments, I realize she's waiting for me to speak.

"My memory's pretty good," I say.

Her smile falters briefly, but she recovers quickly, pulling back her shoulders just a little. No one would notice, unless you'd seen it before and were waiting for it.

"I do hope we can get together for dinner with you and your beautiful new fiancée."

"Jules," I say.

"Jules," she repeats. "She seems lovely."

"She is lovely," I say. None of Jules is a veneer. All her loveliness goes right through to the core of her.

Standing here in front of Caroline, all I can think about is Jules. The only reason she's been living with me, pretending to be engaged to me, is because of the woman opposite me. Nothing makes sense.

Seeing Caroline Thursday night was meant to give me closure, but I'm not sure I got anything at all from it. Today, seeing her one-on-one with all pretenses gone, doesn't make things any clearer.

Maybe I got my closure with Caroline a long time ago.

"Yeah, maybe we'll figure out a time for dinner," I say noncommittally, although I have no intention of actually following through. I check my watch, even though Worth isn't expecting me. "I better go. Don't want to be late."

She smiles her hundred-million-dollar smile. "Send Jules my love."

I can't think of a response, so I just nod and head up the street. I have no reason to be here.

I'M STILL PANTING when Worth opens the door.

"Are you running from the scene of a crime?"

I push past him and head straight to the downstairs restroom, where I throw water on my face.

"Jack's here and we're in the kitchen," Worth calls on his way past.

I brace my hands on the sink and look in the mirror. Why didn't I stop her from leaving? I'm not sure I'm going to be able to go back to my apartment now. Not after having Jules there, in my bed, in the kitchen, watching movies together. It's going to feel so empty.

I push my hands through my hair and head to the back of the house, where there's a kitchen-dining room. It's so moody and sultry in here, like a shady forest floor, it reminds me of Worth himself.

"Hey," Worth says. "Grab a drink and come sit."

Worth has some sodas out on the counter, but I open his fridge and pull out a beer. I need to take the edge off.

"It's five o'clock somewhere, I guess," Jack says.

"Shoot me." I take a seat on the bench opposite Jack and lean my arms on the table.

The energy is off and I know it's my fault.

"Did you have a good time on Thursday?" Jack asks.

I nod. "It was good. I'm glad I went."

"And seeing Caroline," Worth says. "How was that?"

My phone buzzes in my pocket. I pull it out and squint at the email preview, trying to focus on who it is, because I must be reading it wrong. "I just ran into her on the street, and now," I say, tapping the phone before setting it on the table. "She emailed me."

"What?" Worth asks. "Why?"

I let out a half laugh. "I guess because she wants to smooth things over so her father and husband can make money from me." I scan the message. "She wants to go to dinner."

"Just the two of you?" Jack asks. "Does she want something... romantic to happen between you?"

"No, me and Jules, her and Grant."

"A double date!" Jack says. "Not awkward at all."

"Hang on," Worth says. "You haven't answered my question about how it was seeing her. Are you hoping to rekindle something?"

I snap my head up. He can't be serious. I've spent more than a decade hating this woman. "Absolutely not. She's married. And I think she's a terrible human."

"Are you protesting too much?" Jack asks.

"No. I don't find her attractive. She makes me..." I shift uncomfortably in my seat. "She makes me itch." There's something too effortful about her. I can see now that no one gets to see the real Caroline Hammond. Maybe *she's* not even aware of who she is deep down inside. "I don't have feelings for her."

"So, you're not still in love with Caroline," Worth says. "Seeing her makes you itch. Why are you arriving unexpectedly on my doorstep in a mood like you've just murdered someone?"

I shrug and take another swig of my beer.

Worth and Jack don't have the decency to change the topic. Instead, I feel their eyes boring into me, waiting patiently for me to stop evading their questions.

"I just wanted to get out of the flat, that's all." Still, they don't say anything. "Because Jules is moving out."

"Ahhh," Worth says. Jack exhales like they've finally discovered the missing piece of the puzzle. Maybe they have.

"And you don't want her to?" Worth asks.

I think about it. "I've liked having her there. She was fun."

"And you like having sex with her."

Of course I like having sex with her. What a stupid question. "She kinda told me she was using me."

"What?" Jack asks. "Did you two fight?"

I shake my head and slide the beer bottle on the table between my hands. "Nope. She packed up and left. A couple of days ago she said that everyone uses everyone else and that nothing is real. I guess this is the natural conclusion of our arrangement."

I glance up and Jack looks confused. "She doesn't really strike me as that kind of woman. What was the context?"

"We were talking about Caroline. She said I was only pissed off with Caroline using me because I didn't get what I wanted from her."

"Which was?"

"Her to love me, I guess."

"Right," Worth says. "And then Jules said *she* was using you?"

I nod and take another sip of beer, hoping it will ease the rawness in my throat. "For the job at The Mayfair. And I was using her to act like I had a fiancée."

"Well, that's true," Jack says.

"I guess." Except to me, it didn't feel like the trade she made it out to be.

"You guess?" Jack says. "That was your deal, wasn't it? She gets to be manager if you get a fiancée."

"Right," I reply. I feel like such a dick.

"Only, the edges started to blur," Worth says. I can feel him looking for confirmation in my expression.

"Edges?" Jack asks.

Worth sighs. "Between what was in the pact—what was a trade-off or a payment, if you like—and what was real."

"I'm missing something," Jack says. "It was all real. She really did pretend to be your fiancée and she really is the manager of The Mayfair."

"Yes," Worth says. "But they also really became friends and lovers. Our friend Leo here caught feelings along the way and doesn't know what to do about it."

"Ahhh," Jack says. "I get it. So, have you told Jules you like her and want things to continue between you?"

"No," I snap. I'd bloody tried. Or at least I suggested she delay her move-out so we could make time to have dinner and talk.

"He doesn't want a repeat performance of what happened with Caroline when he thought the feelings between them were mutual and found out they weren't."

"I don't even need to be here for this psycho-drama," I

reply, looking between my friends. "You two can play it out all by yourselves."

"But Jules isn't Caroline," Jack says, like I'm not even here. "And you're not eighteen anymore. You've got a better read on people."

I shrug. "It doesn't matter anyway. Life goes on."

"Well, it clearly does matter because you're miserable," Worth says.

"Oh don't worry," Jack says. "It will only last a decade or so and he'll get over it."

He's obviously comparing Caroline dumping me with Jules leaving, but the two events are incomparable. Jules is more important in so many ways than Caroline ever was. That wasn't clear to me until the awards ceremony, when I realized Caroline didn't have the impact or power I thought she did on me. Caroline hurt my ego. Jules has ripped out my heart.

"I hoped things were going to carry on between us," I admit. "We were going to have dinner last night. Talk."

"And you chickened out?" Jack suggests.

"No. I was a little late back from the office, and when I got home, she'd gone back to Jersey."

"So she thought you dumped her and fled? Sounds like a twist on Romeo and Juliet," Jack says.

"With less death involved," Worth says. "Were you late back because you were scared to have a conversation with her?"

"No," I say. "I was stuck on a call and we were texting about sushi and then all of a sudden—" I stop and think. "Everything was fine. She knew I was running late. She was going to place an order for sushi for us both and then... and then I said her dad hadn't shown up for our meeting."

Worth and Jack look confused as fuck, so I fill them in

about Jules' father turning up on the roof terrace and me trying to take the heat off of Jules by offering to meet with him. I explain briefly about their difficult relationship and his frequent disappearing acts.

"So after you told her about her dad not showing up, she split?" Jack asks.

"Yeah. I hadn't made the connection until now."

"And before that she seemed up to continue things with you, or at least talk about it?" Worth clarifies.

"We hadn't talked yet, but yeah, I thought she was open to it. I guess I had it wrong."

"Or she got freaked out by her asshole dad and..."

"And?" I ask. "And what? You think she was embarrassed he didn't show? It doesn't reflect badly on her. She's not responsible for him."

Worth sighs. "Maybe it goes deeper. I'm no shrink, but it sounds like she's used to the men in her life abandoning her. Or at least, one really important man. An easy way to stop that happening again is by not having men in your life at all."

Fuck. Worth might not be a shrink, but that theory fits like a glove. "Shit," I say. "What do I do?"

"I'm not sure," Worth replies.

"It sounds like you're onto something though," Jack agrees. "She's retreating, trying to be an island. Only relying on the people she's sure of."

"But she can be sure of me."

"Can she?" Worth asks. "I mean, how long have you two been sleeping together? It's not like you were going to propose to her."

I stay silent. I hadn't considered proposing, no. But I don't hate the idea.

"Were you?" Jack asks.

"It wasn't part of the plan. Not right now, anyway. But Jules is special. And the more I get to know her, the more I like her. The more time I spend with her, the less time I want to spend without her. She's smart and beautiful and she makes me laugh and she makes me... better. Happy. At peace."

I let my own words sink into my brain. Everything I'm saying is true. Jules is it for me. Or she was.

"Have you told her that?" Worth asks.

"Sushi was canceled, I told you."

"And now it's too late because she's taking a cruise around Antarctica for the next three years."

"No. But she's made her decision."

"Sounds like she was scared. And she hasn't heard what you have to say," Worth says. "She should."

Jack clears his throat. "What I'm about to say is meant with love. It might not seem that way, but... if she's important to you, why'd you let her leave?"

I half snort. "You think I should have handcuffed her to the radiator?"

"No," Jack says. "I think you should have told her how you feel. You know where she lives. You have her number. If you haven't shown up on her doorstep yet, there's a reason."

"It's okay to be scared," Worth says. "Caroline stuck the knife in deep the last time you were vulnerable with a woman. I'm not even going to mention Nadia because she was only around for a nanosecond. But unless you take a risk for Jules, you're going to lose her. You gotta figure out whether she's worth it."

I know she is. As much as I hate to admit it, they're right —I didn't fight for Jules. And maybe that's because I'm scared. Seeing her moving out today hit hard and deep. It felt like she was rejecting me rather than running to protect herself. She needs me to be stronger than my insecurities.

"You're right. I need to tell her. I need to show her that even when she pushes me away, I'll still be right where she left me. I need to fight for her."

"You're a romantic," Worth says.

"Apparently," I reply. "At least when it comes to Jules."

"It suits you," Jack says. "She's lucky to have you."

And I'm lucky to have shrinks who masquerade as the best friends a man could have.

TWENTY-NINE

Jules

This is my chance. I know it, and I'm determined not to fuck it up. I just wish that a pivotal moment in my career didn't depend on my not losing it in front of Leo Hart.

I miss him so much. In the ten days since I moved out of his apartment, I've thought of him constantly. My fingers hover over his name on my phone, desperate to call, to message, to make some kind of contact with him. I thought I'd run back to Jersey and lick my wounds over my dad being an asshole. And I've done my share of that. But I wake up in the morning yearning for Leo. I can't sleep at night for thinking of him. I can barely breathe during the day because I know this whole situation is all my fault. I fucked things up between us so badly.

But there's no going back. Time only moves us on to the next chapter. I at least need to salvage my career out of the ruins of whatever we had. I know he won't deny me that if I can prove to him I'm the right person to be managing The Mayfair long-term.

I'm pacing the roof terrace, looking up at the sky, waiting for Leo. I have the next sixty minutes in his calendar. In an hour, I'll know whether my tenure at the helm of The Mayfair will ever be made permanent.

It's threatening to rain, and if it does, everything is ruined.

The fire door to the rooftop creaks and I spin to see Leo emerge. My heart crawls up my throat, my breath catching there.

His brown floppy curls have grown longer since I last saw him and he looks tired. He's probably working too hard. Or worried about New River. Is it selling? Is construction on schedule? I can't ask him. I've got to keep things on track today or I'm not going to be able to hold it together.

"Thanks for coming," I call as he strides over. Was he always so tall? Was his smile always so dazzling? Thank god I didn't get in any deeper than I already was. My dad leaving knocked me flat. But if Leo left?

I'd never be able to get back up.

"An outdoor meeting," he says. "My first of the day." Our eyes lock and my stomach swirls, full of confusion and need.

Should we kiss? Shake hands? To avoid either, I clasp my hands in front of me and launch into my presentation. "I wanted to show you the space before you make a decision," I say. "I've discovered it's actually bigger than I first thought, which means we have options."

His gaze hits the floor, and I wonder if I've already lost him. I need to plow on. Impress him with my proposal.

"This is a super-special place with fantastic views and would obviously make a great bar. But I think we're underselling ourselves. New York has plenty of rooftop bars. We'd be competing up- and downtown for clientele. I want to use the space for something a little different. I want The Mayfair to offer rooftop weddings and events."

He raises his eyebrows. I can't tell if it's skepticism on his face, but I look away so it doesn't affect my presentation. "There aren't many hotels with the infrastructure and capacity for large-scale rooftop events. The other X factor is weather. All outdoor event reservations need to be safeguarded with an indoor option in case of inclement weather, which means we're reserving two spaces for the price of one." I turn to the table I've set up beside me and swipe open the laptop. "Unless we have an option to cover the space. I've been researching. We could erect a fully retractable gazebo that covers like a permanent structure if it's raining. I've checked with the manufacturer and it would work in all New York weather conditions, other than heavy snow. It makes the space useable for at least nine months of the year."

I glance up at him to gauge his reaction. It's difficult to get a read on him. He seems to be concentrating.

"Let me show you the renderings." I've worked with an architect and designer on 3D renderings.

"I've had estimates from construction companies on the cost of renovations, the impact on the ongoing hotel operations, and timeframe. We can start to take bookings for two years out. Of course it won't just be weddings, but we're charging big money, so it will be big life events that we celebrate up here."

He pulls in a breath and the sound makes my pulse flutter against my neck. I close my eyes in a long blink, trying not to think about his breath on my skin, his fingers in my hair, his mouth on mine.

"Let me take you through the rest of my strategy plans for the next three years." We sit and I hand him a tablet where I've set out the rest of my presentation. I show him the cost savings I want to make and the investments crucial for keeping the hotel in the five-star bracket. It's going to cost money before it makes money, but in three years, this hotel is going to be a jewel in this city's crown.

"It's all very well thought out," he says eventually. He's been borderline silent for the last forty minutes. I can't tell if that's a good sign or not.

He doesn't need to say anything for me to be grateful he's here, despite the fact that his presence is bringing up every emotion I've ever had, all at one time. Seeing him is... everything. And so painful it's like slivers of glass slicing into my skin. How could I think I could just go back to Jersey and get on with the life I had before him? Having him so close satiates something in me. Him being here fills a hole in my heart.

With the comfort of his closeness comes the fear of his absence—the understanding that the more I have of Leo, the bigger the hole in my heart will be if he leaves. I can't survive many more blows.

"Have you thought about permitting?" he asks.

"Yes," I reply, with as much authority as I can muster. "It's all included in the two-year process. The actual construction shouldn't take more than four months."

Leo nods. "I want you to use one of my contractors."

Is he saying yes?

"That's fine," I say.

"It's a small job, but they'll want to do it well and on time because it's me."

"Makes sense," I reply.

He opens his jacket. I look away from the warm skin at the bottom of his throat where his tie might be, if he ever wore one. He pulls out some folded papers and slides them onto the table. "Take a look over these. If you're happy, sign them and send them back to my assistant."

I frown, picking up the papers. I wasn't prepared for Leo to offer me an employment contract here and now, but I'm not going to say no, either. I look closer. When I confirm what I'm looking at, a smile lights me up from the inside out. It's a five-year contract in my role as general manager of The Mayfair.

I feel my whole body exhale. At least I didn't fuck that up.

"You've made some really good decisions about this place. You're organized. Savvy. And I really like what you've done."

I glance up at him, almost scared to look him in the eye in case he sees how much I miss him. "Thank you."

"If we're done," he says, standing.

I get to my feet too. "And I meant to say, I'm really sorry about my dad not showing up for his meeting with you."

Leo pulls his eyebrows together. "You never need to apologize to anyone about your father's behavior. That's on him."

Easy to say. "But you were doing *me* a favor by seeing him. I wasted your time."

"It could never be a waste of my time," he mumbles, but I'm not quite sure what he means. "How are you? It must have been upsetting."

"I'm fine. Kinda. It was sort of... north of upsetting. Honestly, I'm still upset. I've been trying to focus on work."

"It's not my place to suggest this, but have you thought about seeing a therapist?" he asks.

I take a step back at his question. "A therapist?"

"I've been thinking about going myself," he says. "We all have things to work through."

I don't know how to respond. Why does Leo need therapy? He's buried his past with Caroline. Maybe he just wants to manage his day-to-day stress.

An awkward silence passes between us. Leo checks his watch and says, "I need to get to my next meeting, but good work on this. Everything's coming together perfectly."

I smile, but nothing feels perfect. "Thank you."

"I'll see you soon," he replies, then he pauses as if he's going to say something else. But he doesn't, and turns for the exit.

I watch him leave, his words about seeing me soon echoing in my ears. I should be celebrating this moment, and I will, at some point. Right now, all I can think about is how much I've lost.

THIRTY

Jules

The sales launch of the rooftop wedding space opens today. We haven't started construction because we're still waiting for some permits to clear, but at least I can show everyone the incredible view.

The entire roof is covered in pink and white flowers and we have five rows of chairs set out opposite a small podium, so people get a feel for what the space will be like when everything's complete. I've also created a makeshift bar with tall tables so people can see how much room there is for their cocktail reception and their ceremony. The banqueting will all take place in the ballroom, but we're offering the entire city as a backdrop for their vows.

"It looks impressive," Joan says from beside me.

"You think? We're asking people to use their imaginations quite a bit."

"Everyone will be looking at the view. Or thinking about the gift bag."

That's my hope. I've gone all out on the gift bags. They speak to luxury and contain everything needed to relax after a stressful day of wedding planning. From luxurious bath products to designer linens and a bottle of vintage champagne. If the view doesn't make us memorable, I hope the gift bags do.

"How long have we got until people start to arrive?"

"About thirty seconds," she says.

The door is propped open and I tuck my blouse into my pencil skirt just as the first guest arrives. Most of the people we invited today are wedding planners and event organizers. But a few are bringing couples along with them, to see if the space works for their wedding. The website with the renderings and pictures of the view just went live and our calendar is open, ready to accept bookings as soon as they come in.

Joan's cell rings as I step forward to greet our first guest.

"Nancy Franco?" I ask as a woman in her late forties wearing a canary-yellow dress and Chanel jacket comes through the door. I've done my research on this woman. She's one of the most powerful event planners in New York. The Clintons, the Hiltons, and the Gettys have all used her. If I need to impress anyone today, it's her.

We shake hands and I introduce myself just as a waiter bearing a tray of champagne appears beside us. We both take a glass.

"So thrilled you could join us for our launch."

"You have the perfect day for it," she says.

"We absolutely do. But when we start hosting weddings, we won't need to worry about that because of the incredible retractable gazebo we're installing. Can I show you the video?"

Just before I press play on the screen behind me, Joan reappears.

"We just got our first booking," she says, beaming at me.

"We did?" I ask. I was hoping for a few tentative inquiries today, but Nancy's the only person to arrive. "Who from?"

"Margaret Taylor," Joan replies. Margaret Taylor is the second-most powerful event planner in Manhattan. To get a booking from her so quickly is astonishing.

I register the surprise in Nancy's expression. Given she's here so early, I get the impression she likes to have the scoop on opportunities like this. I don't want to offend her by thinking we've given someone else priority access. "So she's booked it sight unseen," I remark. "How wonderful. Is she coming today?"

"She's downstairs, checking out the ballroom with the team down there. She's on her way up."

I nod, then turn my full attention back to Nancy. If I can get two of the most powerful women in New York event planning on board today, I'll have earned my keep here at The Mayfair. "Let me show you this gazebo," I say to Nancy, "before anyone else can catch a glimpse."

The video plays and I explain how easy it will be to set up. She asks a few questions and then gets pulled away by another event planner she clearly wants to catch up with.

Just then, Margaret Taylor comes through the door. I smile and go to greet her—and freeze in my tracks as I see Leo behind her. Did he even know we were having the launch today, or was he coming for another reason and just happened to stumble into this event?

His eyes slice to mine, and he smiles.

"Jules Moore," Margaret says. "So nice to see you."

We exchange air kisses. This is not the first time we've

met. I've dealt with her for a wedding she booked in our ballroom this spring—one of only four in the first quarter of next year.

"Thank you for coming," I say. "I understand you've booked on behalf of one of your clients already."

"Yes, very excited to be able to support you with the wonderful things you're doing with this hotel. Aren't we, Leo?"

It's like a metal claw has grabbed my heart right out of my chest.

He grins. "Yes, very excited," he says.

Leo? My Leo? The Leo standing right in front of me is getting married?

"I must see that video of the gazebo you promised," she says.

Joan takes over and guides Margaret to the table and laptop. And thank god, because I know if I move, I'll crack in two. Leo doesn't move with her. Instead, he puts his hand at the small of my back. Somehow I manage to shuffle to the side of the roof terrace, right by the railings.

"Congratulations," I manage to eke out, although I can't muster a smile.

I glance up to find him looking right at me. I want to disappear through thirty-five floors to the basement. I feel like I'm turning to dust right before his eyes, like my insides are drying up and will blow away in the wind any minute now.

"I booked it for us," he says.

I hold my breath. What did he just say?

"I wanted to make sure we got the first booking. It seemed fitting."

"I don't understand," I choke out. "You're getting married and..."

"Oh god!" It's the first time I've ever heard Leo sound panicked. "No, I'm not getting married. Not to someone else, anyway. We're getting married. I hope. In two years."

I figure I might be hallucinating. Or just plain asleep and dreaming. What is he talking about?

"You ran out on me because you were scared I was going to run out on you. Just like your father did, over and over. I didn't get it at first. I didn't understand that I lost you when I told you about your dad not showing up for our meeting. Eventually, it made perfect sense. I thought you didn't want me. But that's not it. You don't want *him*."

My heart stutters in my chest. I have to pull in a slow breath to settle my pulse.

"I know you love me just as much as I love you," he says.

And from somewhere, I find the strength to put my hand on his chest to stop him galloping further ahead when I'm still so far behind.

"You love me?" I ask him, staring into his eyes.

"So much." He smooths his hands over my shoulders. "And you love me too." I smile at him, and he grins back, sure enough for both of us. "You don't have to say it. I know it. I feel it. We both feel it. You just don't trust it. And I don't think I did either for a minute back there. It took me a beat to catch up. Now that I have, now that I'm *sure*, there's no going back. So I booked our wedding. Maybe we want to do it earlier and cancel. Maybe we want to do it later and just use the date for a big party. Either way, I didn't want to miss out on being the first ones to benefit from the incredible job you're going to do here."

"Have you actually lost your mind?" It's the only thing I can think of to say.

He chuckles. "No. The exact opposite. Take all the time

you need to catch up. I'm here forever, so there's no rush. I'm not going anywhere."

"I thought you were getting married to someone else."

"There'll never be anyone else for me. From our very first meeting, something in me shifted."

"What? When I was blue and rocking a skull belt?"

"Yeah. I'd never felt such a connection before. I was pretty torn up about you not calling. I'm not letting you go again."

"Just like that, this is how it is?" I ask.

"Yup. I'm here to stay. I'm not walking away from you. Not ever."

There's a lump of grief packed in my throat. "You can't say that."

"I *can* say that."

"But we're going to fight."

He laughs. "I know. But I'm not going to run. We're going to work through whatever comes up. You're the person I want to spend my life with. You're the person I want to cook mac and cheese with. You're the person I want to raise a family and grow old with. It's all you, Jules."

I reach for the railing to steady me. Everything he's saying is exactly what I needed to hear, and I didn't even know it.

"I do love you," I mumble. "And I'm so sorry I ran out on you. I shouldn't have done that. I was... scared. Scared that you weren't who I thought you were."

He slides an arm around my waist. "I know. And I know you're going to get scared again and you might try and ditch me, but I won't let you go. I'm here. I'm who you can rely on for the rest of your life."

I exhale. Is it really that easy? He just turns up and promises me everything I've ever wanted in a relationship?

But no—none of this has been simple. What Leo's done has taken a lot of effort, and bravery, and... love.

"I love you," I say, my tone stronger now. "And... I think I'm going to need to take things in bite-sized pieces, but... I want to be with you too. Forever."

"You do?"

"I absolutely do."

EPILOGUE

A week later

Jules

I stare at the tray of rings in front of me and then glance across at Leo, who's also staring at them. Then I look down at the ring I'm already wearing.

"I do like this ring," I say, holding out my hand.

"I know you do," Leo says.

"Then why can't I keep it?"

Leo really wants to buy me a new engagement ring. I keep telling him, there's no need. The ring I already have is gorgeous. And huge.

"You absolutely can," he replies. "But wouldn't it be nice to have a new one as well? I didn't spend long picking that out and it..." He winces and suddenly I get it. The ring I'm wearing is all about Caroline.

"You want this ring to be about you and me and not your past?"

He turns and smiles. I brush the corner of his mouth with my thumb. "You always know what I'm thinking."

"I like this one," I say, pointing to the smallest solitaire on the tray.

Leo rolls his eyes. "I like this one." It's the biggest.

"Leo," I say. "I work in a hotel. I want to be able to wear my ring every day. I can't wear that every day."

Leo glances up at the assistant helping us, as if she's going to tell us what to do.

"I want to go back to Jersey and not have to cover up my ring or take it off entirely. I'd feel like the queen of England wearing that thing on the subway. Next, you'll have me wearing a tiara."

Leo sits back on the sofa, considering. "I don't want you mugged."

"Right," I say. "So what about this one?" I point back to my original choice.

He looks again at my selection and then scans the tray. "This," he says.

I gasp because I know he's found it. It's bigger than the one I selected, but because of the emerald cut and the setting, it somehow looks very solid. "I love it," I say.

"It's perfect," he says. "Try it on."

"Let me help you with that," the assistant says, taking Leo's choice in her gloved hand and sliding it onto my left ring finger. "This is a very special piece. The central stone is a three-and-a-half-carat emerald cut. It's a simple shape with tapered, baguette-cut single-carat diamonds either side. What makes this piece very special is that the stones are flawless. Given what you're looking for, I think this is an excellent compromise. It's not the largest stone on the tray by any means, but because of the quality of the stone, it *is* one of the most expensive."

"A flawless diamond. I like that," Leo says, looking at my finger.

It's a gorgeous ring, and now that it's on, it feels good—like it belongs there.

"Despite its value, it's very easy to wear," the assistant says.

"And then you could have a second to wear when we go out in the evenings," Leo says.

"Absolutely not," I reply. "I like this one. We're not leaving here with two rings, Leo."

He sighs. "I guess I'll have to wait for our anniversary."

I roll my eyes. I can't believe I wrote Leo off as an unrepentant player. He's such a gooey romantic. He likes to take care of me and I like to take care of him. We know each other's hearts are precious and we handle them carefully.

"Can we take it with us now?" Leo asks the assistant as he pulls out his wallet.

"I think they have to have it sized," I say.

"It's actually the perfect size. If you can give me a few minutes to arrange things, you can take it with you."

I take Leo's hand and look at his watch. "Will we be late for dinner?" Bennett and Efa are having a housewarming dinner at their place and I don't want to be rude.

"No, the car's waiting for us. Do you need to go home first?"

I shake my head, and Leo smooths his hand over my red jersey dress. He says red is his favorite color on me. I've invested in some red underwear to surprise him tonight.

"I have a surprise for you tonight," I say.

"That makes two of us. I have a surprise for you too."

"You do?" I grin. He just bought me a flawless diamond ring. I don't need anything from him.

"Yeah. I'm thinking about buying another hotel in New York," he says.

I pull my eyebrows together. "No, you are not."

"I am," he says. He pulls out his phone and brings up The Royal Park website. "This one's for sale."

"Leo!" I'm waiting for him to relent and tell me he's only kidding, but he's urging me to take his phone to look more closely. "You're not buying another hotel. You're not interested in the one you have."

"Well," he says, "speaking of The Mayfair..."

My stomach drops. He's not thinking of selling it, is he? The plans for the rooftop are being drawn up by the architect. I'm really excited about how it's all going to look, and more than that, how it's going to drive business to the hotel.

"You want to manage two hotels?" he asks.

"What?"

"You're doing such a good job with The Mayfair. Oh, that reminds me, I went ahead and transferred that into your name. That's why I need another hotel. The guys will get pissed if I'm not playing their little game."

"Wait a minute, what did you say?"

"I've got to buy another one or I won't qualify for the competition."

"And The Mayfair doesn't count because...?" I think I heard him the first time, but I want to make sure.

"The Mayfair is yours now." He shrugs. "It seemed fitting. If it hadn't been for that place, I would have never got my second chance with you. A second chance that will last a lifetime."

"You gave me a hotel?" I ask. It's like I'm in a real-life game of Monopoly. "You can't just give me a hotel."

"Actually, that's true. I have some papers at home you need to sign to complete the transfer. My lawyers are sticklers. I suppose it's not technically required, as you'll own half of it anyway when we get married."

I roll my eyes. We've been arguing about a prenup. I want to sign one. Leo doesn't want us to. He thinks we should be equal partners. And it's sweet and romantic, but I'm not used to taking things from people. I'm used to being independent, not relying on anyone.

"But," he continues, "this is a transitional time. I get that it's going to take you a while before you allow yourself to need me. I need to prove to you that I won't let you down. During that time, you'll have the hotel."

"I wouldn't have agreed to marry you if I didn't trust you. I hate that you think I'm expecting you to disappoint me."

He smiles at me and pulls me closer. "I know you know intellectually. But it will take a while to unpick what your father did. I know that and I'm okay with it. I'm sure enough for both of us."

This is only one of the reasons why I love him—because he'll shoulder any burden I give him and take care of me no matter what.

"You don't need to be sure for me," I say. "I'm sure of you for myself. You haven't tilted my world *off* its axis, you've done the opposite. Now, I feel right. I feel whole in a way I never have before."

Leo hasn't rocked my world—he's made my world safe. Better. More. His love has filled every space and doubt. I'm the woman I was always meant to be because of Leo.

Another Week Later

Leo

It feels like we're merging families today. More than when I went to Jersey or when Jules and I went to Florida. That felt like Jules was *inducted* into my family. They loved her and I could feel her heart expand as they treated her like the daughter they never had. The stakes are higher today. If our friends don't like each other, then it's a problem.

"We should seat Sophia there, opposite the view," I say to Jules.

"You going to put place cards out for people?" she asks, her eyes sparkling with teasing.

"Maybe," I say. "This is important. Sophia should feel comfortable."

"She's fine. Having a view of Manhattan won't make her feel more comfortable. Although..." Her gaze shoots to mine. "The idea of place cards might not be a bad thing." She rolls back her lips like she's trying to keep a secret.

"What?" I ask.

"Well, Sophia is very single now that Jamie made the break a breakup. I mean, she's not even dating since that last guy turned out to be, you know..."

"The ex-felon who pretended to be an accountant."

"I think he actually used to be an accountant, but was working in Davy's Diner because he wasn't allowed to... account anymore. Since the conviction."

I sigh. What an idiot. First rule of accountancy—don't steal your clients' money and buy a yacht. "Right. So Sophia is single— Oh. I see where you're going." I shake my head. "You're playing with fire."

"But it would be so great if— I mean, she has four to choose from."

"Byron just texted. He's in Acapulco. He can't make it."

"Acapulco? Really? Does he make this shit up?"

I chuckle. "No. His business is just really... international."

"Okay, so she has three to choose from. And they're all good guys, right? You'd vouch for them."

"I would. But not necessarily to a woman who was dating them. Especially to your best friend. What would happen if one of them was more into the other? Or one got pissed off at the other? This could rip our group in half. And it could put us in a very awkward position if we set them up in the first place."

"But, Leo. It could be so nice! And I know Sophia loves a British accent. Fisher is—"

"In the wholesome music industry. He's still a virgin," I say sarcastically.

"They're adults. They know we have nothing to do with it. And if it doesn't work out, they can be civil if nothing else."

Someone bangs on the door, and when I hear voices, I realize I haven't locked the front door again. "Hello!" I call out.

"Hey," Bennett replies.

Efa appears and waves with both hands. "This feels like a big moment," she says. "And... I have a plan." She waves something in the air. "Place cards! I thought we could play matchmaker with Sophia!"

I groan. There's no way I was ever going to win this argument with Jules, but I definitely won't with Efa in on it.

"Fisher?" Jules asks. "I haven't met Byron yet."

"Fisher!" Efa says. "Two British guys and two American girls. It's perfect."

"Exactly," Jules says, throwing me an I-told-you-so glance. Efa and Jules stand over the dining table, putting the place cards down and then swapping them about like this is a state dinner.

"Fisher doesn't need someone to match his energy," I mumble to myself, because no one is listening.

"We could not make it obvious and put her between Fisher and Worth," Efa says. "Have you showed her Fisher's Instagram?"

"No," says Jules. "Sophia would be on to me right away. And she hates being set up. She says it always ends in disaster."

I look pointedly at Jules and raise my eyebrows.

"Have some faith," she says to me.

More voices at the door switch Jules and Efa into warp speed as they make the final changes to the place cards and then start talking like they weren't doing something to feel guilty about.

"Sophia!" I say, trying to sound natural and not like she's just walked into *Love Island*, Manhattan edition.

"Leo," she says, suspicion in her voice.

I wrap her in a big hug, and then go and grab the tray of mimosas that I've completely forgotten about. Sophia's been a fantastic friend to Jules and that puts her at the top of my Christmas card list. I'd like her to meet someone. I'd also like to find my friends their soul mates. They deserve them. Although, the jury's out on whether Fisher really deserves a beautiful, kind, loyal girl in his life. He's broken more than his fair share of hearts over the years.

As I'm handing out drinks, everyone else arrives and Jules makes the introductions. I watch her beaming at my friends with real affection and wonder how I got so lucky. God, I would love Worth, Fisher, Jack, and Byron to have what I have, but it's so fucking rare. Like a one-in-a-billion chance that they could be as happy as Jules and me. I'm not sure it's even worth them trying.

Jules guides everyone to their seats and then asks Fisher what he's been working on. She and I sit next to each other, opposite Sophia and Fisher.

Sophia narrows her eyes at Jules, watching her intently, clearly suspicious. When Fisher finishes what he's saying, she turns to me. "Are you really going to wait two years for that rooftop to be ready to marry this girl?" That's a good way to change the subject and distract everyone.

"Good point," Worth says. "I vote Leo will do anything Jules wants."

"Sounds like a sensible man," Bennett says.

"I definitely want to celebrate at the rooftop," Jules says. We've had this conversation at least eighty times since we picked out her second ring—the real ring.

"Right, but we can do that for our anniversary, or we can pick another reason," I say.

"Yeah," she says. "I agree. We don't have to get married up there. I don't want a big fuss or anything. I don't want it to be... like a business function. I think if we have a big wedding, you're going to feel obligated to invite people for business reasons."

"You need to have a destination wedding," Worth says. "That solves that problem."

"Not really," Sophia replies. "People still invite people to destination weddings."

"An impromptu destination wedding," Fisher says.

"Vegas," everyone around the table choruses.

Bennett looks at his watch. "I could have a plane ready for us in an hour."

My heart begins to race, and I grab Jules' hand. "We could do that. Then we'd be married."

"My mom would kill me."

"No she wouldn't," Sophia says. "So long as you didn't tell her and had a small, town hall ceremony when you got back."

A grin spreads across my face. I really like the idea of being married to Jules by the end of the day. I'm impatient. Being engaged is too easy to fake. I want to be her husband.

"I don't have a dress," she says. "I haven't even started to look. Even though I don't want a big wedding, I do want a pretty dress."

I try not to show my disappointment. I want her to have the wedding she wants. So we should wait.

The table falls silent, until Jules says, "I really like brunch. We should make it a regular thing. I know you guys have your Monday nights, but brunch is a nice couple-of-times-a-month supplement."

There's a rumble of agreement around the table.

"In fact," she continues, "we could host again this time next week. And you never know, someone might bring up an impromptu Vegas wedding. And by then, I might have found a dress."

I turn my head to look at Jules, to make sure I'm picking up on her fairly obvious hints that she's going to marry me next weekend. She beams at me, and I cup her head in my hand and press a kiss onto her lips.

"I'll arrange the jet," Bennett says.

"I'm clearing my week so I can help with everything," Efa says. "I know some really cool places with beautiful dresses."

"Me too," Sophia says. "Although I'm imagining Efa knows better places."

Jules squeezes my hand under the table. And I kiss the side of her head.

We're doing this. This time next week, we're going to be married.

"You think a skull belt would look nice on a wedding dress?" she asks.

Proof, as if I needed any, that I've waited two years too many to marry the woman who I've known is my destiny from the first moment I set eyes on her.

READY FOR SOPHIA'S BOOK? Who does she end up with? Pre order **The Hero + Vegas = No Regrets**

Want Bennett and Eva's story? Catch up with **The Boss + The Maid = Chemistry**

Like fake relationship books? Try **Duke of Manhattan. Read on for a sneak peek!**

DUKE OF MANHATTAN

Ryder

Everything was better on a private plane. Flying private wasn't something the British aristocracy did. My family would consider it too frivolous—*nouveau riche*, as they described it. It wasn't the first or the last thing my family and I disagreed on—I loved everything about the experience. The way the leather seats hugged my ass. The fact that flight attendants' skirts looked shorter and legs looked longer. Even their attention was more flirtatious.

The blonde beauty assigned to this flight dipped low to pour my water and give me a look down her blouse at her high, rounded breasts.

I appreciated the courtesy.

If I'd been going back to London under better circumstances, I might have considered seeing if her attention to detail extended to the bedroom. I liked luxuriating in a blow job and I had the feeling Melanie would be happy to make it last as long as I wanted.

But even gripping this beautiful woman's neck as she buried her face in my lap wasn't going to improve my day.

I glanced at my watch.

"Thirty minutes to landing, sir," Melanie said. It was a shame I'd miss out on her. I didn't normally deprive myself, but I wasn't in the right head space. "Can I get you anything else?"

"No. I'm going to make a quick call." I needed to tell my sister I was about an hour away.

I unclenched my fingers from the soft, cream leather on the arm of the seat. It had been six hours since I'd learned of my grandfather's fall. I didn't often miss being in London but it was times like these where I wished New York was a forty-five-minute drive away from my family.

I had to keep telling myself that there was nothing I could do for my grandfather whether I was sitting next to him by his bed or here in the air.

"Have you landed?" Darcy asked as she answered my call.

"Thirty minutes."

"So you'll be here in a little over an hour. Message me just before you arrive and I'll come down and meet you."

"Why? Is there something you're not telling me?" Had my grandfather's condition deteriorated since I'd last spoken to her?

"No. This hospital is just hard to navigate." She sounded tired, like she'd been up all night. I'd be able to relieve her burden a little when I arrived.

"Is he conscious?" I asked, still unconvinced she was telling me the whole story.

"Yes. He says he's never felt better, but clearly breaking your hip at eighty-two isn't good." Her voice was tight. She was holding herself together. Keeping a stiff upper lip.

"He's going to be fine." This time. "Have you had the results of the CT yet?"

"No. You know it took them a couple of hours to convince him to have it done." The corners of my mouth tried to tug into a smile without my permission. Darcy would hear the amusement in my voice and be furious with me for taking his side. Grandfather was an indomitable character and there was little anyone could persuade him to do if he didn't want to. And vice versa, when people told him he couldn't do something, he found a way. We were a lot alike in that way. He was my hero when I was young. And more of a parent to Darcy and me than our own feckless mother and father. Our father had run off with a waitress before I could remember him and our mother had never recovered and spent most of her time seeking spiritual enlightenment at various places in Asia. Our grandfather was the man who had soothed us when we were upset, who had come to school plays—who we *still* turned to for advice.

"He hates people fussing," I said.

"I know, but after the stroke, we can't take any chances."

My grandfather's stroke two years ago had been a shock to us all. Luckily for us, he was a fighter and he'd regained most of his speech and movement. But he was frail and weak on his left side, which made him vulnerable to falls. "I know. Still it's going to be fine," I said with as much authority as I could muster, but if his fall had created a bleed in his brain . . . I took a deep breath and tried to steady my rising heart rate.

"Victoria called," Darcy said, her words clipped and tight.

I clenched my jaw and didn't reply. I couldn't bear to hear about my cousin's selfish wife.

"No doubt she wanted to know if they could start counting the silver," Darcy said.

I took a deep breath. I had to keep it together or I'd upset my sister.

My grandfather's title passed to the next married male heir. As I was oldest, it should have been me. But as one woman had never been enough for me, my cousin Frederick, and his wife, Victoria would be the next Duke and Duchess of Fairfax.

It wasn't like I needed the money. I'd made more for myself than my grandfather was worth, and I certainly didn't care about the title. I'd never wanted to be the Duke of Fairfax. Frankly, I'd never understood why my sister being a woman precluded her from being next in line. She should get the title, the money and the estate—and all the headaches that went with it.

Frederick and I had never been close, although as he was heir to Woolton and my grandfather's grandson, I saw more of him than I would have liked. He was jealous and mean-spirited as a child and he'd never grown out of it. He seemed to envy everything I ever had—toys, friends and later women. Despite the fact my sister and I had to live with our grandfather because our parents didn't want us, Frederick hated that we lived at Woolton and he didn't. He never missed an opportunity to criticize what Darcy was doing for the estate. And constantly made comments about me *running away* to America. Insults I could have coped with. What I didn't like was the fact that when I called him to tell him of our grandfather's stroke, instead of asking which hospital he was in or about the prognosis, the first thing he did was tell me he'd call me back when he'd spoken to his lawyer.

There was no going back for us after that.

"Well, tell Victoria to speak to me in future. I'll have no problem in telling her to fuck off." The fact was, as soon as my grandfather was dead, the silver would be hers to count. And although I didn't have the same pull toward our family's history as Darcy did, it still didn't seem fair.

"We need to talk when you get here. Properly."

I knew what was coming. We were going to discuss how me getting married would change everything. "Of course."

"I mean about Aurora," she said.

Darcy had hinted that our childhood friend would be a willing wife a number of times. This time she sounded more determined. But I'd have to be clear that Aurora wasn't someone I was going to marry. "I'm going to see the lawyers about things while I'm in London, too." I was still hopeful that we'd find a legal solution to Frederick inheriting the estate.

A couple of beats of silence passed. "You know how I feel about that," she said.

"I don't want to fight over grandfather's estate," I replied. Darcy hated the idea that there would be a battle over our grandfather's assets, because it seemed to somehow taint the importance of our love for the man. However, knowing how he wanted my sister to inherit, I knew he would welcome a solution. "But what's our alternative?"

"I really want you to consider an arrangement with Aurora—she cares about our family, and she'd make an excellent wife."

"I don't want to get married." Certainly not to someone who only wanted me for the title I'd inherit. And the alternative—that she'd want a real husband—was worse. Aurora and I had known each other as kids, first crushes, but she didn't know me now, not as an adult.

"I'm sure most men feel like that. And it's not like you have to . . . you know . . . *live* like husband and wife."

"That's not the point, Darce." *Fucking* Aurora would be the least of my problems. She'd always been attractive. I'd have slept with her before now if I hadn't thought she'd read all kinds of meaning into us having sex. But I knew myself well enough to know I could never be faithful to one woman. There were too many beautiful girls in the world. I preferred the ones I didn't know. It was less complicated.

"It's not like we're talking about the rest of your life." I really wanted to make this better for my sister, but she'd see that I could buy her another property, really similar to Woolton Hall. I knew it wouldn't be exactly the same, there wouldn't be that emotional investment she had in Woolton, but her life wouldn't change significantly. The thing was she was married to the estate—it had been her whole life since we were kids. After university, when Darcy said she was going to work full time on the estate, I urged her to find her own path in the world. But working at Woolton was the only thing she wanted to do. She loved the place.

"I have thought about it. A lot." We'd been talking about this for *years*. My grandfather's stroke had only escalated things. "You know Aurora isn't the right woman for me."

"She's as good as anyone. She'd let you do your own thing."

I wasn't the kind of guy who cheated on his wife. Marriage was a commitment, a promise to be faithful, and I didn't break my promises so I didn't make any that I couldn't keep—I wasn't about to become my parents. I wanted to look back at my life and be proud of the man my grandfather had brought up. I wanted to do my grandfather's sacrifices justice.

"Let's talk when you get here. Whether we like it or not,

Grandfather is eighty-two. You're running out of time to think about this. You need to act quickly or it will be too late."

She thought she could convince me. As much as I hated to disappoint my sister, it wasn't going to happen.

Fucking was my favorite sport, and I'd gone pro a long time ago. I wasn't about to leave the field a moment before the whistle was blown. And I was determined the game would last as long as I had blood in my veins. Besides, who was I to deprive the women of Manhattan?

I tried not to shudder as I opened the door to my grandfather's room. I hated that very particular smell you got in hospitals. I wasn't sure if they all used the same cleaning products or whether death and disease carried their own fragrance.

"What the hell are you doing here?" Grandfather bellowed at me from his bed as I stepped inside.

I chuckled. "Now that's not a very nice welcome. I hope you're being slightly more charming to the nurses." I winked at a girl in her early twenties who was checking blood pressure readings.

"Everyone is making such a bloody-awful fuss, Ryder. I've been falling over for eighty-two years. I'm not sure why everyone's acting like I'm on my death bed."

I shook my head. "You broke your hip, Grandfather. Did you expect no one to care?"

"They're talking about surgery," Darcy said from behind me.

I spun around. "Surgery? What for?"

My sister looked pale as I pulled her into a hug.

"The hip. They're saying he needs a partial replacement," she mumbled against my shirt.

I squeezed and released her. "He's going to be fine. I'll speak to the doctors."

"I already did. They said surgery almost always follows a fall like this."

"Stop fussing," Grandfather called from his bed.

I laughed. If sheer force of will could keep someone alive, Grandfather would live forever.

"You look good." I patted my grandfather on the shoulder.

He shrugged off my hand. "How's business?" he asked, always ready to live vicariously through me and my life in New York. His whole life had been managing the family's holdings, which included Woolton Hall, a large, stately home outside London, the surrounding land and nearby village, which was rented out to villagers, and a townhouse in London. I never asked him if he resented the responsibility that came with the title, or if he might have done something else, had he been given a choice over his future. But he was a man of honor and commitment, a man to be admired. The person I aspired to be.

"It's good," I replied. "I'm trying to buy a small luxury fragrance business at the moment."

"Fragrance? Doesn't really seem like your thing."

"My thing is anything that makes money." I had an eye for spotting growing businesses and buying them just before their loans were called in or their lack of cash flow paralyzed them. "It's a solid business that needs investment to take a step up."

"And you're going to give them what they need?" he asked, pointing his finger at me.

I shrugged. "I'm a generous guy. You know that."

Darcy rolled her eyes. "No doubt there'll be more in it for you than them."

I nodded. "But there'll still be *something* in it for them. And that's the point. I don't screw them. I'm just shrewd." I was excited about the company I was targeting at the moment. The business hadn't been up and running very long and yet they'd done incredibly well. Retail wasn't my sweet spot but this business was worth stretching myself for.

"How are things back at the house?" I asked as I pulled a chair up to my grandfather's bed.

"The stables need a new roof," Darcy replied. "And frankly so does most of the west wing."

"She doesn't know what she's talking about," my grandfather replied.

My sister had taken over the majority of the running of the estate in the last couple of years. She'd worked side by side with my grandfather since graduating and he'd carefully passed down all that he knew.

"Grandfather, Darcy always knows exactly what she's talking about."

He growled and looked out of the large windows onto the Thames. His lack of argument was as much of an admission as we were going to get.

"I'm going to make a phone call," Darcy said. "Do you want anything while I'm gone?"

I squeezed her hand. I knew what running the estate took out of her, especially as she knew eventually she'd have to walk away from everything she'd done. I'd never understood why she didn't leave, find something of her own to put all of her energy into.

She twisted her hand free and shot me a tired smile.

"We need to talk," my grandfather said as soon as Darcy

had gone. I never liked those words coming from anyone's mouth. Bad news always followed.

I leaned back into the chair, ready to take on whatever it was that he had to say.

"I'm getting older, Ryder."

Christ, had Darcy been on at him about me marrying Aurora? We'd agreed to keep Grandfather out of it. I didn't want him to worry that he was leaving behind a big mess for Darcy and me when he died.

My stomach turned over and I leaned forward. "If you're worried about the hip surgery, don't be. You heard Darcy; it's perfectly normal after a break. You're going to be fine."

"I need to tell you something before I go in to surgery." His eyes fixed on mine just like they had when I was a child and I was in trouble. I hated to disappoint him. What had happened? "It's about my investment in Westbury Group."

"Your investment?" My grandfather had given me a couple of thousand pounds when I started up and in return he'd taken a special share. But he'd always refused to take any dividends from the company and he'd never shown any interest in the day-to-day operations. I'd almost forgotten about it.

"We should have sorted this out a long time ago. I guess I just liked the idea of being an investor in your success."

"What are you talking about?" He sounded defeated, and that wasn't the man I knew and loved. "Do you need money for the repairs Darcy mentioned?"

He chuckled and patted the hand I had resting on the side of the bed. I'd never question my grandfather's love, but he didn't show it through hugs and declarations. Darcy and I just knew from the way he was always around, making sure we never needed anything, weren't in trouble, alone or forgotten. He was our anchor.

"No, I don't want your money." He glanced at our hands before nodding. "I'm afraid if your cousin gets his hands on my share, he might have a different view."

I squinted as the early morning sun reflected off the windows and into the room. "I'm not following you. What's my business got to do with Frederick?"

He took a deep breath and began to cough. Jesus, I hated to see him so frail. I poured him some water from the plastic jug on his side table but he waved me away. "I'm fine," he said, wheezing.

"You need to take it easy."

"I said I'm fine." He inhaled and his breathing evened out. I sat back in the chair, trying to look more relaxed than I felt. "Do you remember when I invested in Westbury Group? I took that special share so you wouldn't have the burden of a loan?"

"Yeah, of course." I scanned his face, wanting to get to the crux of what he was saying.

"Well, the money came from the estate, and so the share is in the estate's name."

"I remember," I replied.

"Well, a year or so ago I went to Giles to see if there was anything we could do about this blasted succession thing. It's not right that you should have to be married to inherit. The estate, Woolton, the title. It's all rightfully yours."

I'd been to see our family lawyer and estate trustee to discuss the future, but I'd never had a conversation about it with Grandfather. I didn't like to be reminded that one day he wouldn't be around to keep me in line.

"You know that it's not important to me. I have my own money and I can more than look after Darcy." I hated talking about what happened after. The thought of a world that my grandfather wasn't a part of wasn't something I wanted to think about.

"Well, that's the point. I'm not sure it *will* be yours."

Had I heard him correctly? "What do you mean?"

"The terms of the trust set out that I can't alter or sell any of the assets of the trust after I turned eighty." My grandfather may be the Duke of Fairfax and heir of the Woolton estate, but everything was managed through a trust that governed exactly what could and couldn't be done in order to preserve the estate for future generations.

"Right. I'm not following you." I glanced over at the door, expecting Darcy to return at any minute. Perhaps she'd understand what grandfather was trying to say.

"So I can't transfer that share back to you. You can't buy me out," he said.

I shrugged. "So. Your investment hasn't affected the way I run the business at all. Keep the share."

"But it's not mine. It belongs to the trust. Which means when I die"—I winced as he said the words—"it passes to Frederick."

I still wasn't understanding. I studied his face, trying to work out exactly what he was saying. "So he'll have a minor share. So what?"

"Have you looked at the paperwork we put in place at the time?" he asked, shifting on the bed.

I couldn't remember any of the nuts and bolts of what we'd done. I'd been too excited to get my business off the ground to care. I'd found a small biotech firm in Cambridge I'd wanted to invest in, an opportunity that wouldn't have lasted long. And it had been one of the best decisions I'd made. It had made me a fortune, and opened the door to new opportunities. It was from that investment that all my success had come and I'd finally felt as if I deserved my place in the world. As much as I loved my grandfather, as I child, I still lived with the reality that I wasn't enough for my parents. Westbury Group helped me feel grounded. It was *mine.* And it wasn't going anywhere. "I can't remember the details. But everything has worked out fine. What's the problem?"

"In order to give you the money from the trust, the share needed to have certain powers. So, if I don't like the way you're running the group, I can take control of the company."

"That's never been an issue, though." There was no one in the world who I trusted more than my grandfather to go into business with.

"But when the share transfers to Frederick . . ."

The scrape of my chair echoed around the room as I stood abruptly. I shoved my hands in my pockets, trying to keep calm. "Are you telling me that Frederick is going to be able to take control of my company?" My grandfather was the person I could trust most in the world. Frederick was the person who I trusted least. "That he could take everything I've worked for all these years?"

"I'm sorry, my boy. I never meant for it to be like this."

I paced up and down by his bed. "So we change the paperwork, right? Can't we pass a resolution that changes the rights of that share?" I stopped and gripped the cream metal bar at the foot of the bed, waiting for my grandfather's response. That had to be the solution, right? "I still own the majority of the company."

He shook his head. "I wish it were that simple. Once I turned eighty, no changes to investments can be made. I'm so sorry, I had no idea my investment in your company, in your future, could affect you like this."

My knuckles whitened as my grip on the bed tightened. "This isn't your fault."

"I should have had Giles do a full review of our assets much sooner, but . . ." But the stroke had happened and all we'd cared about was his health.

"Don't think about it." I didn't want my grandfather to worry about it. I could do that for both of us. Westbury Group was everything I'd worked for my whole life. It meant I never had to rely on anyone—it was my independence. Westbury Group ensured I didn't have to be reliant on anyone for anything.

"I'd like to think that Frederick will do the right thing, but . . ."

I sighed. We both knew that would never happen. If Frederick got the chance to ruin me, he'd grab it with both hands. He'd been waiting his whole life to prove to me he was the bigger man. He wouldn't pass up the opportunity.

I had to make this right.

"We'll find a solution. I'll speak to Giles about it."

I might not be the next Duke of Fairfax, but I would do everything within my power to make sure that Frederick didn't end up destroying everything I'd ever worked for.

Scarlett

Dating in New York City was the worst.

I was following all the advice the internet had to offer—not being too available, not having sex too early and not putting all my eggs in one basket. But I just lurched from one disappointment to another disaster. I'd thought the guy last Thursday was super cute in complimenting my shoes until he confessed he liked to dress up in women's clothes at the weekend and would like to see if my pink suede five-inch heels came in his size. Maybe I was being too picky, but I just didn't want to fight with my boyfriend over who wore what when we went for dinner.

And then there was the guy who looked like he'd never had a haircut and didn't look me in the eye once during our entire date. And how could I forget the forty-something, sweaty man who told our waitress she had a nice rack?

I swiped across the screen of my phone to see a text from Andrew—so far no disaster with him. We'd only had one date, and besides getting the feeling he was a neat freak, he seemed relatively normal. I wasn't attracted to him exactly. And he hadn't made me laugh. But he didn't have me wanting to stab him in the eye with a fork after twenty minutes, so I'd agreed to date number two.

Looking forward to seeing you tonight.

I pulled up my calendar and found an entry that said, "*Dinner with Peter.*" I looked back at my phone. Had I gotten the contacts confused? Peter was the one who wore plaid and had a cat. I'd agreed to a third date with dinner because on our second date, he'd tipped our waitress really well, even though it was clear he didn't earn very much. I wasn't exactly attracted to Peter either.

I scrolled through the messaging history. No, the text was definitely from Andrew.

Shit.

I'd double-booked.

The door to my office swung open and my business partner, Cecily, poked her head of corkscrew curls around the door. "Are you free?" she asked.

"Sure, if you can help me solve my dating dilemma." I'd been sharing dating dilemmas with Cecily since college. Roommates our sophomore year, we'd bonded as soon as we'd unpacked our copies of *The Notebook* and abandoned the day for a few hours with Ryan Gosling. I'd been a finance major and her sweet spot had been marketing. It made for the perfect business pairing.

"That sounds like fun. Being married is so boring sometimes." She took a seat in the chair opposite my desk.

I'd never thought that marriage was boring. I'd loved my husband, had looked forward to going home in the evening and hanging out with him. Over two years after our divorce, and I still missed him. Missed having a partner in crime. Missed my best friend. I forced a smile. "That's what Marcus said." Apparently, being in Connecticut with me wasn't enough for my ex-husband. It was the reason I was here looking over the Hudson and living in a one-bedroom apartment in downtown Manhattan with 90 percent of my belongings in storage. As a married woman I'd lived in a beautiful four-bedroom, clapboard house in Connecticut with incredible views of the water and a fifteen-minute commute to my office. The change was still like a knife to the stomach sometimes. Still in my twenties, I should be embracing living in the city that never slept.

Maybe I *was* boring.

When he left me, he told me he hated the idea his life was mapped out for him, but me? I'd been happy. Content. With Marcus by my side, everything had been as I had always imagined my life would be from a little girl. I hadn't thought to wish for anything more.

"I'm sorry. I wasn't trying to be insensitive."

I smiled. "It's fine. It was a long time ago." Except it didn't feel like it on days like today. I didn't want to be dating. I'd much prefer to go home and snuggle into bed with a book than go to some fancy restaurant and try to be engaging and funny.

Dating was exhausting.

"So what's your dilemma? I'll share mine if you'll share yours?" she asked as she took a seat on the other side of my desk from me.

"You have a dating dilemma? Does your husband know?" I said, grinning.

"I'm discreet," she said with a wink. "Come on, spill."

"I'm just double-booked, that's all. I made dinner plans with Andrew and Peter tonight."

"Again?" She cocked her head to one side. "Isn't that the second double-booking in the last couple of weeks?"

Yeah. And exactly how had I let this happen *again*?

"Well I guess it means you're wanting to see them."

The exact opposite, actually. Andrew and Peter were both nice enough, but I couldn't see a future with them. Neither of them were my soulmate.

"It's no big deal. I'll just cancel one of them." Or both of them and have a date with my e-reader. "I assume your dilemma's not a dating one."

Cecily's curls bounced as she laughed. "No such luck, and it's not just my dilemma, either. It's yours too." She widened her eyes. "We've had another approach from Westbury."

Westbury was by far the most enthusiastic investment company we'd been speaking to about stepping in to pay off our loans that were about to become due. But it was also the least flexible in its terms.

"I'm so sorry we're in this situation," Cecily said.

"Don't apologize. We had to have that money and we didn't have any other offers." Cecily Fragrance had become successful almost too quickly and a year ago we had needed a lot of money, fast, to be able to fulfill the orders we were getting. Cecily might have signed the loan documentation because I'd been out of town, but it was as much my decision as it had been hers. "We knew it was a short term thing. Who knew we'd be this successful?" The loans were due to be paid back but we had to keep any cash we had to continue to invest in the inventory. We needed the loans replaced. Next month. If we didn't get them our cash flow would disappear. "And Westbury hasn't changed its offer?"

"It's still all or nothing. They take the whole business, they hire us as employees and we lose our shareholding."

Westbury had a reputation for being shrewd and successful. "The money's better though," she said, sounding more positive.

Most investors were happy to take a minority stake in the company, but Westbury Group wanted the lot. Cecily and I had started this business. We'd handpicked each one of our employees. Hell, I'd even chosen the coffee machine. We didn't want to just walk away. But was Cecily wavering? Was she on the ropes?

"What do you mean, better?"

Her eyes flickered over the surface of my desk. "Enough to pay all the shareholders what we'd hoped to get at the end of year three."

I snapped my mouth shut. That was a *lot* of money.

Cecily and I *could* start again. But I loved Cecily Fragrance. It had become something I never thought a job could be—a passion.

It had provided distraction while I was grieving the loss of my marriage. I'd never understood it when my friends talked about their work like it was a hobby until Cecily and I started our business. It never felt like work for me. I loved it. And Cecily Fragrance had been the only good in my life since my divorce. I had needed a change, to not just see the hole where my husband had been wherever I looked. Marcus walking out had rocked my world, but a drive to prove he'd made the wrong decision had lit a fire in me. It was proof to my husband that I wasn't as predictable, boring and safe as he thought I was—he'd no doubt expected me to stay in a corporate job at an investment bank with a steady monthly salary for the rest of my career. Setting up my own business, with no structure and process unless I created it and taking a chance on getting paid every month was something he never would have thought I was capable of. And not something I'd ever imagined for myself. But when your world is on its ass, sometimes, you'll try anything. I might not have been able to save my marriage, but I wasn't ready to give Cecily Fragrance up.

"What do you think? You want to walk away? Give up everything we've worked so hard on and let someone else reap all the success and rewards?" *Say no. Please say no.*

She winced. "Well, not when you put it like that. But I'm not sure we have a choice. None of the other offers pay off our loans in full."

Had she given in so easily?

I certainly hadn't. My brother was a wealthy guy and would want to help us out if I told him the situation. But I knew his company had taken over a rival recently and he didn't have a lot of cash at the moment. Besides, I wanted to do this on my own. I didn't want my brother to have to save me.

"I understand that you'd rather see Cecily Fragrance continue without you than fail with you." I didn't think it would have to come to that. I knew we could make this work. We'd brought it this far.

As the face of the company, Cecily handled all the major business meetings, while I concentrated on keeping the wheels turning on the day-to-day operations. I'd heard plenty of horror stories of management getting distracted with new investment and I was determined not to let that happen. I'd not dealt with the investors but if Cecily was being beaten down, it was my turn to step into the ring. "We may still get other offers, might even be able to use those to increase some of the offers we've already had."

She picked lint from her skirt. "Maybe. I just really don't want us to go under and we'd still have jobs."

"How about I meet with all the bidders and try to negotiate?" I suggested. "I worked for an investment bank. I might have learned a couple of things on the way." Surely there was a way Cecily and I could keep running this business with the loans replaced.

"You think you might change their minds?" she asked.

I shrugged. "Who knows? But it's worth a try, isn't it? We still have some fight left in us, don't we?" I wanted to know I hadn't lost hers.

"The next instalment on the loans is due in a month—we don't have long."

I nodded, trying to ignore the twitch under my eye telling me it was an almost-impossible task. "We can't give up, Cecily. This is our baby."

She smiled half-heartedly. "It's taken so much energy to get this far, I'm not sure I have enough to finish the race."

"Well, that's why I'm here. I'm going to get us both over the finish line. Whatever it takes."

I was going to save Cecily Fragrance.

And I was going to cancel on Andrew *and* Peter and call my sister, Violet, for drinks. I wanted to have the evening I wanted to have, rather than the one I thought I should have as a twentysomething in Manhattan.

"I hope to God you're banging them both. And at the same time every Tuesday," Violet said as I explained to her about my double-booking. My sister told me nothing but the truth, and she believed in me more than anyone I knew. If I was going to fight Westbury Group to retain a shareholding, then Violet was the perfect pre-match pep squad.

"Shhhh," I said, glancing around to check if anyone had heard her.

The bar, one of my favorites, felt like a private member's club from the fifties with its low lighting, Chesterfield sofas and American standards coming from the grand piano in the corner. It represented how I'd imagined Manhattan would be rather than the realities of dating, long hours and traffic that weren't quite so glamorous.

"Well, really, what were you doing bringing me to a place like this?" she asked.

She was right. This was the sort of place Harper and I came with our best friend Grace. Violet and I normally ended up going for burgers in midtown. "I like it."

"So?" Violet asked. "Are you banging them both? I know it's too much to hope that you're doing them at the same time." She squinted at a party of suits across the bar who I'd noticed had checked her out as she'd wafted in earlier. "I think I'd like to try a three-way before I'm old. Two men, though," she clarified. "I did the two girls and a guy thing in college and it didn't work for me."

I spluttered into my glass, half choking. "Violet. Please. Save me from death by embarrassment. At least for tonight."

"Well if you answer my question, I'll stop over-sharing."

"No, I'm not *banging* them—certainly not both at once."

"Urgh," Violet said. "I might have known. Tell me you've fucked *someone* since your divorce. Please. Tell me your vibrator isn't the only thing to have given you an orgasm in the last two years."

Violet may be teasing, but the way she said it, I felt slightly ashamed that I'd still not managed to take that step of first-time sex after divorce. My sister was so . . . liberal with her relationships with men; I knew she'd find it difficult to understand why I'd not slept with any of the guys I'd dated. I didn't even understand it myself. But none of them had seemed quite what I was looking for. They hadn't been special. I'd dated plenty of men since Marcus, gotten myself back out there. I just hadn't taken that final step.

I'd even dated guys exclusively. Well one guy. For about a week until it became clear that there was no way I was going to be able to avoid sleeping with him, so I ended things.

Violet grabbed my hand. "I know I've said this all along, but what you need is a one-night stand. You're overthinking the sex thing. It's just sex. Like brushing your teeth or exercising. It's a fact of life."

"It's difficult." I understood and I agreed with Violet—sex wasn't such a huge deal. But sex after marriage was terrifying. Perhaps because I'd finally be accepting that my marriage was over and also because sex was a precursor to a relationship—a threshold that I had to step over. If I kept on this side, then I was safe. And when things ended, no one could say the relationship was a failure if it didn't exist in the first place. I didn't want to go through life leaving a trail of disappointment and broken relationships behind me.

"It's really not. And frankly, if you're really nervous you can just lie there while he does all the work. It won't be as good but if that's all you can manage, with your banging body and beautiful face, you don't need to do anything to get a guy off."

"Are we *really* having this conversation?" I wasn't nervous. I missed sex. I just didn't want a relationship that was doomed to failure.

Violet reached out and patted my hand. "We're going to keep having this conversation until you get over this issue you have around your first time, first love thing. Your life isn't a Coke commercial. No one's life is a Coke commercial. And Marcus has gone and he's not coming back. Anyway, you know he's fucking Cindy Cremantes now."

I'd heard that particular rumor last time I was at my brother's house in Connecticut. Cindy was still working at the pharmacy in Westchester as she had since school. I wasn't sure why she was so much more exciting than I was.

"I don't think my life is a Coke commercial."

"I beg to differ. I understand that Marcus is the only guy you ever slept with, but despite this décor, we're not actually in the fifties." She circled her finger in the air. "You're not a housewife. You don't have to pretend you don't like sex. That's not what life is like in the modern world."

"I like sex plenty. I'm not frigid."

Violet sighed. "Marcus didn't leave you because you're boring in bed. You don't have to be afraid."

"Yeah, I know." Marcus wasn't boring in the bedroom, and I enjoyed sex with him. But I would have been open to something . . . new, more. I didn't want to throw our car keys into a bowl at the next country club dinner or anything but maybe he could have fucked me on the kitchen floor or talked a little dirty to me once in a while. Once, when we were newlyweds, I'd interrupted his shower and dropped to my knees all ready to give him a blow job when he awkwardly told me he didn't have time because he was running late for work. "I'm just not ready for a relationship."

"Sex isn't a relationship. You're waiting to see if these guys you're dating are Mr. Right until you fuck them?" she asked, drawing her brows together as if it was the most ludicrous thing she'd ever heard.

I shrugged. "More that I'm avoiding a relationship by not having sex."

She nodded. "Okay. Got it. But you're missing out—having sex with someone doesn't mean you're having a relationship with them. Not always. What you need is sex with a stranger."

I'd never picked up a guy before—barely even flirted with someone who wasn't my husband. Marcus and I had been dating since high school. "So how would this one-night stand thing go? If, in theory, I was prepared to do something like that."

Violet swallowed her sip of vodka before breaking into a huge grin. "Pick a guy." She nodded toward a man sitting at the bar, swirling his drink and staring at the bottom of his glass like he had a lot on his mind. "He's hot. No wedding ring. Get it done."

Get it done? It wasn't highlights or a run around the park.

"Don't be stupid. I can't just pick up a guy." From what I could see the man at the bar *was* attractive—a strong jaw, a nicely cut suit you could tell was handmade. But he could still live at home with his mom or have a fetish for peeing on women . . . or men. I was prepared to push at my boundaries, but there were limits.

"You keep telling me you want to be more adventurous. Now, I think you've got no worries on that score—you've just let dipshit Marcus get in your head. But in theory, if you did want to have a one-night stand, he would be perfect." She lifted her chin toward the hot guy at the bar.

"Just find someone to fuck. Someone you'll never see again and then when you find someone you really like, you can have a relationship *and* the sex."

"I liked Andrew. And Peter, for that matter."

"Maybe you did. But not enough. Maybe it's all the pressure. With a stranger, there's no expectation—apart from that you're both gonna get laid."

Maybe that was it. Maybe I just didn't need to think about it—about anything.

"You're doing that thing," Violet said, frowning at me.

"What thing?"

"The thing where you tap your index finger. It's annoying."

"You're annoying."

She just shrugged as if the idea didn't bother her at all. Violet was always so sure of herself and everything around her. It was almost as if she were wearing super-strength glasses with a prescription straight out of science fiction—she saw things differently, more clearly than I did. Usually, she was right.

"In theory—because there's no way I'm ever going to do it—if I *wanted* to pick up the guy at the bar, what would I do?"

"In theory?" Violet asked.

I nodded while taking the two tiny black straws sticking out of my cocktail into my mouth.

"You wouldn't have to do much. Just find a reason to go to the bar."

"Why would I need to go to the bar? They have table service."

Violet exhaled loudly. "I said *find* a reason. It doesn't

matter what it is. Just go to the bar and order an unusual drink." She paused, her mouth slightly open as if she were midway through a word. "A French 75."

"That's a cocktail?" It sounded more like a paint color or a dog breed.

"A French 75 is *the* cocktail. How do you live in New York City and not know these things?" she asked. "It's not on the menu, which makes you look cool and sophisticated. And it's a talking point."

"So, I go to the bar, order the drink. And then what? I ask him to fuck me?"

"Shhh, this is a nice place," Violet said giggling. "Just go over, stand close to him. Be open to it. Maybe glance sideways at him. In that dress, it's all you'll have to do."

I glanced down at my dress. It was my red one. I'd worn it for work. It couldn't be that sexy.

"Maybe after I finish my drink."

Violet rolled her eyes. "Maybe my ass. You'll never do it."

I kept being told what I wouldn't do. What I wasn't. By Marcus, by recruitment consultants who'd said I'd never be a finance director after working in treasury, by my brother who said I'd never move to the city.

Well fuck it.

I'd done all those things. I could walk up to a bar and order a damn drink.

"Two French 75s coming right up." I slid out of the booth and didn't glance back to see if I'd shocked Violet. I didn't want to lose my nerve. It wasn't like I had to talk to the guy at the bar. If anything, it would be better if I didn't. I could prove to Violet that picking up a man wasn't as easy as she thought it was.

My red patent heels clipped on the wooden parquet

floor, out of sync with the heartbeat pounding in my chest. The guy Violet had pointed out was sitting at the corner of the bar, so rather than slide in next to him, I went to the corner, that way I could check to make sure it wasn't just his profile that was handsome.

I placed my hands flat on the shiny mahogany, deliberately not looking to my right. The barman wasn't behind the bar.

"I think he went out back for a second," the handsome guy said with an accent I couldn't place. I glanced over. Nope, his profile wasn't the only thing handsome about him. As soon as I looked at him, it was as if my eyes were glued to his. He grinned. "Hi."

I sucked in a breath and smiled, curling my fingers under my hands and squeezing my nails into my palms. "Hi." His eyes, a deep chocolate brown, watched me as if I was the only thing in the room.

"Ryder," he said.

"Oh. Scarlett." I nodded, still smiling. "My name that is. I mean, my name is Scarlett."

Get it the fuck together, Scarlett. He's just a man.

Except, he wasn't *just* anything. He certainly didn't look like any man I'd ever met. He looked like a movie star. Even sitting down, I could tell he was tall—taller than Marcus who stood at five eleven. His skin was tan and his hair a shiny chestnut brown. One large hand gripped his glass and the other stroked down his jaw.

He raised his eyebrows. "Scarlett? As in O'Hara?"

"No, as in *King*."

The corners of his lips curled up into a half smile and he nodded. "Scarlett King. I like that."

I like that, I repeated in my head, trying to sound like he did. And then I got it. He was British.

His full, pouting lips.

His almost smile.

His accent.

Wow.

If either Peter or Andrew had been like this guy, I wasn't sure I would have been able to stop myself from sleeping with them, whatever my concerns. But they weren't. They hadn't made the hairs on the back of my neck stand on end. Hadn't gotten me to push my shoulders back and my chest forward. Hadn't made me think about what they'd look like naked.

"Sorry to keep you waiting," a man said to my left. I tried to turn my gaze back to the bartender, but Ryder had captured it.

"Scarlett and her friend over there would like a drink. Put it on my bill," Ryder said.

"That's a bit risky. What if I said I was ordering a bottle of Cristal?" I asked.

"I'd say they don't offer it here but the twenty-o-one Krug is excellent. And put it on my bill."

I didn't know how to reply.

"Martin. The Krug," Ryder said to the barman. He sounded so authoritative. Perhaps it was just the way each word he said was a little clipped because of his accent.

Shit. I didn't want to look like one of those girls that was just after the most expensive drinks she could get. "Oh, no! You don't have—I really just came over for a couple cocktails. The same again if you don't mind," I told the barman. I'd forgotten the name that Violet had given me.

"You're turning down Krug?" Ryder asked with a frown.

"Yeah, this way, I can talk to you without you thinking you bought your time."

Ryder raised his eyebrows. "Now that I can live with. So where shall we start?"

Shit, I had no idea what came next. I'd only gotten as far as ordering a cocktail when talking it through with Violet. He tilted his head slightly and I waited for him to decide. "Tell me what you're discussing so conspiratorially about over there with your friend," he said. "You looked like two girls who didn't want to be interrupted."

Weren't we supposed to start with the basics? What I did for work? Did I live in New York? Something in the way he looked at me told me this guy wanted my soul straight out the gate.

"You first," I said. "Why are you here? Drowning your sorrows? Bad breakup? Lost a trillion dollars?"

He chuckled. "Nothing like that," he said, taking a sip of his drink. "Trying to keep myself awake so I wake up tomorrow without jet lag. I flew in from London earlier today."

London. Interesting.

"You're here on business?" I asked, leaning against the barstool, letting myself relax a little.

"I'm based here and my business is here too. You live in the city?"

I nodded. "So you were just visiting London?"

"Yeah, my grandfather had a fall and so I flew back to check on him."

I rolled my eyes. What a cheeseball. "You were visiting your sick grandfather?" I stood up and looked to see if our cocktails were ready. "Does any girl believe it when you tell them that?"

He laughed. "You're right. That sounded like a line. But it's true. Luckily he's fine and you haven't hurt my feelings." I didn't know if he was playing with me.

"Well, if your grandfather is sick, then I'm sorry."

His eyes seemed to sparkle as he watched me, giving me lots of time to finish what I was thinking. "Thank you," he said finally. "If I was wanting to be cheesy, I'd ask you to tell me something about yourself that no one else knows."

"That's cheesy? I think it's kinda nice-cheesy. Rather than sleazy-cheesy."

"Well it's good to know which box I'm in." His sparkle was back. His eyelashes were so long, I had to look closely to check he wasn't wearing mascara. The city was full of metrosexuals, but I wasn't about to go to bed with a man who wore makeup. I liked a guy who thought anything other than shower gel and shampoo was strictly for people with vaginas.

But Ryder's lashes were bare of any enhancement.

"So, why don't *you* tell *me* something that no one else knows? Something real," I said.

He narrowed his eyes as he looked at me as if he was trying to figure out whether he could be honest. "Sometimes I can't sleep at night because I worry I won't get it all done before I die," he said, looking away and into his drink.

The sparkle left his eyes when he'd spoken and I reached for him but didn't want to touch, didn't know where that would lead, so left my hand resting on the wood next to his drink. "Get what done?" Maybe he was back from visiting his grandfather and contemplating his place in the world.

"Everything I'm here to do." He stared at my hand and I pulled it away. "You never think about it? What's left at the end?"

His expression was so sad, I wanted to make it better.

"Not on a Tuesday," I replied in a matter-of-fact way.

He looked back at me, grinning. "That's a good strategy. I'm going to try it. Now, your turn."

"Something no one else knows?" My family knew me very well and Marcus knew me inside and out. "I'm not sure there's anything *no one* else knows."

"Liar," he whispered.

I was pretty sure this conversation wasn't the sort that led to bed. It certainly didn't feel like foreplay.

"Okay, one thing no one else knows," I said, pulling my shoulders back and picking up the two cocktails the barman set down in front of me. "I think you're a sexy guy."

And before I could catch his expression, I turned back to Violet with our drinks.

Had I just said that? Well, it was true. And no one else knew it except me. I mean, I'm sure plenty of people told him he was a sexy guy. But *I* hadn't told anyone. Not until I'd told him. I wanted to let out a squeal. I couldn't believe I'd actually said it. I was pretty sure Violet would approve.

"Why did you leave him? It looked like it was going well," Violet complained as I sat back down opposite her.

"What did you expect? That he'd flip me over the bar and fuck me in public?"

"Maybe," she replied.

I chuckled. I'd not gotten his full name. And he'd not asked for my number. But it had been fun. And not as scary as I'd expected.

"Well at least you've lightened up. Just think how much lighter you'd be if you'd fucked him."

"Sex isn't the answer to *everything*." It wouldn't save my company or pay the mortgage.

"Yeah but *good* sex makes everything a little bit better," Violet said.

"I couldn't agree more," a man said from beside us.

I snapped my head around to find Ryder standing over our table. How much had he heard?

"I think *you're* sexy," he said, staring straight at me. "And I want your number."

"I'm just leaving," Violet said, grabbing her purse and scooting out of the booth.

"Wait, I'll come with you." It had suddenly gotten very hot in here and I needed some air.

"No you won't," Ryder said. "You're staying here for a little while. With me. I want to get to know you a little better."

Violet's mouth widened in a bright smile. "You heard the man with the accent. Call me later. I love you." And before I had another chance to argue she'd disappeared and I was left sitting opposite the sexiest British guy I'd ever met, who didn't seem to find me boring at all.

BOOKS BY LOUISE BAY

All books are stand alone

New York City Billionaires

The Boss + The Maid = Chemistry

The Player + The Pact = I Do

The Hero + Vegas = No Regrets

The Doctors Series

Dr. Off Limits

Dr. Perfect

Dr. CEO

Dr. Fake Fiancé

Dr. Single Dad

The Mister Series

Mr. Mayfair

Mr. Knightsbridge

Mr. Smithfield

Mr. Park Lane

Mr. Bloomsbury

Mr. Notting Hill

The Christmas Collection

14 Days of Christmas

The Player Series

International Player

Private Player

Dr. Off Limits

Standalones

Hollywood Scandal

Love Unexpected

Hopeful

The Empire State Series

The Gentleman Series

The Ruthless Gentleman

The Wrong Gentleman

The Royals Series

King of Wall Street

Park Avenue Prince

Duke of Manhattan

The British Knight

The Earl of London

The Nights Series

Indigo Nights

Promised Nights

Parisian Nights

Faithful

What kind of books do you like?

Friends to lovers

Mr. Mayfair

Promised Nights

International Player

Fake relationship (marriage of convenience)

Duke of Manhattan

Mr. Mayfair

Mr. Notting Hill

Dr. Fake Fiance

The Player + The Pact = I Do

Enemies to Lovers

King of Wall Street

The British Knight

The Earl of London

Hollywood Scandal

Parisian Nights

14 Days of Christmas

Mr. Bloomsbury

The Boss + The Maid = Chemistry

Office Romance/ Workplace romance

Mr. Knightsbridge

King of Wall Street

The British Knight

The Ruthless Gentleman

Mr. Bloomsbury

Dr. Perfect

Dr. Off Limits

Dr. CEO

The Boss + The Maid = Chemistry

The Player + The Pact = I Do

Second Chance

International Player

Hopeful

Best Friend's Brother

Promised Nights

Vacation/Holiday Romance

The Empire State Series

Indigo Nights

The Ruthless Gentleman

The Wrong Gentleman

Love Unexpected

14 Days of Christmas

Holiday/Christmas Romance

14 Days of Christmas

British Hero

Promised Nights (British heroine)

Indigo Nights (American heroine)

Hopeful (British heroine)

Duke of Manhattan (American heroine)

The British Knight (American heroine)

The Earl of London (British heroine)

The Wrong Gentleman (American heroine)

The Ruthless Gentleman (American heroine)

International Player (British heroine)

Mr. Mayfair (British heroine)

Mr. Knightsbridge (American heroine)

Mr. Smithfield (American heroine)

Private Player (British heroine)

Mr. Bloomsbury (American heroine)

14 Days of Christmas (British heroine)

Mr. Notting Hill (British heroine)

Dr. Off Limits (British heroine)

Dr. Perfect (British heroine)

Dr. Fake Fiancé (American heroine)

Dr. Single Dad (British heroine)

The Player + The Pact = I Do (American heroine)

Single Dad

King of Wall Street

Mr. Smithfield

Dr. Single Dad

Sign up to the Louise Bay mailing list www.louisebay/newsletter

Read more at www.louisebay.com

Made in the USA
Las Vegas, NV
10 October 2024